MRS. JEFFRIES TURNS THE TIDE

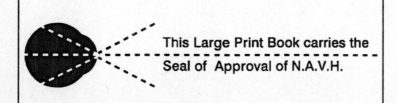

This Large Print Book carries the
Seal of Approval of N.A.V.H.

MRS. JEFFRIES
TURNS THE TIDE

EMILY BRIGHTWELL

WHEELER PUBLISHING
A part of Gale, Cengage Learning

GALE
CENGAGE Learning

Detroit • New York • San Francisco • New Haven, Conn • Waterville, Maine • London

GALE
CENGAGE Learning®

LIBRARY OF CONGRESS CATALOGING-IN-PUBLICATION DATA

Brightwell, Emily.
  Mrs. Jeffries Turns the Tide / By Emily Brightwell . — Large Print edition.
    pages cm. — (A Victorian Mystery) (Wheeler Publishing Large Print Cozy Mystery.)
  N 978-1-4104-6237-4 (softcover) — ISBN 1-4104-6237-4 (softcover) 1. Large type books. I. Title.
52.R46443M748 2014
813'.54—dc23   2013034278

Published in 2014 by arrangement with The Berkley Publishing Group, a member of Penguin Group (USA) LLC, a Penguin Random House Company

Printed in the United States of America
2 3 4 5 6   18 17 16 15 14

MRS. JEFFRIES TURNS THE TIDE

CHAPTER 1

As she reached the heavy wooden gate, Ellen Langston-Jones breathed a sigh of relief. Mrs. Barclay knew today's lesson had been put back an hour — he'd seen to that — but she didn't want to be any later than necessary. Martha Barclay could show displeasure in any number of ways and Ellen didn't want to put up with her cold stares and pursed lips today. Glancing over her shoulder at the gathering fog, now so heavy she couldn't even see the hansom cab that had just dropped her off, she shoved the key into the old lock, turned it, and pushed the gate open. It was silly to be so jumpy on such a day as this. But the combination of joy and apprehension was a potent one and had set her nerves tingling like a schoolgirl before her first dance. Really, get ahold of yourself, she told herself sternly. She hurried in and closed the gate, taking care to hear it click shut.

Tucking the key back into her pocket, she stepped off the flagstone entry and onto the gravel path that rimmed the large, oval-shaped communal garden. She walked briskly toward the far end, her feet crunching loudly against the loosely packed pebbles. She glanced toward the center, but the mist was so thick she couldn't see the lavish greenery bursting into bloom after a long and cold winter. She didn't need to see her surroundings, however. She knew this garden like the back of her hand. Small paths bisected flower beds filled with red tulips and yellow daffodils in the spring and other, lusher blooms now that it was June; trees of ash, oak, and silver birch provided shade for the residents as they sat on the wooden benches on warm evenings; and low box hedges provided miniature mazes that delighted the children. The houses along here were all large and expensive, most of them with kitchen terraces and black or white wrought iron stairs leading to larger, grander balconies used by the family and not the servants. She laughed softly. Soon it would be her turn.

The gate slammed shut with a loud bang. She jerked in reaction and then stopped and took a deep breath. It was probably just a maid or a footman. Many households allowed the staff to use the garden key if they'd been out running errands for the master or mistress. The servants' entrances were all at the back of these big houses, and it was easier to cut through the garden than walk all the way around.

Whoever it was started up the path. Ellen moved on, eager now to reach the house. It was getting late and she wanted to go over irregular verbs with the girls. A tickle built in her nose. She reached into the pocket of her light gray jacket, yanked out her hand-kerchief, and in the process one of her gloves came out and landed on the ground just as she sneezed. She knelt down and picked it up. The footsteps stopped as well. That's odd, she thought as she straightened up. Why did they stop when she stopped? She tucked the glove back into her pocket and continued on, but this time, she cocked her head so she could hear.

The footsteps started again.

Suddenly wary, she increased her pace slightly and felt a surge of relief, as the footsteps didn't follow suit. See, she told herself, it's just like Brandon used to say. You were letting your imagination get the best of you. You were just being silly and those footfalls belong to some footman or tweeny who is nervous about this nasty fog.

But then whoever was behind her moved faster.

The swirling mist suddenly thinned, and she could see that the path ahead was empty. She was alone. Alarmed now, she glanced to her left and made out the shape of the tiny hut used by the gardener. But the half-sized door was closed tight and he wasn't about the place. Where was the fellow? He should be somewhere nearby; he couldn't be digging, pruning, or planting in this miserable weather.

She stopped and turned, squinting hard to see who might be coming up the path so fast, but the whiteness descended as quickly as it had come and she could see nothing.

Just then, the footsteps stopped.

She'd had enough. She was no silly girl. She was a grown woman. "Who is there?" she called. "I'm Mrs. Langston-Jones from the household of Sir Donovan Gaines, and I'll thank whoever is back there to identify him or herself."

But no one replied.

Some trickster was trying to intimidate her on this, one of the most wonderful days of her life, but she was determined not to let them do it. She whirled about and stalked on toward her destination.

The footsteps started again, this time

moving just a tad faster.

She balled her hands into fists. This was beyond a prank now. Someone was deliberately trying to frighten her. One of them must have found out. But how? They'd been so careful. She increased her pace. Her breath was coming hard and fast now, obscuring her ability to hear what was going on behind her. But she knew that whoever it was, they were still there, and they weren't even bothering to be quiet now.

Her anger turned to fear and she broke into a run, not caring how silly or undignified she might seem if anyone happened to come outside. She heartily wished someone, anyone, would appear. She could hear them behind her, and they were gaining on her.

Her feet pounded against the gravel as she plunged onward, uncaring of the damage being done to her new black leather shoes. Her pursuer sped up as well and she would have screamed for help but she couldn't, she could barely get a breath. Mentally, she cursed herself for giving in to her vanity and wearing an old-fashioned corset. But she'd wanted to look pretty for him, wanted him to notice her slim waist beneath the sensible waistcoat and blouse.

A cry escaped her as the black metal frame of the staircase came into view. She was almost there, she'd be safe now. The kitchen would be busy at this time of day and there would be someone to help her. She ran faster, almost sobbing in relief as her fingers brushed the bottom of the railing. A hand shot out and grabbed her elbow, jerking her to a halt.

Her eyes widened at the sight of her pursuer. "It's you! What do you think you're doing?" She gasped. "You're going to pay, what are you doing with that pillow? What's that in your other hand? Oh my God, that's a gun. For goodness' sake, don't." She tried to move away and went backward, stumbling on the bottom step. "Please, please, don't . . . don't."

Her assailant held the pillow in front of her chest and fired directly into it, hitting her in the heart. She collapsed, one arm caught on the bottom railing as she sprawled onto the path.

The killer knelt down, laid the gun on the ground next to her body, checked her pulse, and then did one last thing before disappearing into the swirling mist.

Mrs. Goodge looked up as Wiggins and Phyllis came into the kitchen for their tea. It was a quiet afternoon at Upper Edmonton Gardens, home of Inspector Gerald

Witherspoon.

"Cor blimey, that smells good," Wiggins, the footman, exclaimed. "What are you bakin', Mrs. Goodge?"

The cook chuckled. "It's something called a peach cobbler. Luty sent me the recipe and two jars of her preserved peaches. We'll have it after our dinner tonight." She put the pastry onto a metal trivet on the top of the counter.

"We've got to wait until then?" Wiggins complained. "Can't we 'ave it for tea?" Brown-haired and blue-eyed, he had a face that had only recently lost the plumpness in his cheeks that had made him appear much younger than his twenty-three years.

"We've got the rest of them scones for tea," the cook muttered as she eyed her pastry, looking for flaws. Mrs. Goodge was an elderly, rather portly woman with gray hair tucked beneath her cook's cap and spectacles covering her hazel eyes. "This might not be fit to eat. I've never made it before and I'm not sure the crust is supposed to be that dark."

"Don't be silly, Mrs. Goodge," Mrs. Jeffries, the housekeeper, said as she came into the kitchen. "You know good and well that if you made it, it will be utterly delicious." She was a woman of late middle age whose auburn hair was now liberally laced with streaks of gray. Short of stature and gently rounded, she wore a brown bombazine housekeeper's dress, which rustled as she hurried to the counter and took a deep breath, inhaling the mingled scents of peaches and nutmeg. "This smells heavenly."

Delighted by the compliment, Mrs. Goodge laughed. "It's kind of you to say so, but even I make mistakes. It's different from our usual pudding, but I thought it was high time I tried something new. I hope the inspector likes it."

Phyllis, the maid, put a plate of scones on the table. She was a plump young woman with dark blonde hair pulled back in a bun at the nape of her neck and a face as round as one of Mrs. Goodge's pie tins. "It's too bad that we've got to wait till dinner to have the cobbler." She turned and went to the cooker. The kettle had just whistled. "Betsy and Smythe won't get to taste it unless there's a bit left over for tomorrow's morning tea."

Betsy and Smythe were married and lived close by in their own flat. He was the inspector's coachman and she had been the maid, but since marrying and having a child, Betsy had given up her job. Even though he had no need for employment, Smythe stayed on as the coachman, but as the inspector rarely used his carriage or horses, he did whatever was needed around the house. Mrs. Jeffries knew for a fact that he donated his quarterly wages to charity.

Years earlier, when Smythe had returned from Australia, he'd stopped in to pay his respects to his former employer, Euphemia Witherspoon, the inspector's aunt. He'd found her in a terrible state. Her servants were robbing her blind. She was ill and the only one taking care of her had been a very young Wiggins. He'd tossed the servants except Wiggins into the street, called a doctor, and done his best. But his efforts were in vain. Before she died, she'd made Smythe promise to stay on until her nephew was properly settled into the house. He'd kept his word and in doing so, had caused himself a number of problems. He'd never revealed to the household that he was wealthy and by the time he could have gone, he was too involved with solving murders to want to leave. More importantly, he'd fallen in love with Betsy.

"I miss them bein' 'ere." Wiggins slid into his seat. "Especially since they were gone so long to Canada visitin' Betsy's relations. Seems like forever since either of 'em 'as nagged at me to sit up straight or tuck in my shirt."

"We all miss them, but married couples need their privacy," Mrs. Jeffries reminded him.

"Betsy always comes by for morning tea," Phyllis said.

"And sometimes in the evenings so the inspector can see our godchild," the cook added. Inspector Witherspoon, Mrs. Goodge, and Luty Belle Crookshank, one of the household's friends, served as godparents to Smythe and Betsy's baby daughter, Amanda Belle.

Phyllis grabbed the big brown teapot off the counter and put it on the table next to the pastries. "But still, it's not the same as when they were here all the time."

"That's true." Mrs. Jeffries sat down at the head of the table. "But as I've said before, the only real constant in life is change and we all must adjust."

"At least Smythe is 'ere every day." Wiggins helped himself to a scone.

"Thank goodness for that," Mrs. Jeffries said. "There's plenty of work to be done. This house is so large there's always something that needs repairing or replacing." Even though Gerald Witherspoon was only a mere inspector in the Metropolitan Police

16

Force, he'd inherited both this house and a substantial fortune from Euphemia Witherspoon, his late aunt.

Wiggins reached for the butter pot. "It took us hours to pry off them old brass sconce plates on the third floor. Smythe's got 'is work cut out for 'im findin' somethin' to replace 'em."

Mrs. Jeffries grimaced as she began to pour the tea. As the housekeeper, she was responsible for purchasing household items, but the mere thought of the hours it would take to find something that would fit over those old pipes so daunted her that when Smythe volunteered to do it, she'd gladly handed the job off.

"He said he's got a friend who can help, someone in the business." Phyllis pulled out her chair and sat down.

"I bet 'e went to the ironmongers over on Ladbroke Road," Wiggins said. "His mate owns the shop and the two of 'em go a long way back. They knew each other in Australia."

"Exactly what did he do in Australia?" Phyllis nodded her thanks as the housekeeper handed her a cup.

"Oh, a bit of this and that," the housekeeper replied. This was dangerous territory. The rest of the household had no idea that Smythe had made a fortune when he was in that part of the world. "He worked at the waterfront and then he did some prospecting in the outback. But then he got homesick and came back to England." She passed a cup to Mrs. Goodge.

" 'E scared me to death when I first met him," Wiggins said. "I'll never forget it. 'E come stormin' into Miss Witherspoon's room and old Mrs. Haggerty, she were the housekeeper, come doggin' his 'eels and tellin' him to get out, but he weren't scared of her. He came right over to the bed and asked me what the blazes I was doin'. I were just a lad then and I was doin' my best to take care of the mistress . . ."

"And you were doin' a right good job of it as well." Smythe's voice came from the doorway. "If you hadn't been, I'd 'ave chucked you out the way I did the others," he said. "But we've no time to waste nattterin' about the past." He looked at the housekeeper as he came into the room. He had a brown paper bundle under his arm. "There's been a murder and I'm pretty sure it's in our inspector's district."

The room went silent and everyone sobered. Murder was not something they took lightly. Solving them was what they did best.

Inspector Gerald Witherspoon had solved

more homicides than anyone in the history of the Metropolitan Police Department. But what very few people, including the inspector himself, realized was that he had help he didn't know about, namely, the people in this room and a few of their trusted friends.

None of them had set out to become detectives, but providence or fate or perhaps even the hand of God had set them on a path pursuing justice, and now none of them would turn back even if they could.

It had all begun when Inspector Witherspoon, then in charge of the Records Room at Scotland Yard, had moved into the house. Having been raised in very modest circumstances, he'd no experience running a large household so he'd hired Mrs. Jeffries, the widow of a Yorkshire policeman, as his housekeeper. He'd not needed a footman, but being the decent man he was, he didn't have the heart to show young Wiggins the door, so he kept him on. As he'd also inherited a huge, old-fashioned carriage and the two horses that went with it, he'd asked Smythe to stay as well. Before long, Mrs. Goodge had joined the household and then Betsy had collapsed on the inspector's doorstep and he'd taken her in. Once she'd been nursed back to health, he'd offered her a job as a housemaid. While all this was happening, a series of killings the press dubbed the horrible Kensington High Street murders, were taking place less than half a mile from the inspector's home, and Mrs. Jeffries had encouraged him to ask a few questions here and there. He'd ended up solving the case, and after that, he was reassigned to the local police station, and if a homicide occurred on his watch, he got it. But because of his reputation and his remarkable record, he was frequently called into other districts to solve their murders, especially if the victim was a member of the upper classes.

"Sit down and have a quick cup of tea while you tell us what's happened." Mrs. Jeffries poured another cup.

Smythe put his package down at the end of the table, yanked his chair back, and sat down. "Ta, Mrs. J. I could do with one." He took the cup she handed him. "I'm dyin' of thirst. I raced back here faster than Snyder's hounds."

Everyone waited while he took a quick sip. Then Mrs. Jeffries said, "Right then, tell us everything."

He understood what she wanted. They'd learned over time that no detail, no matter how small it might seem, was to be overlooked. "Milo's had some plates that would fit over them pipes upstairs, so I bought 'em and started for home. When I got to the corner of Clarendon Road, I spotted Constable Evans stationed at the fixed point, so I went over to say hello. Just as I got there, this young housemaid come screamin' up to him that a woman 'ad been shot and was lyin' dead on the staircase at the back of the 'ouse. Evans blew his whistle, signaling for more 'elp, and two other constables showed up."

"How long did this take?" Mrs. Jeffries asked.

"Not more than a minute," Smythe replied. "Remember, the inspector mentioned they'd had a string of house robberies in that area and they'd brought in other constables from K District to 'elp em patrol the area. But the housemaid was jumpin' up and down, babblin' that poor Mrs. Langston-Jones had been shot by a maniac and we 'ad to hurry. Evans isn't a fool, he knows not to hotfoot it to a murder scene without notifying the station, so he made her wait till the others arrived. He sent one of the lads off to the station and took the other one and they raced toward the house. I waited till they were far enough ahead not to notice me and then I went after 'em. They went into a house at number seventeen Portland Villas."

"I know that street, it's about a mile from here," Phyllis muttered. "It's a posh neighborhood, too."

"That means our inspector will definitely get the case," Mrs. Goodge muttered.

"Go on, Smythe," Mrs. Jeffries urged. "Did you learn anything else?"

"Not much, but as you'd expect, once the constables were there, a crowd gathered about the street. But no one seemed to know much, only that the victim was the French tutor and she was found lyin' outside of the house where she worked. The place is owned by a family named Gaines. Once I realized there weren't much else to suss out from the scene, I 'urried back 'ere so we could get started."

"But what if Inspector Witherspoon doesn't get this one? Portland Villas isn't that close, it might be in K District and not on our inspector's patch. Shouldn't we wait until we see if he is going to get the case?" Phyllis asked.

Mrs. Jeffries shook her head. "No, we won't wait. Even if this one weren't in his district, Inspector Witherspoon would get it."

"They always give the ones that might involve or embarrass the rich and powerful to our inspector," Mrs. Goodge explained to the maid. "And you said it yourself, the murder house is in a posh neighborhood. So we'll not be wastin' our time by gettin' a bit ahead on this one." She turned to the housekeeper. "Should we send for Luty and Hatchet straightaway?"

Luty Belle Crookshank and her butler, Hatchet, were special friends of the household. Luty Belle had been a witness in one of their early investigations. Savvy and smart, she'd realized what the household was doing as they snooped about asking questions, and when that case had been over, she'd come to them seeking assistance with a problem of her own. She and Hatchet now insisted on helping whenever the inspector had a murder case.

"Absolutely."

Wiggins was already getting to his feet. "Should I tell them to come right now or first thing tomorrow for our mornin' meeting? It's gettin' late and we don't know very much yet."

"We do," the housekeeper insisted. "We know the victim was the French tutor at the Gaines household, most probably a wealthy man's home. So there's always the possibility that Luty or Hatchet will know something about them." She turned to Phyllis.

"Go across the garden and get Ruth. She'll want to be here as well."

"Let's hope she's in town," Mrs. Goodge muttered. "One of Lord Cannonberry's lunatic relatives might have called her to come and nurse them." Ruth was Lady Cannonberry, the widow of the late Lord Cannonberry and a wonderful woman. Unfortunately, when her husband passed away, he left her a passel of relations that frequently called upon her to play nursemaid to them and their mostly imaginary illnesses.

Phyllis and Wiggins got their hats and hurried toward the back door. Fred, the household's mongrel dog, looked up from his spot by the cooker and gave his tail a hopeful wag. But when the back door slammed shut and it was clear that no one was going to take him "walkies," he went back to his nap.

Smythe rose to his feet. "I'll nip home and get Betsy and the baby. Even if she can't do as much as before, she'll want to be 'ere."

"Tell her to wrap my lambkins warmly," Mrs. Goodge said as he headed for the back door. "Even if it is June, there was a miserable fog today and it's still damp out there."

Inspector Gerald Witherspoon climbed down from the hansom cab and stared at the row of homes while Constable Barnes paid the driver. Witherspoon was a slender man with pale skin, a long, bony face, and deep-set eyes. He pushed his spectacles up his nose as he surveyed the area. Full-sized brown brick town houses, all with cream-colored ground-floor facades, lined both sides of the street. Their doors were all brilliantly painted, there wasn't so much as a hint of tarnish on any of the brass door lamps, and even the stoops looked as though they'd just been scrubbed. He sighed inwardly. Like most Metropolitan Police districts, this was a combination of rich, ordinary, and downright poor neighborhoods. When the summons had come in, he'd been hoping that, for once, he'd get a case that didn't involve wealth or power, but it looked as if he wasn't going to get his wish today. This was a rich man's street and that always complicated matters.

He scanned the street and spotted the murder house right away. A constable stood at the top of a short staircase. Two matrons with shopping baskets on their arms, three housemaids, and half a dozen street lads milled about on the pavement, most of them staring with open curiosity at the closed front door of the house.

"Looks like the news of the murder has

already spread," Constable Barnes said as he nodded toward the small crowd. Barnes was an older man with a ramrod-straight spine, a ruddy complexion, and a headful of curly gray hair under his policeman's helmet.

"Yes, I expect it has. Bad news travels fast," the inspector agreed as they crossed the road and stepped onto the pavement. They went up the short walkway to the stairs.

As they approached, the constable on guard nodded respectfully. "They're waiting for you inside, sir. We've not moved the body nor interfered with anything. The police surgeon's on his way." He rapped on the door, opened it, and moved back as the two men went inside.

Inside the foyer, a tall, gray-faced butler standing beside a round table jerked visibly as they entered.

"Oh dear, we've startled you," Witherspoon apologized as he glanced at his surroundings. Directly in front of him was a broad staircase with a blue and gold patterned carpet. To the right, a polished wood parquet floor ran down a long corridor to the back of the house. The walls were papered in blue and white stripes, and overhead a crystal chandelier hung from the high ceiling. A cobalt blue ceramic umbrella stand was next to the door, and opposite that was a white marble foyer table holding a gold-washed bronze card stand.

"That's alright, sir, it's not your fault. I knew you were expected. We're all just a bit upset over what has happened," he replied. "I'm to take you right out to the er . . . uh . . . place where it happened. You are the police inspector, aren't you?"

"Yes, I'm Inspector Witherspoon, and this is Constable Barnes. If you could take us to the body now —"

The butler interrupted. "It's this way, sir." He turned and scurried down the hallway. "The master is most distressed because the constables wouldn't let us touch anything and poor Mrs. Langston-Jones is in a very undignified position. We all liked her very much and it's dreadfully upsetting to see her just lying there like that."

"We'll work as quickly as we can," the inspector promised. The man moved so fast both he and Barnes were almost running to keep up with him, but as they raced down the corridor, he caught glimpses of ancestral portraits and lushly painted landscapes hanging on the walls.

They came out onto a small terrace that overlooked a huge, communal garden. A dark-haired man dressed in a dark suit, white shirt, and red cravat sat in the corner behind a white, wrought iron table. He stared dully at Witherspoon before looking down at his feet.

A staircase led down to the pathway leading to the garden proper, and that's where the body lay sprawled. Two constables stood guard over the corpse, and another constable kept a smallish crowd of housemaids, gardeners, and footmen from the other houses along the garden well back from the area.

Witherspoon grimaced, swallowed hard, and reminded himself of his duty as he descended the stairs. He was rather squeamish when it came to corpses, but he always did what he had to do.

"Looks like she's been shot, sir." Barnes, who'd followed right behind, went to the other side of the body. "One bullet directly in the chest, I expect it struck her heart. She was youngish, too, not more than thirty-five, I'd say."

The dead woman lay on the ground with her head on the bottom step and her left arm caught in the bottom rung of the wrought iron staircase. She was dressed in a gray skirt and jacket, underneath which was a fitted light blue waistcoat and a white blouse. Her skirt had hitched up enough to reveal her black low-heeled shoes. She had brown hair and a fair complexion with regular, even features. Even in death, she was quite lovely.

Witherspoon knelt beside her and peered at the entry wound for a long moment before shifting his gaze. A gun lay on the ground next to her. "It appears as if the killer dropped the murder weapon and left it here."

Barnes knelt and picked up the gun by the butt, taking care to keep the barrel pointing down at the ground. "This isn't any ordinary revolver, sir," he murmured as he examined it closely. "It's a Beaumont Adams. See." He lifted it so they could both get a closer look. "It's got all this ornate inlaid gold curlicue decoration on the barrel and behind the trigger. These don't come cheap, sir. I wonder why the murderer didn't take it."

"That's a good question, Constable. But do be careful with it. We'll examine it more closely when it's safely unloaded," Witherspoon said. Guns made him very nervous. He got to his feet. He glanced at the closest constable. "Constable Evans, who was first on the scene?"

"I was, sir, and that gentleman over there"

— he pointed to a man standing at the edge of the garden by the kitchen terrace — "was the one who found the body. He wanted to leave, sir, but I told him he had to wait, that you'd want to speak to him."

The man in question frowned irritably and crossed his arms over his chest in a gesture of impatience. Tall, with thinning brown hair and sharp, patrician features, he was smartly dressed in a beige suit with matching waistcoat and white shirt with a wing tip collar and green tie. He caught Witherspoon's eye and waved impatiently. "You there, you in the bowler hat. Are you the one in charge?"

"I am. I'm Inspector Gerald Witherspoon." He started toward him, motioning for Barnes to follow. "Who are you, sir?"

"My name is Lucius Montague, and if it's all the same to you, I'm in a hurry so please be quick with your questions."

Witherspoon nodded politely. "We'll be as brief as possible. Now, can you tell me —"

"Can't we go inside the house," Montague interrupted. "It's damp out here and Sir Donovan wouldn't want me catching a chill. Come along, it's this way." With that he turned and stalked toward the back door, around which a small group of wide-eyed servants had clustered. They parted as the men approached. Montague shoved into the back hall and up the corridor toward the staircase. "There's a sitting room we can use."

"Are you the owner of this house?" Barnes asked as they reached the stairs.

"Goodness no, I live across the garden," Montague said. "And I'm not generally in the habit of using the servants' entrance, but under the circumstances, I thought it best. This house is owned by my dear friend, Sir Donovan Gaines."

When they reached the first floor, he led them into a paneled room furnished with a maroon and gold Empire-style suite of furniture. Montague flopped down on the sofa and took off his gloves. He raised an eyebrow in disapproval as the two policemen took the two chairs flanking him.

Barnes gave him a hard stare and Montague blinked and then looked away. The constable was certain the man had been getting ready to chastise them for sitting down. Well, sod him, he thought as he took out his notebook. The fellow needed to be taught a few manners. "You seem to take a number of liberties with a house that isn't yours. Are you a relative of Sir Donovan's?"

Montague's mouth opened in surprise but he recovered quickly. "No, I'm a friend of the family. A close friend, and I wouldn't call it taking liberties to avail myself of a few comforts when the master of the house is indisposed."

"When exactly did you discover the body?" Witherspoon asked.

Montague gave Barnes one last glare and then turned his attention to the inspector. "It was almost three o'clock. Yes, yes, that's right. I was coming to the house to borrow a book from Sir Donovan's library. When I first saw her lying there, I thought she must have fainted or slipped and hit her head. I was quite stunned when I saw she'd been shot."

"You're familiar with bullet holes, are you, sir?" Barnes asked.

"Certainly not, but I've been grouse hunting and I know what a gunshot looks like," he snapped.

"What did you do then, sir?" Witherspoon interjected quickly.

"I ran to the kitchen door and shouted for help. The servants came straightaway and someone went and fetched the police. Then Sir Donovan came out and, well, he became most upset when he saw that Mrs. Langston-Jones was dead." Montague shuddered. "I've never seen him so distressed. But then I imagine having one of your employees murdered is very upsetting."

"Did you see the gun on the path?" Barnes asked.

"No, once I knew she was dead, I couldn't look at her anymore. I stayed as far away as I could," he admitted.

"What did Sir Donovan do?"

"Do? He didn't really do anything. I think he must have been in shock. He didn't say a word, he simply knelt down and stared at her for what seemed the longest time. I'd gone over to the kitchen terrace by then but I could see he was terribly shocked."

"Did he or anyone else touch the body?" Witherspoon asked.

Montague shook his head. "No, no, he wouldn't let anyone near her. Mrs. Metcalf came out and started down the stairs, but he told her to go back. He said the police were coming and that she mustn't be touched."

Barnes looked up from his little brown notebook. "Exactly where do you live?"

"Number four Baddington Place. It's the next street over running parallel to here. I don't generally use the back door when I come to call, but as it was so foggy today and I had such a lot to do, I took a shortcut through the garden."

"So normally you'd have walked all the

33

way around the street to the front door," Barnes clarified.

"Yes." He pulled a white handkerchief out of his coat pocket and dabbed it across his forehead. "And I really wish I had done so today. I've no wish to be involved in anything as sordid as murder."

"How well did you know Mrs. Langston-Jones?" Witherspoon asked.

"I didn't know her." Montague smiled coldly. "I'm not in the habit of consorting with servants."

"She wasn't a servant." A man's voice had them all turning toward the door. "She was a well-educated woman, the widow of a renowned artist, and she was tutoring my nieces as a favor to me, so she's deserving of your respect."

Montague leapt up. "Oh, Sir Donovan, I meant no disrespect to the dear lady, I was merely trying to explain her position as it pertained to me."

"She had no position pertaining to you." He stepped into the room, his attention on the inspector. "I'm Sir Donovan Gaines." He held out his hand as he introduced himself. "Please forgive me for not addressing you when you came out onto the terrace, but I was still somewhat in a state of shock."

Witherspoon smiled sympathetically as he and Barnes stood up. He recognized him as the man who'd been sitting on the upper terrace when they'd reached the crime scene. The inspector shook hands. "I'm Inspector Gerald Witherspoon, and this is my colleague, Constable Barnes. I'm sorry to meet you under such circumstances and I quite understand how dreadful this must be for you and your household."

Sir Donovan looked to be in his midforties. He was a tall, well-built man without the tummy paunch often seen on men of his age and class. He had black hair shot with gray, brown eyes, a firm jaw, and a straight, patrician nose.

"Please, Donovan, don't be annoyed with me," Montague said. "I truly didn't mean anything untoward by my remarks."

Gaines nodded dully. "I'm sure you didn't and I'd appreciate it very much if you'd give these gentlemen your full cooperation. I want whoever did this to be caught and hung."

"Of course I'll cooperate." Montague turned to Witherspoon. "Go ahead and ask your questions."

"From your previous statements, I take it your relationship with Mrs. Langston-Jones was somewhat impersonal, correct?" the

35

inspector said.

"That's correct." Montague glanced at Gaines as he answered. "Mrs. Langston-Jones was an acquaintance only because she worked here. I had no other relationship with her."

"When you were coming through the garden, did you see anyone?"

"No one, but that's not surprising, it was so foggy I could barely see a foot in front of me," he replied.

"Tell us how you found the body," Barnes persisted.

Montague frowned. "But I've already done that . . ."

"Tell us again."

"I was walking toward the house and, well, frankly, as I said, it was so foggy, that when I saw her lying there, I was sure she'd fallen and hit her head. But then I saw the blood oozing out of her chest and I ran for the kitchen calling for help."

"Who called for fetching the police?" the inspector asked.

"I did," Montague replied. "As I said before, I know a bullet hole when I see one and I knew she'd been shot. I yelled at one of the housemaids to get the police."

"That's when I came out," Sir Donovan interjected. "I couldn't believe it when I saw

36

her lying there."

"I've told you everything I know," Montague said. "I'd like to go home now. This has been terribly upsetting."

"That's all for now, Mr. Montague," Witherspoon said. "Please leave your complete address with the constable at the front door and we'll contact you if we've any more questions."

"Of course." Montague smiled sympathetically at Sir Donovan. "Please don't think ill of me. I didn't mean any disrespect earlier when I spoke about Mrs. Langston-Jones."

"Yes, yes, I'm sure you didn't." Sir Donovan ushered him toward the door. "This has been a dreadful thing for all of us. I'll see you later, Lucius."

As soon as the door had closed behind him, Barnes looked at Witherspoon. "I'll begin taking statements from the rest of the household and organize the house to house for witnesses."

"Thank you, Constable, that would be most helpful." He didn't have to tell Barnes what he needed to do; the two men had worked together for so long they knew precisely what was required in the situation.

"If you'll give me a moment," Sir Donovan said. "I'll ask Mrs. Metcalf, the housekeeper, to prepare the butler's pantry for your use. Will that do?"

A few moments later, Barnes left to take the servants' statements and Sir Donovan was back in the sitting room. "Do sit down, Inspector. We might as well be comfortable while we talk."

Witherspoon sat back down while the other man took the spot recently vacated by Lucius Montague.

"How long has Mrs. Langston-Jones been employed in your household?" he began.

"She's been here since January. Her references were excellent and I knew her from her previous employment."

"How's that, sir?"

"Eight years ago she worked as a governess to the Furness family. They lived a few doors down from here and spoke highly of her character and her qualifications. I often used to see her in the gardens with the Furness children. When she left them, she married and moved with her husband to France."

"I heard you say he was an artist?" Witherspoon said. He'd no idea where this line of inquiry might be leading, but as Mrs. Jeffries had on many occasions encouraged him to trust his "inner voice," he decided not to concern himself with why he was asking certain questions, but just to go along with whatever popped out of his head.

"That's correct. When he passed away, Mrs. Langston-Jones and her son came back to England."

"And she contacted you for a position?" Witherspoon asked.

He hesitated. "Not exactly. I happened to meet her by chance one afternoon and she mentioned she was looking for work as a tutor. It was serendipitous as my niece and I had just decided to get her twin girls a French tutor." He smiled. "My niece and her two daughters moved in with me when my wife passed away. It worked out nicely as her husband has gone to the Far East to work."

"So your household is yourself, your niece, and your two great-nieces." Witherspoon wanted to ensure he had the facts of the matter straight.

"Not quite, my nephew also resides here."

"Your household is quite large then," the inspector commented.

"It's a very big house, Inspector, and once my wife died, I wanted company."

"Yes, I can understand that," he replied. "What are their names?"

"Neville Gaines, he's my nephew, he works for a firm of commercial estate agents in the City. His sister is Martha Gaines Barclay, and her two twins are Eugenia and Cecily."

Downstairs, Barnes had settled in the butler's pantry with the housekeeper, a red-haired woman of late middle years. "May I have your name, please." He looked up from his little brown notebook and gave her an encouraging smile.

"Anna Metcalf," she said. "I've been the housekeeper here for fifteen years."

"Did you hear or see anything around the time that Mrs. Langston-Jones was shot?" he asked bluntly.

She shook her head. "No, but one of the scullery maids said she heard a funny popping sound and that would have been just a few minutes before Mr. Montague come running in here screaming for us to get the police."

"What time was Mrs. Langston-Jones due here?" Barnes asked.

"She generally came in the afternoon." The housekeeper sighed heavily. "The lessons for the young mistresses were supposed to begin at two o'clock sharp. But the master told Mrs. Barclay at breakfast this morning that Mrs. Langston-Jones wouldn't be here until later and the lessons would begin at three o'clock. Mrs. Barclay wasn't happy about the arrangement and told him that she had planned to take the girls shopping after their French lesson, but the master said that he'd asked Mrs. Langston-Jones to do an errand for him and that Mrs. Barclay wasn't to say anything to her for the lesson being delayed."

Barnes nodded in encouragement. It was always good when people volunteered more information than you asked. "So everyone in the household knew that Mrs. Langston-Jones wasn't going to be coming at her usual time?"

She thought for a moment. "Well, I'd not say everyone knew it, but certainly Mr. Gaines and the young mistresses knew it. They were all together in the dining room. Oh, and Mr. Montague was here as well. Mrs. Barclay had invited him to breakfast."

"She'd invited him to breakfast?" He was no expert on social etiquette, but from what he knew, a breakfast invitation was generally given out for special occasions like a wedding or a trip to the country.

The housekeeper made a face. "Mrs. Barclay felt sorry for him. Mr. Montague's cook quit last week and he's hired another from a domestic agency, but he complains that she doesn't do his eggs to suit him. Mind you, I'm not sure he'll find anyone who'll put up with him. He's gone through six cooks in the past three years and word gets about, you know."

"Did Mr. Montague know Mrs. Langston-Jones? I mean other than just as an acquaintance."

"He must have, mustn't he? You don't have nasty screaming matches with casual acquaintances, do you?"

Barnes looked up from his notebook. "What do you mean?"

"I mean he pretended like she was just an employee here and would barely acknowledge her existence if he happened to see her. But he knew her from somewhere else, I'm sure of it, and he didn't like her. Last week, I overheard them having a terrible argument. They were in the library. He called her a social climbing upstart and said that she was a fool to think anyone would accept it. She shouted back that he ought to mind his own business and that if he were any kind of gentleman, he'd pay what he owed and be done with it. He got really angry then and told her that if she repeated such things, he'd make her sorry she was ever born." She broke off and leaned toward the constable. "Looks like he kept his word, doesn't it."

CHAPTER 2

Amanda Belle didn't wake up as Betsy settled onto the chair between Luty Belle Crookshank and Mrs. Goodge. It wasn't her usual place at the table, but she wanted to give both godmothers equal access to the baby.

"Oh dear, is our meeting going to wake her up?" The cook looked at the sleeping child, her face creased in worry. "My darling needs her nap. Shall we put her in her cot? I'll make sure Samson isn't in there." Mrs. Goodge had bought an infant's bed from Liberty's Department Store when she'd become godmother to Amanda. When Wiggins had first put it up, Samson, whom the rest of the household considered the world's nastiest cat, frequently tried to sleep in it but had lately been thwarted by Smythe tying a fitted piece of heavy cloth over the top so the animal couldn't reach it.

Betsy shook her head. "She'll be fine on

my lap. I'm hoping we do wake her up —
otherwise she'll be up all night. This is her
third nap today."

"I can hold her if you want," Luty Belle
offered. "That'll wake her up."

"Madam, Miss Betsy has said she's fine
where she is," Hatchet, Luty's butler,
interjected. "And it's getting late and we
must get on with the meeting. You've an
engagement this evening and you'll need
time to get back to Knightsbridge and
change into something more formal."

"Oh, alright," Luty said reluctantly. She
was an elderly white-haired American with
more money than most of the crowned
heads of Europe. But despite her advanced
years, her mind and her tongue were both
razor sharp. She wore a bright red day dress
trimmed with black lace on the high color
and cuffs. Black onyx earrings hung from
her lobes, and a triple strand of pearls
dangled around her neck. Practical and
plainspoken, her wealth and colorful person-
ality gave her access to bankers, aristocrats,
captains of industry, and most members of
the Prime Minister's current cabinet. Using
a combination of charm, intelligence, cun-
ning, guile, and sheer bravado, she used her
considerable resources to ferret out all manner of information about victims and sus-

pects. "Who got murdered?"

"A woman named Ellen Langston-Jones," Mrs. Jeffries said. "It happened this afternoon. Smythe was speaking with Constable Evans at the fixed point on Clarendon Road when a housemaid raised the alarm." She told them the rest of what they knew thus far. "Smythe and Wiggins have gone back to the area to see if they can find out anything else," she finished.

"Sir Donovan Gaines," Ruth repeated, her expression thoughtful. "I've heard that name before, I'm sure of it." An attractive slender blonde of late middle years, she was the widow of a peer. She'd been brought up in a country parsonage by a vicar who raised his daughter to take Christ's admonition to love her neighbor seriously. Consequently, she fed the poor, clothed the naked, and gave comfort to the oppressed. A firm believer that all souls were equal in the sight of the Almighty; she insisted the household call her Ruth when they were together. She was, however, sensitive to the fact that none of them would be comfortable using her Christian name in front of outsiders; in which case, they addressed her by her title. She worked tirelessly for the rights of women and held back on the more radical aspects of the cause only to avoid embarrassing Gerald Witherspoon. It would upset him greatly if he were forced to arrest her for chaining herself to a railing in front of Parliament. "Yes, yes, that's right. I met him at a luncheon for the Orphans' Hospital in Hammersmith. His late wife was on the Board of Governors. He's a widower and rumored to be very, very wealthy. Now that the mourning period for Lady Gaines is past, he's considered very eligible."

"How did his wife die?" Mrs. Jeffries asked.

"I think it was cancer," Ruth replied. "I can't recall the specifics, but she was ill for a long time before she passed away."

Mrs. Goodge tapped her finger on the table. "That name sounds familiar to me, too, but I can't quite place where I've heard it."

"Don't worry." Betsy shifted the sleeping baby. "It'll come to you soon." She glanced at the housekeeper. "And we're sure the victim was shot?"

"That's what Smythe said," the housekeeper replied.

"And that's not the sort of fact he'd get wrong, but it is curious, isn't it. If she was shot, then the murderer was taking an awful risk. The killing took place in the middle of the day and guns, even small ones, make a lot of noise."

Mrs. Jeffries frowned. "True, but some murderers plan their crime carefully. Perhaps the shot was timed to coincide with some other loud noise in the environment."

"You mean they'd pull the trigger just as a church bell tolls or a foghorn blasts or a factory whistle blows?" Phyllis said.

"That's precisely what I mean," Mrs. Jeffries replied.

"We've had one or possibly two murders where that was the case," Hatchet added with a nod of his head. "So it certainly isn't out of the realm of possibility. I wonder if there's anything near Portland Villas that would make a sound loud enough to mask a gunshot."

"It'd have to be something pretty noisy," Luty said. "Like Betsy said, even a little gun like a derringer would make a racket and that's a quiet neighborhood. But wait a minute, there's a church just around the corner, so like Phyllis said, it could've been the bells."

Mrs. Jeffries could see that they were getting into the spirit of the hunt, perhaps too much so. "As we all know," she began. "Speculating is dangerous this early in the game. We've fallen into that trap before."

"Indeed we have," Hatchet agreed. "For

all we know, dozens of people could have heard the fatal shot. It's been so foggy someone could easily have eluded being seen."

"We'll know more by tomorrow," Mrs. Jeffries said. "Smythe and Wiggins should be home before long, and I'll see what I can get out of the inspector tonight."

"Does that mean you don't want us doin' anything yet?" Luty asked.

"No, no, of course not. We have enough to get started, I just didn't want us to get ahead of ourselves." Mrs. Jeffries smiled self-consciously. "I'm the worst — give me one piece of yarn and I'll knit a whole sweater before I even know what size was wanted. We should begin gathering information as soon as possible."

"Do you want me to do the shops?" Phyllis glanced at Betsy, who gave her a reassuring smile. Betsy was too busy being a mother to go "on the hunt," and Phyllis had taken over her job. She wasn't as good as her predecessor about getting shop clerks and housemaids to chat, but she did her best, and Betsy was always encouraging her and insisting she have more faith in her abilities.

"Yes, but wait until tomorrow morning," Mrs. Jeffries said. "Most of the shops near

Portland Villas will be closing by the time you reach that neighborhood. Besides, by tomorrow morning we ought to know where the victim lived, and if it's close enough to the Gaines house, you might be able to kill two birds with one stone."

"Alright." Phyllis looked at the clock on the pine sideboard and got up. "But there is one thing I can do to get a bit ahead. I'll run up and do the inspector's room. Now that he's got a murder, he'll be late home. I was going to do it tomorrow morning but I've plenty of time before supper." She nodded respectfully at Ruth, Luty, and Hatchet; gave Betsy a grin; and blew a kiss at the sleeping baby before disappearing up the back stairs.

"We've a dinner party tonight." Hatchet stood and went to the coat tree. He grabbed Luty's shawl and his shiny black top hat. "Perhaps Madam will be able to learn something useful while I have a chance to speak with the menservants in the butler's pantry. Lord Billington always sends down a bottle of something to keep us occupied, and even his bad whiskey ought to loosen a few tongues."

"Thank goodness I didn't send my regrets," Luty admitted as she stood up and pushed back from her chair. "Billington is a nice man but his dinner parties are so stuffy you want to heave a dish through the window just to get some air in the room. I'll see what I can find out tonight. Now the name of the victim was Ellen Langston-Jones and she was murdered outside of Sir Donovan Gaines' back door, right?"

"That's correct," Mrs. Jeffries confirmed. She turned to Ruth. "Are you home this evening?"

"I'm afraid so." Ruth smiled ruefully as she rose. "I've no social engagements tonight. But there's a luncheon tomorrow at Mrs. Penworthy's home — she's the recording secretary at our Women's Suffrage Alliance — so I'll have a chance to see if anyone there knows anything useful."

"I'll get notes out to some of my old colleagues," Mrs. Goodge muttered. "Them names all sound familiar so one of us should know something. The dry larder is full so there's ample supplies on hand to bake treats for my sources."

Unlike the others, the cook did her investigating without leaving the kitchen. She'd come to the household after being sacked from her previous employment for being "too old." After a lifetime of working for the rich and powerful, she'd felt it was demeaning to take a position with a policeman, but she'd needed a roof over her head so she'd taken the job. But once they'd started investigating murder, she'd changed. She no longer felt that one should stay in one's place and be grateful for the chance to work fourteen-hour days and tug their forelocks at their masters. Working for justice had given her life more meaning than she could ever have imagined. Even better, once here, she and the others had become "family," and for the first time in her life, she knew what it was like to be with people that you cared for more than you cared for yourself.

She did her part by using her vast network of old colleagues for information. She and others of her generation had cooked, cleaned, sewn, gardened, repaired, painted, and labored most of their lives in houses that weren't theirs. There were few stately homes, town houses, or mansions in England that hadn't employed someone she'd once worked with. But she didn't stop there. She also had a small army of delivery boys, laundrymen, fruit vendors, tinkers, and other tradespeople trouping through her kitchen. She loosened their tongues with tea and freshly baked treats, asking them questions and stroking their vanity to get every morsel of gossip out of each and every one of them.

It was amazing how much one could learn by talking to ordinary working people, and that was something the rich and the powerful didn't understand. If you treated those lower than you as if they were nothing more than pieces of furniture instead of humans, then there were consequences. Housemaids, tweenies, cooks, and footmen all had ears with which to hear, eyes with which to see, and mouths with which to repeat everything they'd seen or heard. Mrs. Goodge took great pride in her work, both as a cook and as an investigator in the great cause of justice. She'd become an expert at wheedling secrets out of her sources and doing it so well that they always came back for more.

Lucius Montague stared at his hostess. "Please, you've got to help me. I know that you've some sort of connection with the police and they need to understand that, despite what anyone may think, I've nothing to do with this woman's death."

Fiona Sutcliffe smiled politely at her unwelcome guest. She was a tall, slender woman closing in on late middle age. Her brown hair, dressed by her maid in an elegant coiffure, was liberally threaded with gray, and there were fine lines etched around her eyes and thin mouth. But despite her years, beneath her lavender day dress, her back was as ramrod straight as Her Majesty the Queen's and her manner just as regal.

She'd received him in her morning room and now she wished she'd taken him into the drawing room. John was due home any moment now and his appearance would save her a great deal of trouble. But her husband was a true gentleman, and once the butler told him she had a guest, he'd never think of barging into what was her private room. More's the pity. She wasn't quite sure what to do and a timely interruption might alleviate what was becoming a most uncomfortable situation.

Lucius Montague was related to the British royal family by an obscure connection with one of the Eastern European dynasties. She couldn't recall precisely how closely he was kin to Her Majesty, but she did remember some gossip about his mother being a minor princess. Socially, she couldn't afford to offend him. On the other hand, she and John had only recently managed to avoid a scandal themselves, so she wasn't sure she wished to involve herself with his troubles. "Lucius, I've no idea why you've come to me —"

"Don't be ridiculous," he interrupted. "I've already told you why I'm here. Everyone in London knows you've some influence with the police. For God's sake, you were almost arrested when that man who worked for your husband was shot."

"He wasn't 'that man.' He was John's brother-in-law as well as the deputy director at our company. Furthermore, the reason I wasn't arrested was because I'd nothing to do with his murder," she snapped. Honestly, did he think that being related to minor royalty gave him leave to be so rude?

His eyes widened and he paled visibly. "Oh dear, I've offended you, haven't I. I certainly didn't mean any—"

"You haven't offended me," she interrupted. "But I would thank you not to go about London reminding my friends and acquaintances about what was a most distressing time for myself and my family. As for any influence with the police you think I might have, then I must disabuse you of that notion immediately. The police didn't arrest me because I was completely innocent."

Panic flashed across his face. "Fiona, please, forgive me, I've handled this badly but I'm at my wit's end. I've no idea what to do."

"Find a good solicitor." She started to rise, but when she saw the tears pooling in his eyes, she relented and sat down. She'd been there herself and understood what it meant to feel so very threatened. "Oh, Lucius, you do look a right mess. Would you like a drink? I think you could use something stronger than tea." Without waiting for his response, she got up and yanked the bellpull by the door. "Will a sherry do?" she asked as the door opened and the butler appeared.

"I'd rather have a whiskey."

"Please bring in the decanter of whiskey from the drawing room and two glasses," she instructed.

"While we're waiting" — Fiona took her seat — "why don't you tell me the truth?"

"I don't know what you mean."

"Please, Lucius, if you want my help, you'll need to be honest with me. Despite your aristocratic sensibilities, merely discovering a dead body shouldn't have put you in such a state of agitation. There's a reason you think the police are going to be looking your way and I want to know what it is." She wanted to know exactly what kind of situation might result if she used what little influence she had in certain quarters. If he had anything to do with that woman's murder, Fiona would wash her hands of him and not worry one whit about the social consequences. He looked at the floor, staring hard as if he were trying to memorize the pattern on the elegant rose and green carpet. "If I tell you, will you help me?"

"I don't know," she replied. "Did you do it? Did you commit murder?"

His head jerked up. "Certainly not. How could you even think such a thing? I'm a gentleman —"

"And lots of gentlemen have killed when it suited them," she shot back. "Especially the sort that think they have a God-given right to do as they please."

"But I'm not like that!" he cried. "I'd never do such a thing . . ." He broke off as the butler returned carrying a crystal decanter and two cut-glass whiskey tumblers on a silver tray.

He put it on the small rosewood table beside the sofa. "Shall I pour, madam?"

"No, thank you, that won't be necessary," she said.

"Very good, madam." He retreated through the double doors, closing them softly.

She poured their drinks and handed one to Montague. "Alright, I'll take your word that you're innocent in this matter. That being the case, why are you so frightened of the police?"

56

He gulped his drink and then held the glass out to her. "Please, another one."

She raised her eyebrows but took his glass and poured another shot. She handed it to him. "Stop avoiding the question. I can't do you any good if I don't know what is going on here. Did you have a romantic relationship with Mrs. Langston-Jones?"

"Of course not." He sniffed disapprovingly. "She was only a French tutor, hardly the sort of person I'd be involved with, but I did know her to some extent. As a matter of fact, I had a disagreement with her last week, which is one of the reasons the police will be looking at me."

"If you had no relationship with her, how could you possibly have quarreled with the woman?" Fiona demanded. "Listen, Lucius, this is no time for you to be reticent. Tell me what happened and tell me quickly. We don't have all day. It's getting late and I need to change. We've a dinner party this evening and John hates to be late."

"Yes, alright, but this isn't easy for me. She is or was a widow and her late husband was an artist by the name of Brandon Langston-Jones."

Fiona took a sip from her glass. "I can't say that I'm familiar with the name, but go on."

He nodded. "He was an English artist, but they've lived in France for the last seven or eight years so that he could paint. Last year, I saw one of his paintings in a small gallery in Paris and I bought it. I think if the fellow hadn't died, he'd have become somewhat famous. At least that's what the count said, and he was somewhat of an expert on art."

"Yes, yes, I know all about your friendship with the Count de Mornay. What does any of this have to do with his widow being murdered on Sir Donovan's back stairs?" she asked impatiently. Lucius was a terrible name-dropper. Generally, she found it amusing, but today she was in no mood to put up with his ridiculous and exaggerated sense of self-importance.

He drew back in surprise. "I'm getting to that. Once the count mentioned that he was sure Langston-Jones' work was going to increase in value, I decided I'd buy more of it, and I did. I purchased two more paintings from the same gallery and took them back to my hotel. I was going to pay for them the following week when my letter of credit arrived by post from my bank."

"You mean they let you walk out of the gallery with the paintings?"

"The count vouched for me." He took

58

another gulp from his glass. "In some circles, my name and background still mean something. But that's beside the point. The paintings were expensive and I intended to make good on the debt when it was convenient for me. Unfortunately, by the time I had my financial matters in hand, I got a telegram from my uncle in Budapest about my late mother's estate. I had to go there straightaway."

"So you paid the gallery at a later time?" she ventured. She suspected she knew exactly why there had been words between the deceased and her friend.

"I meant to, of course, but the incident was of such small consequence, that I'm afraid I forgot all about it. Mama was of royal blood, you know, and I couldn't neglect settling her estate properly."

"You never paid them what you owed?"

He had the good grace to look embarrassed. "I'd not put it quite like that. As I said, it was a small incident in my life. Mama's affairs took me across the continent, and even in these modern times, that's not an easy journey. I was there for months haggling with lawyers. You know how long I was gone. I didn't get back until April. The fact that I'd not paid the gallery for those wretched paintings simply slipped my mind."

"But it didn't slip her mind, did it," Fiona guessed.

He sighed, sat back, and closed his eyes. "No, it most certainly didn't."

"And because you'd not paid the gallery, they hadn't paid her."

"I imagine it went something like that." He took another drink.

"When you returned from the continent, you must have been surprised to find her employed at the house just across the garden from you," she said softly.

"Oh yes, very much so." He laughed harshly. "When I saw her, I was stunned. She was with Sir Donovan's two nieces. Apparently they were having a lesson as she was pointing out all the trees and bushes and identifying them in French."

"I take it she saw you as well."

"That she did," he replied. "She didn't approach me or anything like that. She came around later that afternoon to my home and demanded payment."

"Why didn't you explain what had happened and arrange to take care of it right then?" Fiona asked. "Surely that would be the simplest way of handling the matter."

He looked down at the floor again. "Be-

60

cause I didn't have the money," he admitted. "So I asked if she'd give me some time to get my finances in order. I told her I was just back in town and that my cash reserves were low. She agreed and said she'd give me until June fifteenth. Unfortunately, some of my investments haven't done as well as I'd hope, and even by our agreed-upon date, I couldn't raise the money."

"If you were having financial difficulties —"

"That's not the case here," he interrupted. "I'm simply a bit behind in selling off some stocks."

"Well, whatever your reasons, why didn't you give her back the paintings?" Fiona asked. She wasn't sure what to make of this. Lucius was supposedly a very wealthy man and the paintings in question weren't Rembrandts or Botticellis.

"I couldn't." He shrugged. "I'd already sold them. As a matter of fact, I sold them as soon as I acquired them. I needed money to finance my journey to Budapest."

"Oh dear God, I must go, Inspector." Sir Donovan leapt to his feet. "Forgive me, sir, but I must go. Mrs. Langston-Jones has a seven-year-old son. He'll be home by now and worried about his mother. I've got to

61

tell him what happened."

Witherspoon was puzzled. "Excuse me, sir, but isn't that the sort of news that is best delivered by a relative of the deceased?"

Gaines shook his head and headed toward the closed double doors. "No, I must do it. Her relations live in Dorset and Mrs. Langston-Jones wasn't close with any of them. They were somewhat estranged. I'm sorry, Inspector, but I really must go. I'll bring the boy back here with me. I don't want him alone at a time like this. You can finish interviewing me either later this evening or tomorrow morning. I'll put myself completely at your disposal." With that, he pulled open the door and disappeared.

Witherspoon wasn't sure what to make of this development. By Sir Donovan's own admission, Mrs. Langston-Jones hadn't been in his employ for a long period of time, yet he seemed to know where she lived and that she didn't get along with her family. It also seemed strange that he was taking it upon himself to break what must be awful news to a child. Why? And why bring the boy back here? Did Gaines feel guilty about something? The inspector stopped himself. He mustn't speculate at this stage in the investigation. Besides, it was quite possible that Sir Donovan Gaines felt sorry for the lad. Perhaps he was simply a decent man doing the decent thing.

The butler stuck his head into the room. "Pardon me, Inspector, but Sir Donovan wanted me to ask whom you'd like to speak with next? Both Mr. Neville Gaines and Mrs. Barclay are available."

"Mrs. Barclay, please," he replied.

"Very good, sir."

Witherspoon studied his surroundings while he waited. You could learn much about a person by the way their home was furnished. He spotted a stack of magazines lying in an oval brass basket next to a balloon-backed green velvet chair. The walls were papered in a pale cream with a gold and green pattern of entwined leaves. Fringed fabrics of deep green and lavender draped the tops of curio chests and book-cases, and a glass-fronted rosewood cabinet housed an eclectic collection of interesting objects. Witherspoon got up and crossed the room for a closer look. An ancient pair of eyeglasses, a very old book, and an antique blue cobalt snuffbox were on the top shelf. The center shelf held a carved marble chess set, and on the bottom shelf stood two green, gold, and red Chinese vases.

"I understand you wanted to speak with me," a woman's voice said. "I'm Mrs. Barclay."

Witherspoon whirled around. He'd been concentrating so hard he'd not heard the door open. He smiled politely. Brownhaired, of medium height, slender, and with ordinary features, she appeared to be in her early thirties. "Yes, ma'am, I'm afraid I must. I'm Inspector Gerald Witherspoon. Your uncle very kindly offered this room for my use. Would you like to sit down? This may take a few moments."

"I don't see why it should. I know nothing about what's happened here." She moved to the settee and took the spot her uncle had relinquished only moments earlier.

"I understand that Mrs. Langston-Jones tutored your daughters in French." He took the chair across from her.

"That's correct. She came Monday through Friday at two in the afternoon." She crossed her arms over her chest. "Except for today. Uncle Donovan sent her to do an errand. He informed me at breakfast that she wouldn't be here until three o'clock. It was most inconvenient. I'd planned to take my daughters shopping. Cicely and Eugenia go to St. Catherine's

Day School for Young Ladies until noon each day. St. Catherine's offers French classes, of course, but Uncle Donovan insisted they have a private tutor and so Mrs. Langston-Jones was engaged."

"What kind of errand was it?"

"He sent her to a bookstore." She gave a sour smile. "He said he wanted her to pick out some volumes on art history for the library. I don't know why he thought she was capable of such a task; it was her late husband who was the artist."

"Which bookstore was it?" he asked. He watched Mrs. Barclay closely, trying to determine whether she had disliked the victim, or whether she was simply a snob.

"Macklin's on Charing Cross Road."

"How long had Mrs. Langston-Jones been employed here?"

"She came just after Christmas. One day Uncle Donovan popped into the drawing room and announced he'd hired her to be the girls' tutor."

"He didn't consult you before engaging Mrs. Langston-Jones' services?" Witherspoon asked.

She stared at him coldly. "Of course he consulted me. He'd told me that he wanted to get them private tutoring, but at the time she was hired, I wasn't aware he'd moved so quickly with the plan, that's all. Uncle Donovan leaves the rearing of my children to me."

"I see," he said. "How long have you been living here?"

"What's that got to do with anything?" she asked. "My personal situation has nothing whatsoever to do with Mrs. Langston-Jones and most certainly not with her murder."

"It's a routine question," he replied. "We like to get a clear picture of how a household is run if a murder has occurred on the premises."

"We came a little over a year ago. It was the middle of May, right after Lady Gaines passed away. My husband's company sent him to Malaysia, and he wanted me and the girls to stay here," she explained. "The climate there is dreadful, and Patrick and I didn't think it would be healthy. I simply cannot stand heat, and as you know, it's always warm there."

"So your husband is far away. That must be very hard for you."

She gave him a tight smile. "We write, of course, and he was here for two weeks at Christmas. Inspector, what does my situation have to do with this matter? Patrick doesn't even know Mrs. Langston-Jones.

He left before she came here."

"As I said, ma'am, I'm simply trying to understand how the household runs," he said. "Where were you earlier this afternoon?"

"You mean at the time of the murder?" She laughed. "I was here, Inspector. I was upstairs in my room having a rest. I often rest after lunch."

"And where is your room? Does it overlook the back stairs or the communal garden?"

"No, it's in the front so I neither heard nor saw anything." The ornate clock on the mantelpiece chimed and she turned to look at it. "Inspector, is this likely to take much longer? I've an engagement and I'd like to get ready."

"It'll not be much longer," he promised. "Was there anyone in the household that disliked Mrs. Langston-Jones?"

She shrugged. "None of the family is likely to have had a personal relationship with the woman. She was, after all, the hired help. As to whether or not any of the servants disliked her, you'll have to ask them."

"What about your daughters? Did they have an opinion about their tutor?" he pressed.

"She was their teacher and I assume they

liked her well enough." She started to get up.

"I'll need to speak to them," he said.

"You'll do no such thing." She flopped back down, giving him a good glare. "I'll not have my children upset about this matter."

"They were home, weren't they?" he continued. "They might have seen or heard something or someone. I presume they do look out the window or go out into the garden."

"They were in their room when it happened," she snapped. "And furthermore, I don't see why our household should be inconvenienced just because Mrs. Langston-Jones has got herself murdered."

Her attitude didn't surprise him; this was usually the way the upper class reacted when faced with something completely outside of their control. "I'm certain the victim had no wish to be murdered, Mrs. Barclay." He paused and gave her the briefest of smiles. "Even the hired help love life, ma'am, and I understand she has a young son. I'm sure she would have wanted to be here and see him raised to manhood."

Witherspoon was generally predisposed to be very gentle with the fairer sex, but her attitude about the murder victim annoyed him greatly.

She flushed and looked away. "Forgive me, Inspector. That was most unkind. I didn't mean to imply that I wasn't sorry Mrs. Langston-Jones was killed. As you say, she had a child. I'm sure losing his mother will be awful for the lad. But this is a very upsetting event. It's not the sort of thing that happens to people like us."

"I assure you, madam, it does," he countered. "But I do understand that this must be very difficult for you. Do you know of anyone who might have wanted to harm the victim?"

She shook her head. "No, but I know very little about her, as I've already explained. My uncle hired her to tutor my daughters."

"Didn't she have references?"

"According to my uncle, she did."

"You didn't check them?"

She sighed. "No, I did not. Why should I? I trusted my uncle's judgment implicitly. He's a good and generous soul who very kindly offered his home to us when Patrick took the post overseas. What's more, Mrs. Langston-Jones spoke French fluently. Of that I was certain."

"You speak French yourself?" he asked.

"No, but when she came for the interview, Mrs. Linthorp, she's a friend of the family, was here for tea. She does speak French. They conversed for a good half hour, and when Mrs. Langston-Jones had gone, Hester informed me that her command of the language was excellent. Besides, years earlier Mrs. Langston-Jones had been a governess to the Furness family." She pointed to her left. "They're our neighbors and they spoke highly of her character. That's why I felt no need to check her references, though perhaps, considering what has happened, I was remiss in my duties."

"What do you mean by that?" he asked.

"Isn't it obvious, Inspector." She gave a delicate, lady-like snort of derision. "The woman was married to an artist and everyone knows what they're like. She was probably killed by one of her husband's wild-eyed bohemian friends."

Downstairs, Barnes smiled at the young woman who stood in the doorway. She was a slender blonde with a thin face, blue eyes, and a largish nose. She was visibly nervous as she crossed the narrow space and eased into the spot just vacated by the housekeeper.

"What's your name?" he asked kindly.

"I'm Susan Carey, sir, the downstairs maid." She clenched her hands together on the tabletop and bit her lower lip. "I don't know what I can tell you, sir. I was cleanin' the master's study when poor Mrs. Langston-Jones was done in."

"I know it's hard to understand why we need to question you, but it's important that we know as much as possible about her and this household," he said gently. The poor girl looked as if she were going to burst out crying. "There's no reason to be frightened or upset. You're not being accused of anything."

She unclenched her hands, took a deep breath, and stiffened her spine. "You're right, sir. Mrs. Langston-Jones was always good to me and I liked her. The least I can do is help a bit in findin' the one who killed her. She didn't deserve to die like that."

"No, she didn't," Barnes agreed. "Was there anyone in the household that didn't like her?"

"We all liked her," she blurted out. "I mean, us servants. Like I said, she was always good to me and the other girls. She always treated us decent like and spoke to us like we weren't stupid. When she found out that Alma, she's the upstairs maid, liked to draw, she gave her a box of drawing pencils and a paper tablet. Alma was ever so grateful, she even offered to pay for them, but Mrs. Langston-Jones wouldn't let her.

She said they'd belonged to her late husband and he'd have wanted someone to use them."

"But there was someone in the house that didn't like her, wasn't there," he pressed.

An expression of panic flashed over her face as he spoke, and Barnes realized her earlier burst of courage had faded.

"Oh, sir, I don't know that I'd like to say such a thing. I shouldn't have put it like I did." She glanced over her shoulder at the closed pantry door.

He knew what had her so worried. "I'll not repeat what you tell me to your employer," he assured her. "You have my word that I won't."

She stared at him long and hard, as though she were trying to decide whether he could be trusted. Finally, she shrugged and said, "Mrs. Barclay didn't like her and Mr. Neville claimed he had nothing against her, but he was lyin'. Both of them were always finding fault with every little thing she did. Then they'd go runnin' to the master, trying to make trouble for her."

"In what way?"

"Well, Mrs. Langston-Jones didn't always use the schoolroom to teach the young mistresses. Sometimes she took them out to the high street and had them repeat everything they saw in French, and she did the same thing belowstairs. She'd bring them down to the kitchen and dry larder when the groceries come in and point to the meat and vegetables and teach them the French words. She'd do the same out in the garden."

"That sounds like a very reasonable way to teach another language," he murmured. "But I take it Mrs. Barclay objected."

"She did indeed. She said Mrs. Langston-Jones didn't know the first thing about teaching another language and that a proper tutor would use the schoolroom upstairs for lessons. But the master simply called the girls in and started speaking to them in French, and before you knew it, they was chattering like magpies. Then the master said to Mrs. Barclay that Mrs. Langston-Jones had only been here a few months and already the young mistresses were doing ever so much better so her methods must be working."

"Did you witness this incident directly?" he asked.

"Yes sir, I was taking up the rugs from the hallway in front of the drawing room. The door was wide open and I could hear and see everything. Mrs. Barclay wasn't happy when the master had them girls chattin'

73

away, but there weren't much she could say, was there?"

"Perhaps she resented Sir Donovan's interference in her daughters' education?" he pressed.

She shook her head. "No, sir, she was always runnin' to the master and asking his opinion about every little thing when it come to the young mistresses. Like I said before, she just didn't like Mrs. Langston-Jones. She was always making unkind remarks about her hair and how she dressed and the fact that she only had one pair of shoes. When that Mr. Montague or Mrs. Linthorp was here, she gossiped about the poor woman something terrible, but mind you, she watched her tongue in front of the master."

"She spoke to Mr. Montague about Mrs. Langston-Jones," he said, hoping to lead her in the direction he wanted her to go.

"Indeed she did, sir." Susan leaned closer. "And Mr. Montague gossiped worse than an old woman. What's more, sir, he didn't like Mrs. Langston-Jones, either. You should have seen his face when he first caught a glimpse of her out in the garden with the young mistresses. I was cleaning the foyer when he come burstin' in, demanding to speak to Mrs. Barclay. Well, she came flying

74

downstairs wondering what on earth he was on about."

"What did Mr. Montague say?"

"He asked Mrs. Barclay what 'that woman' was doing with her daughters and Mrs. Barclay replied that she was the new French tutor. Right then they noticed me so the mistress took him into the small sitting room and shut the door. But they were in there together for a good half hour."

"Have you ever heard Mr. Montague have words with Mrs. Langston-Jones?"

"You mean like an argument?"

"That's right, have you ever seen them quarrel?"

"I've heard him shoutin' at her," she said. "Just the other day."

"Where were they when you overheard them?"

"Out in the garden, sir. It was my afternoon out so I was using the back gate as a shortcut. They was standing in the center by the bench with their backs to me. That's when I overheard them goin' at each other like cats and dogs."

Barnes was silent for a moment. Anna Metcalf stated that she had overheard the victim and Montague having heated words in the library but the argument Susan overheard had taken place outside in the garden. Had Montague had two separate rows with Ellen Langston-Jones within a few days? If so, that meant the man was lying his head off. "Were you able to hear what they were saying?"

"You mean what were they squabbling about?" She laughed. "Oh yes, I slowed right down because I didn't want to miss any of it. I ducked down behind a hedge so they wouldn't see me."

Barnes' eyes narrowed. He hoped she was telling the truth here and not exaggerating. "You don't care for Mr. Montague, do you?"

"None of us do, sir," she admitted. "He's always finding fault and pointing out our mistakes. He's here all the time, and if there's so much as a smudge of dirt on the banister or a chair railing, he's making sure Mrs. Metcalf or, even worse, Mrs. Barclay takes note of it. But I'm not tellin' tales just because I don't like the man. I wouldn't lie, sir, I'm a Presbyterian and I go to church every Sunday. I did overhear them goin' at it the other day. I'm not makin' it up."

"There, there, lass, I'm sure you're tellin' the truth," he soothed quickly. "Go on, then, finish telling me what you heard."

"I don't remember the exact words —"

"Just do the best you can," he interrupted. She rubbed her chin. "Mrs. Langston-

Jones said she was tired of waiting and that she'd give him another week and then she was goin' to take legal action. She said she'd already engaged a solicitor and all he was waiting for was for her to tell him to file the papers at the court."

"And what did Montague say?"

"At first he didn't say anything and I was afraid he'd gone, so I peeked over the hedge, but he was still there. He was just staring at her with his mouth hanging open. It was like he was shocked or something. Finally, he said she had no grounds for a court case because she couldn't prove anything and she snapped right back that she could prove she was the legal owner because he'd never paid the gallery. He started blusterin' that he'd hire a solicitor as well but she interrupted him and said that she was tired of givin' him chances. That he was rude and nasty, and instead of the money he owed, she wanted the paintings back." She paused and took a breath. "That's when he shouted that he'd see her dead and in hell before she got anything from him."

CHAPTER 3

Smythe stepped through the door of the Twin Ravens. Noisy and crowded, it was a good working-class pub and the one closest to the Gaines home. Footmen jostled shop clerks for a spot at the bar, empty baskets belonging to a trio of bread sellers sitting at the table closest to the fireplace were stacked haphazardly on the hearth, and along the walls, the benches were fully occupied. People with glasses of gin and beer huddled together as they laughed and talked.

"This might not be a good idea," Smythe yelled to make himself heard over the babble of voices. "Bloomin' Ada, they're packed so tight in 'ere, we won't get close enough to 'ear any gossip."

"Let's try anyway," Wiggins shouted as he pulled the door shut. "I don't want to go back without learnin' somethin' and we've not 'ad much luck so far."

Smythe nodded. "You'd 'ave thought one of them neighbors 'angin' about and gawkin' at the police would have heard somethin' useful." He started toward the bar.

There had been plenty of locals hanging about the street in front of the murder house, but none of them knew anything Smythe and Wiggins hadn't already heard. To top it off, they'd almost been seen by Constable Griffiths from the Ladbroke Road Station. He knew them. They'd had to duck and run before either of them could get close enough to identify the police surgeon that Griffiths was escorting through the front door. It was too risky to stay near the Gaines house; there were too many constables who knew them by sight. So they'd decided their best bet was a local pub. Murder was always the kind of news that traveled fast in any neighborhood.

Wiggins was right on Smythe's heels as the crowd parted for the big man. When they reached the bar, the coachman wedged himself into a tiny space at the end, turned, and craned his neck, scanning the area. But the people standing about were planted like oak trees, the bread sellers looked like they were going to be nattering till last orders were called, and no one had vacated any spots on the benches.

He leaned close to the footman's ear. "Let's try somewhere else. We're not goin' to find out anything 'ere. None of this lot is in any 'urry to leave." Annoyed, Smythe glared at the crowd. They'd gotten a fast start on this case and it was ruddy irritating to be held at the gate now just because the blooming pub was too crowded to have a decent conversation.

"Give it a minute," Wiggins replied, his attention fixed on the door. Just then it opened and a bearded fellow wearing the heavy greatcoat of a hansom driver stepped inside. The cabbie stood there for a moment, his gaze flicking along the people at the bar. He suddenly moved, elbowing his way through the crowd and stopping at the far end. He spoke to two men, and a few seconds later, all three of them headed for the door.

"There's a spot." Wiggins lunged toward the empty space.

The barman, who'd been corking a keg, shifted toward Smythe. "What'll you have?"

"Two pints, please, but we'll 'ave 'em down there." Smythe pointed to the left as he hurried after the footman.

Wiggins flattened himself against the wooden railing, taking up as much space as he dared. The elderly gent on the very end gave him a quick glance, and Wiggins, mindful that they were on the hunt, nodded respectfully. Smythe eased in on his other side but there wasn't enough space for his broad shoulders and he bumped the arm of the woman next to him.

"Watch what you're doing!" she cried. "You've spilled my drink."

Smythe smiled apologetically. "Beggin' your pardon, ma'am. I'm not generally so clumsy. Please let me buy you another."

Her eyes narrowed as she looked him up and down before nodding in agreement. "Seein' as you've spilled half of mine, that's only fair."

"Sorry, ma'am, sometimes I forget how big I am," he said. She was past her youth and had a face that had once been pretty but was now worn out from a hard life and too much gin. The barman put their pints on the counter and Smythe handed him the coins he'd taken out of his pocket. "Another drink for the lady, please."

"Ta." He took the money, then reached under the counter and pulled out a bottle of gin. She drained her glass and shoved it toward him.

"Here you go, Maggie." He poured her another one. "Don't drink it all in one gulp."

She laughed as he moved off to serve someone else. She lifted her glass to Smythe. "Ta, you're a nice one, aren't ya. You've done right by me."

He lifted his beer and inclined his head. "It was the least I could do. I'm not generally so bad mannered as to spill a lady's drink. Forgive me." He could pile it on when he had to, and as the publican had known her name, that meant she was a regular here. She might know something so he wanted her happy, willing to chat but not so drunk that she didn't make any sense.

She eyed him warily. "I've not seen you in here before."

Smythe took a quick sip from his glass to buy a bit of time. He cocked his ear toward Wiggins, trying to hear what was being said. The lad was having quite a chat with the older fellow on his other side and it wouldn't do to give out differing stories.

Wiggins, who'd glanced over and noted that the coachman was eavesdropping, raised his voice. "My newspaper sent us 'round here. They don't know that it's much of a story, but they wanted to be the first to get the goods, if you know what I mean."

"You're a clever one, aren't ya." Smythe grinned broadly, and Maggie, thinking he was flirting, smiled and fluttered her eyelashes. "You've not seen me 'round 'ere," he said, "because I've never been 'ere before."

"What brings you here now?"

He jerked his thumb toward Wiggins, who was still talking excitedly with the elderly gentleman. "I'm with 'im. 'Is newspaper sent 'im when they found out there'd been murder done here."

"You mean that tutor from that toff house on Portland Villas?"

"So you've heard about it."

"Don't be daft. 'Course I've heard. News travels fast 'round here and I've got a lot of friends."

Smythe held her gaze as he debated his next move. He was a married man and he loved his wife more than his own life, but he needed information, and as long as he flirted a bit, he sensed Miss Maggie here would keep on talking. "A woman like you always 'as a lot of friends."

Delighted, she laughed and took another sip of her drink. "Oh, go on with you."

He jerked his thumb toward Wiggins. " 'Is guv sent 'im to get the facts of the case before the other papers find out what's what."

"What do you do then, carry his pencil case?" She laughed heartily at her own wit.

"Nah, 'e carries 'is own pencils, I'm

the . . ." He allowed himself a wicked grin. "What you'd call the muscle. 'E's a right handy one with words, but not so good with 'is fists, if you get my meanin'."

She chuckled. "This is a good neighborhood. I don't think he'll be needing your services. But then again . . ." She suddenly sobered. "That poor woman didn't expect to get killed so I guess it's not as safe as I thought."

"We 'eard she were shot in the private garden," he ventured.

"She was, but with so many houses round the garden, there's lots that has keys and can get in."

"But I thought them communal gardens only give out one key to each household," he said. That was what happened at Upper Edmonton Gardens, and furthermore, each year every householder had to produce his key to the garden committee to ensure they'd not lost it or passed it along to anyone else.

"That's generally true, but on Carleigh Road, two or three of them houses has been converted into flats, and my sister, she's the housekeeper for Mr. Chapman, the gentleman who owns two of them converted properties, she says that he's had duplicate keys made and gives them out to all the tenants of the flats." She took another sip. "Now I ask you, if you give keys out to anyone who can rent a room, you've got no control on who comes and goes, do you."

"That's what it sounds like." He leaned closer. "Did you know the dead lady?"

She gave a negative shake of her head. " 'Fraid not. The only thing I know about her was that she'd not been in London long. I only know that because I overheard the clerk at the chemist's talkin' about her."

"Which chemist?" he asked quickly.

"The one on Clarendon Road." She drained her glass, cocked her head to one side, and grinned coquettishly. "Buy me another, then."

"It'd be my pleasure." Smythe kept his smile firmly in place and sincerely hoped that Wiggins was having an easier time than he was.

"I thought you ought to see this before I took it to the station, sir." Constable Griffiths stepped into the room. He carried the wooden evidence box.

Witherspoon waved him closer. He was glad to have a break from taking statements. Truth was, he had a bit of a headache. "What have you got in there?"

"You've already seen it, sir." Griffiths put

the box down on the table. "It's the gun." He reached in and picked it up. Handling it carefully, he held it toward his superior and tilted the weapon so that the base was in Witherspoon's line of sight. "If you'll look closely at the bottom of the handle, there's a small 'LM' etched in gold. The engraving is so ornate that the initials are easy to miss, sir."

"Gracious, Constable, you're right. How very clever of you to have noticed this."

Delighted, Griffiths grinned. "It wasn't so much cleverness, sir, as it was experience. When I first joined the force, I was on a burglary case and one of the objects stolen was a gun like this, a Beaumont Adams. When it was recovered, we were able to identify it because the owner's initials had been engraved on the bottom, just like this one."

"This is done by the manufacturer?"

"Yes, sir. It's not standard on all of them. They charge extra for it, but if you're willin' to pay, they'll not just give you a fancy firearm with golden curlicues, they'll do initials as well. Whenever I see a gun like this, I always check the bottom." He shook his head. "The rich do like putting their names and initials on everything, don't they, sir."

"Yes, I think they must." Witherspoon thought for a moment. "LM," he muttered. There was only one person he could recall that had those initials. "Can you check with the police constable on the door and get me the exact address of Lucius Montague."

"Yes sir." He started for the door.

"Wait a moment, what's this?" The inspector reached into the box and pulled out a small pillow. It was upholstered in green with a darker green fleur-de-lis pattern on the fabric and had tufts of stuffing poking out of a rip in the middle.

"It's a cushion. One of the lads found it under a bush across the garden." He stepped closer and pointed to the center. "Look closely, sir. That's a hole."

Witherspoon held it up and poked his finger through the opening. "It goes all the way through."

"And there's a strong smell of gunpowder as well," Griffiths continued.

He put it up to his nose and sniffed. "Indeed there is," he muttered. He thought for a moment. "This might have been used to muffle the sound of the gun being fired. There was an article about it last month in the *Policeman's Gazette*. Apparently, many criminals have come up with a variety of methods to stifle the noise of a weapon being fired. The examples from America were especially interesting. Someone in Texas stuck an ear of corn on the end of the barrel but the article didn't mention whether it actually worked."

"They seem to have a lot of guns over there."

"I believe it's in their constitution."

"I'll just check on that address, sir."

"Exactly where was this found?" Witherspoon called just as the constable reached the door.

"By the houses along Babbington Place, directly across the garden. Constable Clutter noticed it sticking out of a hedge, sir."

Witherspoon frowned at the evidence box. Why on earth had the killer left the murder weapon by the body but then disposed of the cushion he'd used to muffle the sound of the shot? How did that make any sense?

Constable Griffiths returned. "Sir, it appears that Mr. Montague didn't do as you requested. Constable White reports that he didn't come out the front door, sir." His bony face broke into a broad grin. "But not to worry, the housekeeper was in the foyer and overheard me. She gave us his address. He lives just across the garden, sir, right behind where the pillow was found at number four Babbington Place."

"Good, they're back," Betsy said as she heard the back door open. Fred scrambled to his feet and raced down the hall. She and Mrs. Goodge were in the kitchen. The cook was putting the finishing touches onto a joint of roast beef and Betsy was peeling potatoes. Even though she no longer worked for the inspector, Betsy was determined to help. Both Mrs. Jeffries and Phyllis were upstairs tending to the housekeeping and she'd decided to do her part. "It's getting late and I was starting to worry that something had happened."

"We need to get you out and about." Mrs. Goodge gave the pepper grinder one last twist. "Stayin' in with the baby has set you to worryin' too much. You know good and well that both our lads can take care of themselves."

"I know." Betsy giggled. "But I still worry and so do you. I saw you sneaking glances at the clock."

"Who's been sneakin' glances at the clock?" Smythe asked as he and Wiggins came into the kitchen. Fred was dogging their heels. "What on earth could possibly 'appen to two grown men out on the 'unt?"

He stopped and grinned at his wife. He never tired of the sight of her. "Where's our daughter?"

"She's in her cot having another sleep," Mrs. Goodge said. "And before you raise a fuss like your wife here did and claim she'll be awake all night, I'll tell you what I know. I may not have had children myself, but I know that when they're teething, they need a lot of rest so I'll thank you not to wake her. My poor lambkins is hurting."

Betsy smiled and looked at her husband. Honestly, she'd never have thought that the cook, a horrible snob when she'd first come to Upper Edmonton Gardens, would take such delight in being godparent to the child of a housemaid and coachman.

Smythe winked at his wife. He'd looked forward to holding the baby, but as a wise man, he held his tongue. "Right, then, we'll let the little one sleep. Where's Mrs. Jeffries and Phyllis?"

"They're upstairs. Phyllis is cleaning the inspector's room and Mrs. Jeffries is turning out the drawing room," Betsy said. "They wouldn't let me help."

"They want to get everything shipshape and Bristol fashion before we get too involved in the hunt." Mrs. Goodge put a sheet of brown paper over her roast and tucked it underneath the edge of the platter. She grabbed a clean tea towel from the counter and draped it on top of the paper. "There, that should keep this warm until the inspector gets home."

"It's not quite shipshape yet, but we're well ahead of the game," Mrs. Jeffries said as she hurried into the kitchen. "But we really must have our meeting. Phyllis will be down in a moment; she's almost finished."

"But we're not supposed to have a proper meeting until tomorrow," Betsy protested. As someone who was now relegated to the sidelines, she was somewhat sympathetic to how it felt to be left out. "That's what we agreed."

"Don't worry about that, love. There's not that much to tell," her husband muttered as he pulled out his chair.

"It's not a proper meeting, Betsy." Mrs. Jeffries gazed at her with sympathy. She understood how Betsy felt.

"But we don't want anyone to feel left out." She slipped into the seat next to her husband. "That wouldn't be fair."

"I agree but there's no reason we can't find out a few bits and pieces if they're available. We'll make sure the others are told tomorrow."

"I suppose so," Betsy muttered. "It's

justice we need to be concerned about, not people feeling like they've been pushed to the side."

"You've not been pushed to the side," Wiggins protested. "You've 'ad Amanda Belle and you need to take care of the lass. That's right important."

"That's true," Betsy agreed. She knew she was being overly sensitive. She wasn't a disgraced child sitting with her nose in the corner. She'd made the decision herself to step back and let the others take on her tasks. "And just because I don't get out and about much anymore doesn't mean I can't contribute."

Smythe grabbed his wife's hand and gave it a squeeze. "You do your fair share, my love."

" 'Course you do, Betsy, especially at our meetings," Wiggins added. "Sometimes you point out things the rest of us, even Mrs. Jeffries, 'as missed."

Everyone, even Mrs. Jeffries, laughed.

Footsteps thumped down the stairs and Phyllis raced into the kitchen. "Sorry I'm late down," she apologized as she sat down. "But there was a bit more dust up there than I'd thought. Honestly, I don't know where it all comes from. We give all the rooms a thorough clean every week."

The housekeeper looked at Smythe. "Now, what did you find out?" she asked.

"Not enough to shake a stick at," he admitted. "The only bit we 'eard from the people 'anging about the Gaines house was what we already knew. But when we moved on, Wiggins had a bit of luck."

"You mean no one had any gossip or tidbits about the Gaines family?" Mrs. Goodge demanded, her expression incredulous. "That's hard to believe."

"But it's true. Mind you, we weren't there very long. We were almost spotted by Constable Griffiths, so we 'ad to hightail it out of there. This murder is in the inspector's district so the streets were crawling with coppers that know us by sight. So we went to the local pub to see what we could suss out."

"There's a surprise." Betsy snorted delicately.

"It's a bloomin' good thing we did," Wiggins said. "If we 'adn't, I'd never 'ave found out so much about Mrs. Langston-Jones. Mind you, the one that I was talkin' with didn't know her so much by that name as he did her maiden one."

"Which was?" Mrs. Goodge inquired.

"Arden. She was Ellen Arden back then and worked for the Furness family as a governess. Mr. Calder, that's the old gent I was talkin' to, was the gardener at the communal gardens there and he knew 'er. He said she was a right nice lady and had only come up to London after her mother died."

"Where was she from originally?" the cook persisted.

"Mr. Calder thought she was from somewhere in Dorset, but he couldn't remember exactly where. But he did say that she used to spend a lot of time in the garden, especially early in the morning. He used to find her walking there before everyone else was up and about. He said that 'e was surprised when she up and left to get married."

"Why?" Phyllis asked. "What's so surprising about a woman getting married?"

"Because she was a spinster lady and she liked bein' single."

"How on earth did your Mr. Calder know that?" Betsy demanded. She cocked her head toward the cook's door, thinking she heard a whimper.

"Because that's what she told him. She said she liked bein' free, that after all them years of taking care of her mother, she loved bein' able to do as she pleased. She loved London, she loved the art galleries and the museums and the trains. He said she made it a point to go somewhere every week on

94

'er afternoon out. Kew Gardens, the British Museum, Hyde Park. She always went somewhere interestin'."

"Sounds like they had quite a close relationship," Mrs. Jeffries murmured.

"They did. She was the only person, exceptin' for Sir Donovan Gaines, who used the gardens early of a mornin'. Mr. Calder said he looked forward to their morning chats and he missed her when she left. Even in summer, most people didn't like to come outside until they'd 'ad their breakfast and the dew had gone from the benches. But Miss Arden was out there every morning just as the sun come up."

"Why did he go to work so early?" Phyllis asked. "The gardeners here don't start work until eight o'clock."

Wiggins shrugged. "I don't know, I didn't think to ask. Why? Is it important?"

Phyllis's shoulders slumped and she looked down at the table. "I don't know, maybe."

"At my previous employer's, the gardeners often started well before seven," Mrs. Goodge said. "They liked to get heavy work done before it got too late in the day. Oh dear, my lambkins is waking up. She's starting to cry."

Betsy was already on her feet and heading

toward the cook's rooms. "I'll get her."

"Mr. Calder's not workin' there now," Wiggins continued. " 'E retired five years ago and 'e's very old. I can't for the life of me see 'im stalkin' the poor lady and shootin' 'er."

Mrs. Jeffries noticed the way Phyllis shriveled. The girl's confidence rose and fell like the tides on the Thames, and one wrong word was enough to crush her spirits. She wasn't having that. "Nonetheless, Phyllis has made a valid point. Your Mr. Calder apparently once had a close relationship with the victim. It wouldn't hurt to find out where he was at the time of the murder."

"That should be easy enough." Smythe got to his feet as Betsy reappeared with the baby.

She stopped just short of the table and smiled ruefully at the others. "I think we'd better be off. The little one isn't in a very nice mood." She held her up so they could see her. Amanda Belle's wispy blonde curls stood up in tufts around her head, her little hands were balled into fists, her face was red, and one foot kicked its way out of the elegant lace baby blanket that Luty Belle had ordered from France. "She wants her dinner and a warm bath."

The cook got up, her gaze locked on her

goddaughter. "Her little gums are sore. I hate seein' her suffer so."

"And if we don't get her home soon, she'll make sure we suffer as well." Smythe went to the coat tree and grabbed Betsy's shawl. He draped it over her shoulders. "But she's worth it. We'll see you tomorrow morning. Wiggins, if ya want to find out about Calder, try goin' back to the pub. The lady I was chattin' with said he was there all the time."

"You spoke to someone?" Betsy shifted the baby, cradling her close. Amanda screamed at the top of her lungs and kicked her feet.

"It doesn't seem right that she's got to hurt like this." Mrs. Goodge looked as if she was going to cry. "Poor little mite is miserable."

"She'll be fine once she's home and fed." Betsy shifted her onto her chest and patted her back but the baby continued to wail.

"The woman didn't know anything, but I'll give a full accountin' tomorrow morning." Smythe ushered his family toward the hall. "Come on, we've got to go before Miss Belle here screams the house down."

The afternoon had turned to evening and the inspector was tired. Nonetheless, despite his fatigue, he had to take the last of the

97

statements. Barnes had completed questioning the servants and met Witherspoon in the foyer. "Almost finished, sir?"

"Neville Gaines is the last one." He stretched and rolled his shoulders to ease the cramp in his lower back. "And hopefully, his won't take too long. He's waiting for me in the drawing room. Anything useful from the servants? Were there any witnesses?"

"Not really, sir. The kitchen was noisy and the windows were shut. Apparently, someone in the house next door has a trumpet lesson every afternoon, and according to the scullery maid, *'blows away at the ruddy thing hard enough to wake the dead.'* They shut the windows every day to keep the noise down and don't open them again until teatime. But one of the girls did report hearing a loud popping noise a few minutes before Lucius Montague came screaming for help."

"A trumpet lesson at the same time every day," Witherspoon murmured. "That's very interesting."

"I thought so, too. Could be the killer used the lesson to muffle the sound of the gunshot."

"Which would mean the murderer was someone who was familiar with the victim's movements as well as the routines of both this household and the one next door," he mused. "We'll have to look into this further, Constable."

"Every household on the garden probably knew about the music lessons," Barnes said.

"I imagine so." He glanced toward the drawing room door. "I'd better get to it. Mr. Gaines didn't strike me as a patient sort of man."

"Do you want me to check with the constables doing the house to house?" Barnes asked.

"Please do. Perhaps we'll get lucky and someone will have heard or seen something. I'll meet you outside as soon as I've finished here."

Barnes disappeared down the corridor and Witherspoon went to the drawing room, knocked once, and then stepped inside.

A man wearing a navy blue frock coat and matching trousers stood by the fireplace with his back to the inspector. He turned. "I'm Neville Gaines. I understand you wish to speak with me."

Witherspoon crossed the room. He'd overheard the housekeeper speaking to Gaines and then seen him as he'd come down the hallway, but they'd not been formally introduced. "That's correct, sir.

99

I'm Inspector Gerald Witherspoon, and as Mrs. Metcalf told you, I need to take your statement."

Short and portly with a square, jutting jaw and an upturned nose squashed between his bulging brown eyes, Neville Gaines reminded the inspector of a bulldog. Witherspoon banished the unkind thought and concentrated on the task at hand.

"Ask your questions, then. But I don't know what I can tell you. I wasn't even here when the incident occurred," Gaines said.

"I understand that, sir, but we interview everyone who lives on the premises and your uncle has told me that you do reside here." He wondered if the man was going to ask him to sit down.

"I still think this will be a waste of both our times, but if you must, then get on with it." Gaines moved to the sofa and flopped down on the end.

Witherspoon remained standing. "Did you know Mrs. Langston-Jones prior to her coming to work here?" he asked. "I understand she once worked for the family that lives next door."

"She was the governess there," Gaines said. "But that was years ago and I didn't live here at the time. I didn't know her."

"The first time you met her was when

100

your uncle employed her as a tutor for your nieces? Is that correct?"

"That's correct."

"Did you get along with Mrs. Langston-Jones?"

Gaines shrugged. "I barely saw the woman, Inspector. She was here during the day and I was at my office. I had no relationship with her whatsoever."

"Were you at your office this afternoon, sir?" Witherspoon asked.

"No," he replied. "I went to look at some property. My company invests in a number of enterprises here in London."

"Where are you employed, Mr. Gaines?"

"At Mason and Tynley. The offices are in the city. I'm one of the directors."

"What time did you go to work, sir?"

"My usual. I arrived there at half eight, worked until lunchtime, and then went to Fulham to see a block of freehold properties."

"How did you find out that Mrs. Langston-Jones had been murdered?" he asked. Witherspoon had no idea why that particular question popped into his head.

Gaines looked surprised. "I found out when I arrived home. Mrs. Metcalf met me at the front door with the appalling news that the French tutor had been murdered on our garden steps. It's not exactly the sort of information one wants or expects to hear when one arrives home. Furthermore, having policemen all about the place is most disconcerting, not to mention disruptive to the household routine. Apparently dinner will be late tonight."

"Did you go back to your office after seeing the property in Fulham?"

"No, the assessment took far longer than I'd originally anticipated, and it was almost half past four when I was done, so I came directly home."

"When was the last time you saw Mrs. Langston-Jones?" he asked.

"I'm not certain. I think it might have been last week when I came home for luncheon and passed her on my way out." He sighed. "Is this going to take much longer? I'm tired and I'd like a drink before dinner."

"We're almost finished, sir. I've only one more question. Do you know of anyone who might have disliked Mrs. Langston-Jones? Anyone who might have wished her harm?"

"Of course not, Inspector, as I said, I didn't really know her at all." His voice trailed off as they heard the front door slam and then Sir Donovan Gaines' distinctive voice. "Send one of the footmen out to the hansom for the child's case, Mrs. Metcalf."

"What on earth?" Gaines muttered as he leapt to his feet and rushed into the hallway. Witherspoon hurried after him.

Sir Donovan Gaines was at the foot of the staircase with a dark-haired little boy who couldn't be more than seven or eight. The child's eyes were red and his face streaked from crying.

Sir Donovan was awkwardly patting the lad's back. "Now, now, you go right on and let it all out. It's horrid, I know." He looked in their direction. "Good evening, Neville. Oh good, Inspector, you're still here."

Gaines fixed his eyes on the boy. "Is that Mrs. Langston-Jones' son?"

Sir Donovan ignored him and spoke directly to Witherspoon. "Mrs. Langston-Jones' son will be staying here."

"Yes, sir, you mentioned that when you left." The inspector had no idea about what the law might be on custodial issues, but surely it wasn't kidnapping if the police were fully informed of a minor child's whereabouts. "Uh, er, perhaps you ought to let the young man's family know of this arrangement."

"My solicitor is taking care of the matter. Young Alexander will be staying here for the foreseeable future."

Footsteps pounded down the staircase and Martha Barclay descended into view. "What do you mean, he'll be staying here? What is happening? Why is this person here?" She stopped on the bottom step and stared coldly at Alexander. The boy shrank back against Sir Donovan.

"I wasn't aware I needed your permission to invite people to my home," Sir Donovan said to his niece. His stare was even chillier than hers.

"Of course you don't," she said quickly. She put a hand to her throat and closed her eyes. "That was most presumptuous of me, please forgive me. This has been a very upsetting day. I'm not myself."

Sir Donovan smiled. "It's been a terrible day for all of us, but most of all for young Alex here. I shall expect everyone" — he glanced around the foyer, his gaze taking in both his niece and his nephew — "to treat him with the utmost respect and courtesy."

"Naturally." Martha Barclay swallowed heavily and tried to smile. "You're doing a kindness, Uncle, and he's your guest. I was a bit surprised, that's all, and to be perfectly frank, a bit concerned."

"Concerned?" Sir Donovan's eyebrows rose. "About what?"

Witherspoon leaned against the wall. It

was almost as if they'd forgotten he was there. He glanced at Neville Gaines, who'd begun to scowl as soon as his uncle's attention had turned to Mrs. Barclay. He caught the inspector looking his way and the frown disappeared and was replaced by a serene smile.

"We don't know this young man, Uncle, and I do have my daughters to consider." She looked toward her brother, hoping for support, but Neville held his peace.

"Oh for God's sake, Martha, this child is seven years old. He's just lost his mother and as such will be made welcome in my house, is that clear?"

"Yes, of course it is," she said quickly.

"Uncle, don't be too hasty." Neville Gaines paused and cleared his throat. "There may be legal ramifications to taking the boy into your home. He does have relatives. I believe there's an uncle. He may object to the boy coming here."

The inspector wondered how a person who claimed to barely know the victim now knew so much about her family.

"Don't be absurd. I've already said my solicitor is taking care of those details," Sir Donovan snapped at his nephew before looking down and giving the boy a wide smile. "Don't worry, Alex, despite this rather odd greeting, you're going to like it here. I'll see to that."

There was a sharp knock on the front door, but before anyone could move, it flew open and a slender middle-aged woman burst into the foyer. She had brown hair, brilliant blue eyes, and an exquisite bone structure. Trailing behind her was a young footman carrying a wicker case.

"I came as soon as I heard," she gushed as she hurried toward Sir Donovan and then almost skidded to a halt as she saw the child. "What's going on here? Has something else happened?" She looked from the boy back to Sir Donovan.

"Where do you want the case to go, sir?" The footman hefted it up to his shoulder.

"Into the room next to mine," he replied.

The lad started down the hall but Sir Donovan called him back. "Use this staircase," he ordered. "It'll be quicker."

"Donovan, I don't understand. I came because I heard there'd been a shooting," the woman said.

"There has been. Mrs. Langston-Jones was murdered and Uncle Donovan has invited the boy to stay here, Hester," Martha Barclay answered. "He's her son."

Mrs. Metcalf, her arms loaded with linens, appeared from the hallway, saw the crowd in the foyer, and then turned to leave. But Sir Donovan had spotted her. "Mrs. Metcalf, come here please. Are you going up to Alex's room?"

"His bed's been airing since you left, sir, and I was going up to change the linens," she replied.

Sir Donovan nodded and looked at the lad. "Alex, why don't you go off with Mrs. Metcalf and have a look at your new bedroom. I want to make sure you like it."

His eyes filled with tears. "If you don't mind, sir, I'd prefer to stay here with you."

"Then you shall, my boy." Donovan looked at Witherspoon. "Inspector, will it be alright to postpone your interview with me until tomorrow? I don't want to leave Alexander on his own."

Witherspoon smiled at the terrified-looking child and nodded in understanding. "Tomorrow will be fine."

"Good, then it's settled. Oh dear, where are my manners?" He gestured at the woman who'd just arrived. She was staring at Alex as if she'd never seen a child before. "Inspector, this is Mrs. Linthorp, she's a dear friend of our family. Hester, this is Inspector Gerald Witherspoon, he's in charge of the . . . uh . . ." His voice broke and he looked down at Alex.

"The matter at hand," Witherspoon finished. He understood that Sir Donovan was trying to spare the child any more pain.

Hester Linthorp gave him a brief nod in acknowledgment of the introduction and then turned her attention to Sir Donovan. "Well, I must say, when I rushed over here, I didn't expect this."

"Nor did we," Neville Gaines interjected. "But uncle is a kind and generous man. Will you stay to dine with us, Hester?"

"That would be lovely." She smiled and again focused her gaze on Alexander. "This poor young boy has had a dreadful day. I expect he'll want to have a quick supper in the nursery and then straight to bed."

"No, no, that won't do at all. I don't want him to be alone." Sir Donovan took Alex's hand and started down the hallway. "Neville, you and Martha take Hester to the drawing room for an aperitif. I won't be able to join the three of you for dinner. Alex and I will be dining in my study."

"Here's your sherry, sir." Mrs. Jeffries handed the inspector his drink and sat down opposite him. They often shared a drink together when he got home in the evenings and tonight was no exception. "You were home very late, sir. I imagine you're dreadfully tired."

"I am," he admitted. "But it couldn't be helped, because as I told you, it was a homicide. Poor woman was shot going into her place of employment."

"Oh dear, where did she work?" She had to pretend she knew nothing about the case. It hadn't even been reported in the evening papers. She'd sent Phyllis out to get the evening editions and the murder wasn't in any of them.

"She was a French tutor at a private home." He took a quick sip and then told her the details of his day. She knew Witherspoon enjoyed sharing the specifics of his cases with her because, as the widow of a policeman herself, she understood how difficult police work could be. So she listened carefully, occasionally making a comment or asking a question.

By the time he'd finished a second glass of sherry, she was fairly certain she'd learned everything. But even if he forgot something pertinent, she wasn't worried. Constable Barnes would be stopping by the kitchen tomorrow morning, and a quick word with him usually closed any gaps.

Barnes had realized what the household was doing and instead of getting cross about "amateurs" poking their noses into police business, he'd understood they had access to people, places, and circumstances that he didn't. There were some in London who wouldn't give a "copper" the time of day, let alone answer any of his questions. Constable Barnes became an ally and not an enemy. He was also the perfect conduit for getting much of the information the household learned back to Witherspoon.

"Gracious, sir, no wonder you're exhausted. It sounds as if you've taken statements from half of London. With so much territory to cover, what are you going to do tomorrow?" She got up and put their empty glasses on a tray.

"The first thing we'll do is search Mrs. Langston-Jones' flat," he replied. "And after that, we'll keep on with the interviews. But I've a feeling this case won't be like my others. I think it'll be very simple and straightforward."

She froze. But the inspector was staring off in the distance, so he didn't notice her reaction. "Why is that, sir?"

"We've already got a very strong suspect."

She picked up the tray. "Who would that be, sir?" She was fairly sure she already knew what he was going to say.

"Lucius Montague. I'm certain the gun we found belongs to him." Witherspoon rose

110

to his feet.

"Wasn't he the one who found the body?" She knew perfectly well he was, but she had to pretend she didn't. The inspector nodded and she continued, "But surely, sir, unless the man is a complete fool, if he were the one that murdered her, he'd have had ample time to get rid of the weapon before raising the alarm."

Witherspoon shrugged as he walked out into the hall. "Not all killers are intelligent, Mrs. Jeffries. As a matter of fact, by and large, criminals are rarely clever."

"Did Lucius Montague strike you as being particularly stupid?" She almost banged into his back as he stopped just outside the dining room door.

"I don't know," he mused. "I can't determine his level of intelligence, but I do know that he was a very arrogant man."

"Arrogant, sir?" she repeated. Her mind worked furiously. Unless there was an out-and-out confession by the culprit at the scene of the crime, she knew from past experience that it was very dangerous to pinpoint one person as the killer. It was especially dangerous for the police to do this, because when they did, they stopped looking at anyone else.

Witherspoon smiled. "You know what I

mean, Mrs. Jeffries. Lucius Montague is one of those wealthy, privileged types that feel they're above the law. I suspect he's the sort who thinks we'd never look in his direction."

CHAPTER 4

Witherspoon and Barnes stood outside number 14 Valentine Road in Hammersmith. Ellen Langston-Jones had lived in a slightly shabby, three-story gray brick house in a decent, but working-class, neighborhood.

"I don't enjoy this aspect of our job very much." Witherspoon pushed open the black wrought iron gate surrounding the tiny front garden and stepped inside. "Searching a victim's home seems like the final insult."

"It would be more insulting to let Mrs. Langston-Jones' killer go free, sir." Barnes closed the gate and walked the few steps to the front door. He reached up and banged the knocker. "And having a good hunt around her rooms might give us a clue as to who wanted her dead."

"Let's hope so, Constable. I felt so sorry for her son, but the only thing we can do for the boy is bring her killer to justice."

"And I've no doubt we'll succeed, sir. At least the lad is being well taken care of for the moment." Barnes cocked his head closer to the door.

"Yes, I suppose so," Witherspoon murmured. "Sir Donovan seems to have taken quite an interest in the child."

"It's awfully quiet, sir. I hope someone's home." Barnes banged the knocker again. "Wait a second, I hear footsteps."

Just then, the door flew open and a woman wearing a floppy cap stuck her head out. She was breathing hard and carried a feather duster. "Oh dear, I'm so sorry, I was upstairs when you knocked. You must be the police." She held the door wider and waved them inside. "I'm Cora Otis. I'm the landlady here. Come in, then, I've been expecting you. Sir Donovan Gaines told me what happened and I was shocked to hear of it. Mrs. Langston-Jones was a nice woman and an excellent tenant. We shall all miss her very much. Come along, then," she said. Barnes closed the door behind him.

"We'll be more comfortable in here." She tossed the duster on a small table as she led them down the short, dim hallway to the room at the end. "Would you like some tea?" she called over her shoulder.

"No, ma'am. But it's very kind of you to offer. I'm Inspector Witherspoon and this is Constable Barnes," he said quickly.

They entered a parlor furnished with two straight-backed armchairs and an over-stuffed brown horsehair sofa draped with crocheted cream-colored antimacassars on the headrests. Pale ivory paint covered the walls and cheerful yellow and brown striped curtains hung at the two windows of the far wall. A painting of brightly colored blue and red birds hung over the wooden mantel-piece.

"I suppose you need to ask me some questions," she said. She gestured at the two chairs as she took the center seat of the sofa.

"We do." Witherspoon sat down. "And then I'm afraid we need to search Mrs. Langston-Jones' room."

She nodded. "That's fine. As soon as I heard what had happened, I notified Mrs. Langston-Jones' next of kin by telegram."

"That would be Mr. Jonathan Langston-Jones." Barnes pulled out his notebook and flipped it open.

"That's right, she put his name down on the rental application," Cora replied. "I make all my tenants give me the name of a relative that can be contacted in case something happens. I once had a tenant that hadn't done that, and when the poor woman dropped dead of a stroke, I had the worst time trying to determine who, if anyone, ought to be notified. So even though Mrs. Langston-Jones didn't much care for her brother-in-law, I insisted she give us his address. I got an answer back from him this morning, and I must tell you, I'm in a bit of a state as to what to do." She paused to take a breath.

"How so, ma'am?" Witherspoon interjected. He wasn't sure whether he ought to interrupt and ask specific questions or just let her keep talking.

"Mr. Langston-Jones said he'd come up and fetch her things, and I don't mind telling you, I'm not sure what to do. Sir Donovan Gaines, nice man, isn't he, have you met him?"

"Yes, ma'am, we have. Please go on with what you were saying. What are you not sure about?"

"What to do, of course. Yesterday when Sir Donovan came to fetch young Alex and get his clothes, he told me he'd take charge of her possessions and that I wasn't to let anyone but the police into her rooms. But now she's got her husband's kin wanting to come for them and it's a bit of a muddle, isn't it."

116

"I shouldn't worry if I were you," Witherspoon said. "Sir Donovan told us that he'd instructed his solicitor to deal with the matter." In truth, the inspector had no idea if Sir Donovan's actions were legal or not, but as it was a civil and not a criminal matter, he'd decided not to be unduly concerned.

"I hope you're right and that there won't be a problem. I'd not like to get caught in the middle. Sir Donovan was most adamant that no one disturbs her things. He even paid the rent up until the middle of next month. He said he wasn't sure how long it would take to get matters settled and he didn't want to be rushed. I don't know what I shall tell Mr. Langston-Jones when he arrives today, and I don't mind admitting he'll not take kindly to being thwarted."

"What time will he be here?" Witherspoon asked.

"The telegram just said he'd be here this afternoon," she said. "And I won't let him take anything away."

"No, absolutely not," the inspector replied. "The constable and I will search her rooms and see if there's any sort of will or legal documents with instructions about her estate."

"You've met Mr. Langston-Jones before?" Barnes asked.

117

"Indeed I have and I must tell you that he struck me as a rather disagreeable sort of person," she declared. "Self-important and rather overbearing, if you know what I mean. Now, what else do you want to know?"

Witherspoon thought for a moment. She'd already given them several avenues of inquiry, but he decided to proceed with the basic questions. "How long have Mrs. Langston-Jones and her son lived here?"

"Since right after Christmas." She frowned. "They arrived the second of January. They have two connected rooms and a small sitting room on the top floor. I provide meals. We've two other lodgers, both women. Mrs. Deacon and Miss Martin both have rooms on the second floor. I only rent to ladies." She smiled. "Young Alex is the first lad we've had about the place in years. But he's such a sweet young man, neither of my other lady lodgers objected to his presence."

"Do you know if she was frightened of anyone?" Barnes asked.

She shook her head emphatically. "She wasn't one to be intimidated by life. She was a strong woman, but then, she had to be. She was widowed and not in the best of circumstances, if you know what I mean."

"I'm afraid I don't," Witherspoon admitted.

"She was getting ready to defend herself in a lawsuit, Inspector." Cora Otis pursed her lips. "And that's one of the reasons I was so grateful Sir Donovan Gaines showed up and took the boy. I don't think his uncle is going to look after his interests, not after he threatened to take the lad's mother to court. Goodness, sir, please pay attention. I've already told you, I've met Mr. Langston-Jones and he certainly isn't a gentleman."

"He was going to sue her?" Barnes clarified. He wanted to be absolutely certain the woman knew what she was talking about.

"Indeed he was," she said. "I heard him myself. He was here just last week and they had a frightful row. When gentlemen are in the house, I let my tenants use this room," she explained.

"How do you know they were arguing?" the inspector asked. "Were their voices raised?"

"No, I heard them through the door." She laughed merrily. "I wasn't trying to eavesdrop. I came up with a tray of tea, and when I stopped in the hall to shift it so I could turn the handle, I overheard their voices. They weren't shouting but I could tell they were having a terrible row. His voice was low and harsh but I could hear every word. He told her she'd be sorry if she didn't sign the paper, and that once he got her into a courtroom, there were all sorts of things that he could bring up."

"Could you hear how she responded?" Witherspoon leaned forward.

"Indeed I could," she declared. "She laughed and told him to do his worst. She said she wasn't a poor widow that could be pushed around by the likes of him, and that if he took her to court, he might be in for a surprise himself."

"Where's my Miss Belle?" Luty demanded as she took her seat.

"She's having a nap." Betsy yawned. "Neither of us got much sleep last night. I'm sorry, Luty, maybe she'll wake up before we leave."

"Fiddlesticks! I wanted to give her a cuddle." Luty shot Mrs. Goodge a quick frown. "Unlike some people around here, I don't git to see her that often."

"You see her all the time and I didn't raise a fuss when everyone started calling her 'Miss Belle' as a pet name instead of Mandy or Amy." The cook sniffed disapprovingly. The baby had been named after both women and Mrs. Goodge was still a bit miffed that Luty Belle had won the nickname race. The two women had a good-natured but serious rivalry over their mutual godchild.

"No, you didn't raise a fuss. You just rushed out and bought a baby cot and had it put in your rooms." Luty snorted and took her seat. "That was downright childish if you ask me."

Mrs. Goodge burst out laughing. "When you get to be our age, you can be as childish as you like."

"Do restrain yourselves, ladies," Hatchet said as he took his own place. "As I have noted on several occasions, our Miss Belle will grow up to adore both of you."

"Well said, Hatchet," Mrs. Jeffries said. "Let's get started. Now that we're all here, Mrs. Goodge and I want to tell you what we've learned from the inspector and Constable Barnes."

"You ain't the only one that's got somethin' to report." Luty smiled smugly. "I got me an earful last night. But you go first."

"The inspector's first day on the case was very busy." Mrs. Jeffries told them everything she'd heard. "He was happy with the progress they've made. They've already found the murder weapon and a pillow that

121

might have been used to muffle the sound of the fatal shot," she finished.

"Did he say where he was goin' to be this mornin'?" Wiggins asked. "I'd like to know if he mentioned goin' to the Gaines house. I don't want him catchin' a glimpse of me when I'm workin' that area."

"He will be there sometime today," she said. "But I don't know exactly when."

"I saw him this morning," Ruth said. "He and Constable Barnes went past as I was showing the builder a crack underneath the front windows. We chatted for a moment while the constable went to the corner to get a cab, and he specifically mentioned going to the Gaines house today. He also said they were going to search the victim's flat."

"He needs to finish interviewing Sir Donovan and he wanted to have another chat with Neville Gaines," Mrs. Jeffries mused. "He was somewhat suspicious that a man who claimed he barely knew the woman would know that the child had an uncle."

"What's so suspicious about that?" Phyllis asked. "He might have heard it in conversation. I guess what I'm sayin' is that I don't know Mary Williams well enough to do more than nod at her when I pass her on the street, she works at Mrs. Barker's house down the road, but I do happen to know that she's got a great-aunt Greta that lives in Plumstead. I was waiting in line at the grocer's shop last week and she was standing in front of me, chattin' with her friend about a party at the great-auntie's house and how wonderful it had been because a young man had walked her back to the train station."

"You're right, of course," Mrs. Jeffries agreed. "Nonetheless, I do think the inspector is wise to follow up on his idea. Now" — she turned to Mrs. Goodge — "would you like to tell everyone what Constable Barnes told us?"

The cook was only too happy to oblige. She took her time in the telling and made sure she repeated everything. "So it looks like Lucius Montague was lying to our inspector when he said he barely knew the woman. You don't have two separate quarrels with strangers."

"His initials was found on the gun," Betsy reminded them.

"But we don't know for certain they are his initials." Mrs. Jeffries reached for the teapot. "Those letters could belong to hundreds of people in London."

"But hundreds of them weren't arguing with her only days before she was shot," Ruth said. "What's more, the pillow used to muffle the sound of the gunshot was found under a bush outside his house."

"Let's not jump to conclusions," Mrs. Jeffries warned. "These are, at best, circumstantial kinds of evidence that could easily be manipulated by someone else. We must keep an open mind until we learn more."

"Not to be adding fuel to the fire, Hepzibah," Luty said. "I'm afraid it's not lookin' good for Mr. Lucius Montague. When I was at Lord Billington's last night, I heard somethin' right interestin'. It seems that our victim had been to see a solicitor about the fellow."

"How did you hear that, madam?" Hatchet stared at her suspiciously. "I knew you'd heard something from the way you cackled to yourself all the way home. But surely you're not saying a member of the legal profession would announce to all and sundry at the dinner table details of a murder victim's visit to him."

"Don't be silly. 'Course he didn't make any announcement, and what's more, I don't cackle, I chuckle, but that's beside the point. The lawyer was half drunk and braggin' to the boys in Billington's study about bein' in the know."

"What were you doing in Lord Billington's study?" Hatchet demanded. "He'd never have invited you in with the men."

" 'Course he didn't. I was eavesdroppin' at the door." She grinned broadly as everyone but Hatchet laughed. "You know how the ladies always leave the table and the men go off to smoke a cigar and drink good whiskey."

"Yes, yes, madam, we all know that is the custom in civilized households," Hatchet said impatiently. "Get on with your story."

"At dinner, when I'd brought up the murder, I'd noticed that Hamish Todd grinned like a fox who'd found the henhouse unlocked. So when the men went off with Billington, I waited a few minutes and then excused myself from the ladies. By the time I got outside the door, Todd was braggin' that he warned her to be careful, that some people didn't take kindly being taken to court and havin' the whole world know that they were thieves." She paused and took a breath. "The fellow he was talkin' about was none other than Lucius Montague."

"Lucius Montague, now why does that name sound so familiar?" Mrs. Goodge muttered more to herself than the others.

"Cor blimey, the murder only happened yesterday before teatime and we've already got a good suspect," Wiggins said happily.

"Maybe this one will be easier than the others."

"I do hope so," Ruth agreed. "Poor Gerald works so hard, it would be nice if this one turns out to be a simple matter."

"But we should still get out and about, shouldn't we?" Phyllis asked. She looked at Mrs. Jeffries. "You want me to do the shops, don't you?"

"Of course. Even though it appears this man might be the killer, we won't know for sure until all the facts are known," she replied.

"I'm goin' back to that pub and find out about Mr. Calder," Wiggins announced. "Then I'll 'ave a go at findin' a servant at the murder 'ouse. No, wait, I'll 'ave a go at findin' someone from the Montague 'ouse."

"Do both of them," Mrs. Jeffries said quickly. "Really, we mustn't assume this man is guilty."

"Don't fret, Mrs. Jeffries, I'm just 'avin' a go at you." Wiggins laughed. "I know the dangers of makin' up our minds too early in a case. Once we do that, we only go 'untin' for facts that fit our theory."

"We're all well aware of that particular pitfall," Hatchet said. "As for me, I intend to spend the day tracking down some of my sources." He looked at Luty. "I trust, madam, that I can safely leave you to your own devices."

"Oh, your nose is out of joint because I found out more than you did last night." Luty chuckled. "Mind you, a housemaid caught me eavesdroppin', but I took care of her. I gave her a few coins and she was happier than a hog in an apple orchard. Speakin' of hogs, I'm goin' to see a couple of lawyer fellows today. First thing we ought to do is find out who benefits from her death."

"Most likely that would be her son," Mrs. Goodge said. "I can't see that she'd have much of an estate. She was workin' as a tutor."

"But her late husband was an artist." Betsy tapped her finger against the handle of her mug. "Maybe his paintings are worth more than anyone thinks. Doesn't the value of an artist's work go up after he's dead?"

"Only if he's any good," Smythe muttered. "I've got a source I can ask. What was the name again?"

"Brandon Langston-Jones," Mrs. Jeffries said.

Betsy looked at her husband. "What else are you going to do today?"

"As I said, I've got to see someone about the dead artist, then I thought I'd talk to

127

the hansom drivers in the neighborhood," he said. "Whoever killed her had to have got there somehow." He also planned on taking a trip to the Dirty Duck Pub to have a word with his very best source.

"Not if they were already there," Betsy said. "The killer might be someone in the Gaines household or someone who lives around the communal garden."

"I've an old colleague coming by today," the cook announced. "Soon as I heard we'd a murder, I sent her a note inviting her to tea. Mind you, I doubt she'll know anything directly about the victim, she retired from service years ago, but she might know something about the Gaines family or Lucius Montague."

Everyone pushed back in their chairs to get up, but Luty beat them all. "I'm just goin' to have a quick peek at my Miss Belle before we go." She dashed toward Mrs. Goodge's quarters. "I'll not wake her, I promise."

Betsy cringed, hoping her morning wouldn't be spent with a fussy, teething baby who'd not had enough sleep. She caught her husband's eye and he gave her a rueful smile and a quick hug. "Let her have her way," he whispered in her ear. "Miss Amanda Belle's the only godchild she's got."

By the time they reached the top floor, Witherspoon and Barnes were both breathing hard. The inspector leaned against the banister to catch his breath while Barnes used the keys he'd gotten from the landlady to open the door at the end of the short corridor. There were two other doors, but according to Mrs. Otis, they were permanently bolted from the inside because access to both rooms could be had from the sitting room.

"It's a bit warped." Barnes shouldered the door open and stepped inside. He looked around while he waited for the inspector. A green upholstered love seat was directly across from the door, and a bookcase with stacks of magazines on the top shelf and books on the lower rung stood in the far corner. A blue and green oval braided rag rug covered the floor, and emerald curtains hung from the small solitary window. A walnut secretary with a badly scratched wood panel and a cane-backed chair completed the furnishings. The room should have seemed cold and sterile and would have save for the colorful paintings on every available space along the walls.

A series of three laughing harlequins hung over the love seat, a lush pastoral country scene with a rustic wooden frame held pride of place over the bookcase, and two brilliant blue-toned seascapes hung vertically on the wall beside the connecting door.

"I wonder if those were done by her husband," Barnes said as Witherspoon stepped into the room. He pointed at the harlequins. "I'm not an expert, but they're good. They make you want to smile."

"They do, don't they," Witherspoon agreed. "They make a rather dreary sitting room look delightfully cheerful." His gaze moved to the secretary. "I'll start there, Constable. Why don't you begin in the bedrooms?"

"Right, sir, I'll give a shout if I find anything useful," Barnes said as he disappeared through the door.

Witherspoon was relieved when the secretary opened. He'd feared it might be locked. Inside was a ledge with a row of cubbyholes that held a short stack of letters, two pens, four pencils, a bottle of ink, two brass buttons, and a box of cream-colored stationery. He pulled out the correspondence.

Opening the first one, he frowned when he saw it was written in French. He put it aside. He'd take it to the station, and if no one there could read it, they'd send to the Yard for a translator. He opened the second one and saw that it was from a solicitor confirming Mrs. Brandon Langston-Jones' appointment at their offices for the following Monday at three in the afternoon. It was signed Hamish Todd and gave an address of 35 the Strand. "I wonder what this is all about," he muttered to himself. He made a mental note to have a word with the solicitor as soon as possible. The third letter was from Arnold and Boxley, Art Dealers, and said they'd be pleased to handle the sale of the late Brandon Langston-Jones' paintings. They inquired when it would be a convenient time for either Mr. Arnold or Mrs. Boxley to see the inventory. The letter was dated May 28. He put the documents into his coat pocket and had another good look at the desk, but there was nothing else of interest.

"Inspector, you might want to have a look at this," Barnes called.

Witherspoon closed the secretary and went toward the back of the suite of rooms. The first room contained a narrow iron bed, a chest of drawers, a toy box, and a small trunk. It had obviously belonged to the boy. He passed through the connecting door into the last room, the victim's bedroom.

Barnes stood next to a brass bed that was shoved against the wall. Witherspoon stopped in the doorway, blinking at the sudden, vivid swirls of color crowding his field of vision. Paintings of all sizes were everywhere, propped on the dressing table, along the walls, on the top of the large trunk under the window, and even along the wall atop the neatly made bed. "Oh my word, this is amazing. How many paintings are in here?" he asked.

"More than a dozen, sir, but this is what I wanted you to see." He waved a sheet of paper in the air. "I found it in her dressing table along with some brochures from Thomas Cook. It's a letter from Lucius Montague." He handed it to the inspector.

Witherspoon scanned the contents quickly and then read it again, this time more slowly. When he'd finished, he looked at the constable. "Good gracious, we'll need to have another word with Mr. Montague. The evidence against him appears to be mounting very quickly."

"What about Sir Donovan? We've still to finish taking his statement."

Witherspoon sighed. "I know. I also wanted to have a word with her solicitor. There's a letter in the secretary from him confirming an appointment. But after reading this, I think both Sir Donovan and the lawyer can wait."

Barnes jerked his chin at the paper the inspector held. "That last line, sir, the one where he's says that if she pursues him in court, she'll be sorry. That's very close to a threat, and look at the date, sir, it was two days before the murder."

"I'd like a pound of carrots, please," Phyllis said to the clerk at the greengrocer's. She was less than a quarter mile from the murder house doing the shops on the local high street. So far, she'd been to the baker's, the butcher's, the chemist's, and two grocers, and she'd not learned one thing. No one knew anything about the victim, anyone from the Gaines household, or Lucius Montague, or if they did, they weren't sharing the gossip with her. But she wasn't going to give up, no matter how much her feet hurt.

She smiled at the young man. He was a beanpole of a lad, with slicked-down brown hair and a long, bony face. He gave her a shy grin as he dumped a handful of vegetables onto the scale.

"I heard a woman was murdered around here," she began.

He glanced over his shoulder at a closed

door behind the counter on the far side of the shop. "It was just around the corner, miss, at one of them posh houses on Portland Villas. The poor lady was shot on Sir Donovan Gaines' back steps. Some said she'd had her head blown off."

Phyllis pretended to be impressed. "Oh dear, how awful. Have they caught the one who done it?"

"Not yet." He tipped the basket and the carrots spilled onto the sheet of newspaper spread beneath the scale. "Mind you, there's many around here that think the police won't have to look very hard to find the one that did it."

She gasped. "You don't say. Who do they think it was?"

"Some around here is sure that it were that miserable Mr. Montague that done it. They've had words, you know, lots of words. He didn't like her at all. He told Mrs. Bailey who lives in the last house on Babbington Place that he knew for a fact she was a liar and an adventuress, and if Sir Donovan weren't careful, she'd try to ruin his good name as well. Those were her exact words — I know because my sister Minnie works for Mrs. Bailey and was serving them their tea."

"My goodness, you do know so much."

She flicked a quick look at the door and saw that it was still firmly closed. Whoever he was worried about coming in was still safely in the back room, and maybe, if she was very lucky, she could get more out of him. "Did your sister hear anything else?"

He shook his head and began wrapping the carrots. "Not that she said." Again, he looked over his shoulder. "But none of us 'round here would be surprised if Mr. Montague turned out to be the killer. He's a nasty one, he is."

"He's hurt someone before?"

"I don't know that he's hurt anyone, but I wouldn't put it past him." He pursed his lips. "Last month he tried to get me sacked. He marched in here and told the guv that I'd sent a short order. I'm not the first one that works in the shops 'round here that he's complained about either. But lucky for me, it had been Mrs. Victor who did his order that day and she's the owner's wife so I didn't get shown the door. But fancy claimin' that we'd shorted him by over two pounds of produce. Mind you, I think he was just carpin' in the hopes that Mrs. Victor would reduce his bill — he's been late paying the last few months — but she didn't. She held her ground and told him he'd been charged for exactly what he was sent."

"You're fortunate your Mrs. Victor was the one who did his order; otherwise, you might have lost your job. Did he take his business elsewhere?"

He laughed. "He threatened to, but there's only one other greengrocer in the neighborhood and they've refused to let him put his goods on account." He leaned closer and lowered his voice. "I overheard Mrs. Victor tellin' her husband she's worried the fellow's going to be arrested, and if that happens, they'll have a devil of a time gettin' what they're owed. Mr. Victor agreed with her. He said that startin' today, they'd best get paid before he gets his order."

Wiggins rounded the corner onto Portland Villas, slowing his steps as he scanned the pavement across the road, looking for constables that might recognize him. He'd already been to the pub and found out that, at the time of the murder, Mr. Calder had been in his usual spot at one of the tables enjoying a pint.

He came abreast of the Gaines house and saw that the front steps were empty. But he still needed to be on his toes — just because there weren't any constables on guard at the house itself didn't mean they weren't close by. He knew the inspector's methods. Witherspoon believed in being thorough. Wiggins would bet his next hot dinner that he had constables doing another house to house looking for witnesses or searching the area for clues.

He continued down the road, keeping a sharp eye on the servants' entrances of the houses he passed. There'd been murder done in this neighborhood, so he had to be careful not to call attention to himself. He strolled leisurely enough to hear the opening or closing of a door, but not so slowly as to arouse anyone's suspicions. But he saw no one, no housemaids, no footmen, not one person who might be willing to stop and chat. "Blast a Spaniard, you'd think someone would be out and about," he muttered as he reached the far end.

Thinking he'd risk going back the way he'd just come, he turned, but then a constable stepped into view halfway up the block and headed his way. Wiggins did a quick about-face and rounded the corner onto Babbington Place.

Fearing that the policeman he'd spotted might follow him, Wiggins walked as fast as he dared. If the constable did come around the corner, it wouldn't do to be seen running.

The houses here were four-story redbrick and set closer to the pavement than the ones on Portland Villas. He passed one halfway down the block that had a FLAT TO LET sign in the upper window. He glanced over his shoulder and then slowed his pace. The constable had disappeared. A door slammed and he turned just in time to see a young housemaid come out of the walkway of a house he'd just passed. She carried a shopping basket on her arm.

Wiggins rushed toward her, lightening his steps as he drew close so she wouldn't hear him approach. "Oh, miss, I was hoping you could help me," he said. He had a story at the ready and took care to pronounce his words correctly. He'd also put on his best shirt and jacket today.

She turned and glared at him then lifted her hand and swiped at her cheeks. "What are you bothering me for?" she demanded. "Can't a person even walk down the ruddy street without being troubled by strange men?" Her eyes were red and her face stained with tears.

Shocked, Wiggins gaped at her. "Cor blimey, I'm sorry, miss. I didn't mean to disturb you or intrude upon you when

138

you're troubled. But I couldn't see your face so I didn't know you were upset."

"Upset?" she repeated. Her eyes narrowed. "Is that what they call walkin' down the road weepin' these days? I'm a bit more than upset, I'm so angry I could spit. We've just been told our wages are goin' to be late this quarter, and not just a day or two late, either, but weeks late." She snorted in derision. "And I'm not all that sure we'll get them at all. He's such a bloody liar. What am I supposed to tell my mam and dad when I can't send 'em money? That his nibs will pay us when he bloody well can and we can complain to the bloomin' Home Secretary if we don't like it? Good Lord, what am I to do? Mam and Da depend on me to help pay the bills, to keep a roof over their heads and a bit of food on the table." Her voice broke and she looked away, but not before he saw that she was crying again.

"Please don't cry, miss." Hesitantly, he touched the arm holding the shopping basket. "Please let me buy you a cup of tea. It's the least I can do. My name is Clarence Stevens, and I promise, I'm a respectable person. There's a nice café just up the street. Please, miss, I'm a decent sort, really, and I'm a good listener."

She turned to face him and he realized

139

she was very pretty. Despite the tearstains on her cheeks, her complexion was smooth and lovely, the hair tucked under her cap was dark brown, and she had a heart-shaped face. Her eyes were cornflower blue. She was slender without being skinny and the same height as he was.

She studied him for a moment, taking his measure. Finally she said, "Alright, a cup of tea sounds lovely. I was so angry when he announced we'd have to wait to get our money that I don't much care if I'm late gettin' back."

"It's just up here." He pointed toward the end of the block.

"I know the place." She started off and he hurried after her.

"I'd not like you to get into any trouble," he said as he caught up with her.

"Don't worry about that." She smiled cynically. "I'll take as long as I want. Despite his big talk and stupid airs, he'll not be sackin' me or anyone else. The stupid git can't keep servants. He's not just a cheap bugger, he's mean and nasty to boot."

"Montague, Montague." Winnie Roberts frowned as she repeated the name. "I know I've heard that name before."

Mrs. Goodge reached for the teapot and

poured her guest a second cup. She'd been pleased when Winnie had accepted her invitation; they'd worked together years earlier. Winnie had been the upstairs maid, and normally, she'd not have had anything to do with Mrs. Goodge, who'd been the cook. In those days, the rigid structure of their old positions had ensured they'd never be friends, but luckily, both Mrs. Goodge and the times had changed. When she'd heard from a mutual friend that Winnie lived in Ealing, Mrs. Goodge had made it a point to renew her acquaintance. But it had been almost a year since Winnie had last come for tea and Mrs. Goodge was glad for her company.

Winnie had left service years earlier, married, and with her husband, opened a tobacconist shop. Mrs. Goodge genuinely liked her. She was intelligent, observant, and most of all, she had an excellent memory.

"Me, too, but I can't for the life of me remember where."

"Is it important?" Winnie eyed her curiously. She was a small, thin-framed woman with steel-rimmed spectacles and hair that had once been auburn but was now more gray than red. Her business had done well, and she was fashionably dressed in a brown wool skirt and white high-necked blouse beneath her brown and gold plaid jacket. A small gold broach in the shape of a butterfly was on her lapel. "Something to do with one of your inspector's cases. Ida Leacock mentioned that you tried to help him with his work."

"I don't know that I'd call it 'helping with his work.' " Mrs. Goodge laughed. "But I do try to pass on any information I can find. Let's be honest now, given the number of years we both were in service, we saw and heard quite a bit. But you're right — Montague's name has cropped up in the inspector's latest case. These days my memory is so tricky, sometimes things come to me easily but sometimes they don't. Have another scone." She pushed the plate toward her guest.

Winnie helped herself. "Thank you, I will. These are delicious; you always were a wonderful baker."

"It's kind of you to say so." Mrs. Goodge poured herself a second cup of tea and added milk and sugar.

"I remember now!" Winnie cried around a mouthful of scone. "Lucius Montague was the one that Miss Pargeter chased out of the house. Surely you remember, the Pargeters lived up the road from his lordship."

"That's right, they had the estate next to

the river," Mrs. Goodge murmured. "I remember them now. They were very, very rich."

"I should think you ought to." Winnie laughed. "Old Richard Pargeter was always trying to steal you away from Lord Rutherford. He was often a dinner guest and he loved your cooking."

Memory flooded back as wave after wave of images, snatches of conversations, and even feelings washed over her. For a brief moment, she was back in the kitchen of Lord Rutherford's estate, stirring a béchamel sauce and issuing orders to the scullery maids. "Oh my gracious, now I remember." She started to laugh. "What a to-do it caused; everyone talked about it for weeks."

Winnie chuckled. "We most certainly did. It isn't every day that you hear of a guest chased out of the house by his own hostess, and Lottie Drummond, remember, she was the scullery maid, she saw the whole thing."

"I was supposed to disapprove of kitchen gossip, but I couldn't help but listen when Lottie told it." Mrs. Goodge laughed harder. "Lady Rutherford had sent Lottie over to the Pargeters with a basket of gooseberries from the garden. Just as Lottie got there, she saw Abigail Pargeter chasing Lucius Montague out the front door."

"She was bashing him with her umbrella." Winnie snickered. "And screaming for him to get off the property and not come back. When Lottie got to the kitchen, she found out that Miss Abigail had seen Montague kick a stray puppy down the back stairs."

"That's right and the poor thing was badly hurt. I remember Lord Rutherford going on and on about how it should have been put down. It was a little spaniel mix and Miss Pargeter wouldn't hear of it being shot. She nursed it back to health."

"It did end up with a limp, but it became her pet. It went everywhere with her. The Pargeters were all animal lovers."

Ruth found Valentine Road easily enough. The Executive Committee of her Women's Suffrage Group was meeting nearby for luncheon, but as she was early, she'd decided to have a quick look at Ellen Langston-Jones' lodging house. She walked down the street, looking for number 14. At the first house she passed, a housemaid was scrubbing the stoop and had her rags and mop propped against the house numbers. It was the same at the house next to it, where two workmen were plastering the front. She finally spotted an address on the third house and realized that number 14 was on the other side of the street. Stepping off the pavement, she waited till a hansom cab went past and then continued to the other side. A well-dressed matron followed by a footman carrying packages glanced her way as she came around an empty wagon and stepped onto the pavement.

In front of the gate of number 14 a stout woman wearing a floppy cap stood with her hands on her hips. She was arguing with a balding, slender man wearing a blue suit and holding a bowler hat. Ruth slipped past them, taking care to keep her eyes straight ahead as if she hadn't noticed they were in the midst of a quarrel.

"I'm sorry you've gone to the trouble of hiring a wagon for her things, but the police have told me I wasn't to let anyone inside."

"Mrs. Otis, be reasonable. The police have no right to tell you who you can or cannot let into her rooms."

"Mr. Langston-Jones, I know it's inconvenient for you, but I'm going to do what they said. You'll have to come back later, when the police are finished gathering their evidence."

"This is outrageous!" he cried. "I'm her only relative and I've got a right to look after her possessions. Furthermore, you've already said you allowed Sir Donovan Gaines into the premises. You'd no right to do that. Did he take anything?"

"He came for the boy and all they took was a case for the lad's clothing," she said. "What's more, the police hadn't been here then so I didn't know I wasn't supposed to let anyone into her rooms."

Ruth walked as slowly as she could.

"Mr. Langston-Jones," the driver called from the wagon. "We've not got all day if we're goin' to make the four o'clock train. Are we goin' to be loadin' up or not?"

Ruth yanked a handkerchief out of her pocket, dashed it across her nose, and then dropped it. As she knelt down, she glanced at the wagon and saw HINTON'S REMOVALS written in bold red letters along the side. It had a flat, open bed with high metal frames along the sides. Two bundles of newspapers tied up with string and coils of rope were stacked in the corner. A man wearing a flat cap and heavy work boots was standing next to one of the horses, holding on to the harness. He saw Ruth looking in his direction and smiled.

She grabbed the handkerchief and straightened up.

"You'll not be loading anything from this house!" the woman yelled at the driver.

"Please, Mrs. Otis, I just want to get in

and take the paintings," the man pleaded. "They belonged to my brother."

"And now they belong to his widow." The woman pointed to her left. Both the workmen and the housemaid had stopped and were watching the drama unfold. "Now look what you've done. This is a decent house and you've got my neighbors and everyone else out gawking. I'll thank you to go along and leave me in peace."

"Give it up, guv, she's not going to let us in," the driver called. "Come on, time's awastin' and we've got another job this afternoon."

Ruth saw Langston-Jones clench his hands into fists. "Do you know how much this is costing me?"

"I'm sure I don't, sir, and I'm sorry for all the trouble you've gone to, but you'll have to come back when this is all settled." She folded her arms over her chest.

"Hey, guv, either get us in there or come on," the man holding the harness called.

"I shall hold you personally responsible for all my expenses," Langston-Jones said. He turned on his heel and stalked to the wagon. "You'll be hearing from my solicitor." Then he climbed into the seat next to the driver. The other man leapt into the empty bed and the wagon pulled away.

The woman watched until they turned the corner, then she marched into her house, slamming the door hard enough to make the windows rattle.

Ruth let out the breath she didn't realize she'd been holding. She continued walking, this time moving quickly. She couldn't wait till this afternoon's meeting.

CHAPTER 5

Smythe stared at the barmaid, his expression incredulous. "What do ya mean 'e's not 'ere?"

Amused, she raised her eyebrows and set the glass she'd just dried on the counter. "It means exactly what I said, Blimpey's not here. He's takin' a holiday. His Nell wanted to go to Brighton to see the Royal Pavilion."

Smythe couldn't believe his ears. Blimpey Groggins, owner of the Dirty Duck Pub and supplier of information to those who could afford his big fat fees, was always here. "But he never takes a holiday," he protested. "What's got into 'im? 'E's got a business to run."

The barmaid, a buxom thirtyish woman with curly brown hair and a wide mouth, shrugged. "They've only gone for the day. He'll be back on the nine o'clock train. I'll tell him you were here. Now, do you want a pint or not?" She glanced up as the front door opened and a man wearing a gray checked fedora cocked at a jaunty angle and a matching suit jacket stepped inside. "I'll be with you in a minute, Henry."

"I don't have time for a drink, I want to see Blimpey," the man called Henry replied, his gaze fixed on her as he crossed the room toward the bar. "I've got some information about that murder over on Portland Villas, and it's hot, but I need him right quick, my paper's going to press in less than two hours."

"Then you're out of luck, Henry. He's gone to Brighton."

"Brighton?" He stopped, his expression crestfallen.

"That's right and he won't be back until tonight." She turned her attention back to Smythe, but he was already heading for the door.

"Tell Blimpey I'll be back tomorrow," he called over his shoulder as he left.

Smythe stepped off the dusty pavement, dodged a brewery wagon loaded with kegs, and sprinted in front of a four-wheeler and a hansom as he made his way to the far side of the road. He scanned the buildings along the street, spotted what he needed, and then raced toward a recessed alcove between a grocer's shop and a baker's. Wedging himself into the space, he kept his gaze on the pub. He didn't have to wait long before the reporter emerged and turned to his left.

Smythe went after him. He followed him for several blocks, staying on the opposite side of the street, then he crossed again and came abreast of him. He gave a polite nod as the fellow glanced his way. "Can I 'ave a word with ya?"

"What about?" he asked, his eyes narrowed in recognition. "Didn't I just see you in the Dirty Duck? Are you following me?" He stopped in front of an estate agent's office. "What do you want?"

Smythe came to a halt and smiled slowly as he saw the panic flash across Henry's face. He had him now. There was fear in the man's brown eyes as he realized that he'd been overheard and, even worse, that Smythe had understood exactly why he'd come bursting into the Dirty Duck looking for Blimpey. He didn't know which paper Henry worked at, but he knew good and well that if the man's guv found out he'd been flogging news *before* it was printed in their papers, he'd get the sack. "I just want to talk to ya. I was at the pub for the same reason you were, to see Blimpey. Only I was there to buy a bit of information, not sell it."

"Have you gone daft?" he blustered. He puffed himself up, standing straight, taking deep breaths and trying to look as if he were offended. "I don't know what you're on about. I only stopped in to have a pint. There's no law against that."

"Don't be stupid. I heard you tell the barmaid you didn't want a drink. You 'ave information about the Langston-Jones murder and you were goin' to sell it to Blimpey. Come on, then, let's be civilized about this. You've got somethin' of value that I want and I've got a pocketful of cash."

Henry hesitated a moment, then he said, "How much cash?"

"I can afford Blimpey's prices, can't I." He pointed toward another pub on the corner. "Let's go 'ave a sit-down over at the Three Angels. I'll buy you a pint and we can discuss the matter."

"The barmaid will tell Blimpey I stopped in and he's got eyes everywhere." He laughed harshly. "If he finds out I've cut him out of this, he'll not like it."

"I'll take care of 'im. If someone spots you and runs tellin' tales, I'll make it right with Blimpey. Take my word for it, you'll not be 'ard done by. Can we get a move on, I've not got much time."

"Why should I take your word for anything," he protested. "I don't know you from Adam and I've a nice bit of business going with Groggins. Why should I risk that by sellin' my information to you?"

"Because I'll pay for it right now." He pulled a roll of pound notes out of his pocket and held it under the reporter's nose. "By the time Blimpey's available tomorrow, some or all of it will 'ave been published in your paper so I'll not need to buy it then," he said. "But if you're not interested, I'll be on my way." He turned away and started walking.

"Wait a minute," Henry called. "I suppose there's no harm in having a quick drink."

"Come on then." Smythe glanced over his shoulder. Good old Henry was right behind him. That was one of the nice things about doing business with people who could be bought; waving a few quid under their noses always paid off.

"I'm still puzzled by those brochures and timetables," Barnes said as the hansom pulled up in front of Lucius Montague's house.

"Timetables?" the inspector repeated. "You mean the ones from Thomas Cook. Well, it's not surprising she'd have them; she did travel here from France." He

153

grabbed the hand strap as the cab lurched to a stop.

"True, sir, but these weren't cross-channel train or ship schedules. They were sailings to the Far East and America. She'd circled two of them. One was from here to India and the other was between Singapore and San Francisco," he said.

Witherspoon stepped out and pushed his spectacles up his nose while he waited for Barnes to pay the driver. "But surely if she were serious about leaving the country, someone would have mentioned it to us. Mrs. Otis said nothing about her giving notice."

"Maybe she didn't know. The sailings were for late August and September, sir. From what we've learned, Mrs. Langston-Jones was a strong, independent woman, you know, the sort of person who keeps her own counsel."

"She certainly seemed to be a very modern kind of woman," he mused. He smiled as the image of another progressive lady, his own dear Ruth, flashed through his mind. "Perhaps she felt her future plans weren't anyone else's concern."

"We need to have another search of the flat, sir. If she was going to leave England, that might have some bearing on her murder."

Witherspoon frowned. "But if she was going away, why would she be threatening lawsuits? Those things take ages to come before the courts, and we know from Montague's letter that she was going to sue him."

"Maybe she didn't know how long civil cases can take," he suggested. "She might have thought it would be over and done with before she left. I've got a feeling, sir, we don't know for sure that she was going anywhere, least of all sailing off to foreign countries, but if those timetables mean anything, it's worth looking into."

"I take your point, Constable. There could be any number of circumstances pertaining to her plans that we simply don't know." He looked toward the house. "But one thing we do know is that Lucius Montague made what could be construed as a very definite threat against her. Let's see what he's got to say for himself."

They went up the walk and climbed the stairs. Barnes banged the brass knocker. "But there is one thing I don't understand. If Mrs. Langston-Jones was leaving England, where would she get the money? Travel like that doesn't come cheap."

"Indeed it doesn't," the inspector agreed.

155

"But perhaps there was more to her husband's estate than we know. She had his paintings shipped here for a reason."

The door opened and a stern-looking woman in black glared out at them. "May I help you?"

"We'd like to see Mr. Lucius Montague." Witherspoon smiled politely. "I'm Inspector Witherspoon and this is Constable Barnes."

"He's not here." She crossed her arms over her chest. "He sent me out to fetch him a cab over an hour ago even though that's not my job. I'm the housekeeper."

"Do you know when he'll be back?" Barnes studied the woman. Her mouth was set in a grim line, her deep-set hazel eyes were flashing with anger, and her comments along with the way she held herself suggested she wasn't fond of her employer. A nice long chat with Montague's housekeeper might be very useful. He bet she'd have plenty to say. "Forgive me, ma'am," he began before she could respond. "It was rude of me to ask such a question." He nodded apologetically. "You're not responsible for Mr. Montague's comings and goings."

Witherspoon flicked a quick, assessing look at his constable. He wasn't sure what he was up to, but he trusted Barnes implicitly and followed his lead. "Yes, please do

156

forgive us. This must be a very difficult time for you and all of the household. Having a murder on your doorstep is most unpleasant."

She lowered her arms and smiled tremulously. "You're very kind." Her eyes filled with tears. "He's not the easiest of employers, and since the murder happened, he's been even worse. He came tearing in here yesterday afternoon as though the devil himself were chasing him. He locked himself in his study and banged around like a madman for what seemed like hours."

"What do you mean, ma'am?" Barnes asked softly. "Banged around how?"

"It was awful, Constable, and it so frightened the housemaids that they came running into the kitchen to find me. When we got up there, we could hear things thumping against the floorboards and then drawers slamming open and shut. Then he came flying out and just stopped long enough to scream about how someone had been in his study and who was it? I told him I'd no idea what he was talking about, that none of us had been in there since the previous week. We're only allowed into the room to clean on Thursday mornings when he's at his club."

"What happened then?" Witherspoon asked.

"He shouted that we were all useless and ordered us to tidy up his study and then stormed out of the house. When the girls and I went in, it looked as if he'd gone mad. The books from the shelves were on the floor, his desk drawers were open, and there was an open leather case he'd kicked into a corner."

"Case?" Barnes said sharply. "What kind of case? Can you describe it?"

She drew back and stared at them for a long moment, as if she'd just realized she'd said too much. Then she shrugged and held the door wider. "What do I care?" she muttered. "There's naught he can do to me now. Come in, I'll show it to you."

Witherspoon took the lead as they stepped inside and followed her. He told himself they weren't doing anything wrong. Even though Montague wasn't under arrest and they had no definitive knowledge that he was guilty, they'd been invited into the home by a legitimate member of the household, so if the case reached a courtroom, even the cleverest of barristers couldn't claim they'd overstepped their bounds or deprived Mr. Montague of any of his rights.

The black and white tiles of the corridor

stretched past a wide staircase carpeted in green. Landscape paintings and ancestral portraits hung along the pale coral walls, and overhead, three small brass chandeliers were spaced evenly along the ceiling. The housekeeper stopped at the last door along the hallway. "It's just in here," she said as she went inside.

They followed her into the study. The walls were a deep forest green, and the floor covered with a fading but beautiful Persian carpet. Heavy gold damask curtains framed the windows on each side of the marble hearth, and a gilt-framed mirror hung over the mantelpiece. Floor-to-ceiling shelves filled with books and knick-knacks covered the walls flanking the fireplace and a massive desk with an overstuffed green leather chair was in the corner. A gray and green settee and a table with ceramic figurines on a jade and gold fringed runner made up the remainder of the furnishings.

"There, that's the one he kicked." She pointed at a black leather case sitting on the edge of the desk.

Barnes looked at his superior. "Should we have a look inside, sir?" he asked. But even from this distance, he was fairly sure he knew what it was.

"Oh, I think so," Witherspoon agreed.

"Considering what kind of weapon was used to murder Mrs. Langston-Jones, we've cause to examine it closely." He crossed the room and snapped it open. "Just as I thought, it's a gun case."

Barnes came up behind him. "And the gun is gone. Take a look at that, sir." He pointed to the inside of the lid. "Those initials printed there, they belong to Lucius Montague" — then he gestured to the inside of the case — "and a Beaumont Adams would fit perfectly in the gun rest."

"So it seems," Witherspoon said. He looked up and smiled at the housekeeper. "What's your name, ma'am?"

"Jane Redman," she replied. "As I said, I'm the housekeeper here, but not for much longer. I've given my notice and I shall be leaving within a fortnight."

"Why, exactly, did you give your notice?" Barnes had the feeling there was more to this than a temper tantrum from Lucius Montague.

"I don't mind an employer getting annoyed every now and again," she said. "But I'll not be spoken to the way he spoke to me yesterday. He was upset and that's understandable because it certainly isn't pleasant to come across a body, but that's no excuse for how he talked to us when he came out of here yesterday afternoon. I gave him my notice last night, and after what happened today, I imagine the housemaids and the cook that was just hired will be giving theirs as well."

"What happened today?" Witherspoon asked. The information was coming so fast it was difficult to take it all in. He hoped he wouldn't forget any pertinent details.

"He told us we'd not be paid our quarterly wages," she snorted. "We're due them at the end of this month, and right after breakfast today he called us all in and said we'd not get them, that we'd have to wait. Everyone was most upset but did he care, he most certainly did not, and when one of the housemaids complained that it wasn't fair, he told her she'd not be getting much anyway because she'd lost the pillow that goes on that stupid thing." She pointed to the settee opposite the desk. "And that it was an expensive cushion, hand sewn in Belgium or some such nonsense. Then he said he'd take the cost of it out of her wages. She started crying and said she'd not touched his ruddy pillow, that none of us had been in the stupid room since we'd cleaned it last week."

"What color is the missing pillow?" Witherspoon asked. He glanced at Barnes.

161

"Green."

"Have you taken legal advice?" Fiona asked her visitor. She glanced at the clock and saw it wasn't even three yet, so she didn't offer to ring for tea.

"Not as yet," he admitted. "But I've sent a note telling my solicitor to come and see me today. I told him I'd be free at half past four."

Fiona couldn't believe her ears. "Lucius, have you lost your mind?" She got up and began to pace the drawing room. She'd hoped that he would have heeded her words and gone immediately to the best criminal defense lawyer in London, but instead, the fool had gone home and sulked.

He drew back in surprise. "Whatever do you mean? You told me not to worry, that if I was innocent, which I am, that inspector person wouldn't arrest me."

"I also told you to get legal help," she snapped. She took a deep breath and brought herself under control.

"And I'm going to do just that." He clasped his hands together. "I've told you I'm seeing my solicitor this afternoon. Ah, I've a question to ask you."

She stopped in front of the window and turned to face him. She wished she'd told the staff to say she wasn't receiving when he turned up this afternoon, but she'd felt sorry for him. "Go ahead."

"When that man was murdered at your husband's office, did the police snoop about unduly?"

"Unduly?"

"You know, look through his correspondence, read his mail, go through the dustbins, that sort of thing," he explained.

"Yes, they searched his office quite thoroughly and I imagine they also had a look around his home, why?"

He closed his eyes and swallowed heavily. "Oh dear, I was afraid of that. Well, perhaps it will be alright, perhaps she didn't keep the letter."

"Letter, what letter?" Fiona felt her temples begin to throb. "I can't be of any help to you unless you tell me everything. What on earth are you talking about?" She had a horrible feeling his situation was about to get worse.

"Several days before she was murdered, I wrote Mrs. Langston-Jones and told her that I wasn't going to pay her what she felt I owed. Why should I have paid? I didn't buy the paintings from her, I bought them from a gallery in Paris."

"You're splitting hairs, Lucius. You've

already admitted the gallery had the paintings on consignment so you actually do owe her the money. Was that all you wrote?"

He looked down at his feet. "I'm afraid not. I also said that if she took me to court, there would be dire consequences." He straightened his spine, lifted his chin, and looked Fiona directly in the eye. "I wasn't having it. I wasn't going to allow someone like her, a nobody, a tutor for goodness' sake, to threaten my reputation."

"And you put this in writing?" she pressed. Dear God, as much as she felt pity for his predicament, he was a complete fool.

He nodded. "I fear that might have been a mistake. I only meant that I'd go to Sir Donovan if she kept pursuing the matter. Upon reflection, the police may see the contents of the letter quite differently."

"I'm sure they will."

"Furthermore, after I'd sent it, I realized that her influence with Sir Donovan was far greater than mine. I'm a regular guest at their table, but it's usually Mrs. Barclay who sends the invitations."

"Let me make sure I understand this. You had a public disagreement with the woman a week before she was killed, you owed her money which you weren't in a position to return, and when she pressed you to make good a perfectly legitimate debt, you threatened her with 'dire consequences.' On top of which, you now admit that she was killed with your gun. By heavens, if you can't understand that you're in need of a good lawyer, then nothing I can do will help you."

His face paled and he collapsed onto the chair. "Dear God, Fiona, I don't know what to do. I'm not just worried about the police. Even if they don't arrest me, if Sir Donovan suspects I had anything to do with that woman's death, he'll never speak to me again. He'll cut me dead publicly."

Fiona stared at him. She'd always known he was the worst of snobs and, possibly, not the most intelligent man of her acquaintance, but she'd never realized he was so dense he couldn't understand how much danger he was in at the moment. This country was changing, and just because one had power, aristocratic friends, and a few royal relatives didn't make them immune from the laws of the land. "Lucius, listen to me and listen well. I know whereof I speak. Being cut dead by Sir Donovan is the least of your concerns. Right now, the only thing that matters is making sure the police don't arrest you."

"But I didn't kill her. I didn't do it!" he wailed.

She tried to think of what to do next. Lucius was his own worst enemy, but considering what had happened to her, she couldn't in good conscience abandon him now. "You may well be as innocent as you claim, but the evidence against you is formidable and appears to multiply every time I see you." She laughed harshly as memories of her own brush with the inexorable arm of the law washed over her.

"I'm a gentleman!" he cried as he leapt up. "My mother is the first cousin of the King of Bulgaria. My godfather is a cabinet minister, and one of my great-aunts was a lady-in-waiting to Queen Adelaide. Surely that counts for something. I've power and influence."

"Of course it counts for something," Fiona snapped. "But not when the press starts screaming for your blood, and believe me, they will. You can't keep these things quiet anymore. Your servants hate you; surely you realize they'll be only too happy not only to tell the police everything they know, but also the papers. Once that happens, no matter how much influence you think you have, the police will have no choice — you'll be arrested, tried, and probably convicted."

■ ■ ■ ■

Luty was the last to arrive and late to boot. She could hear the others talking and laughing as she raced down the hallway. Reaching the doorway, she stopped and put her hands on her hips as she surveyed the kitchen. "Where's my godchild?" she demanded. "I've waited all day to give her a cuddle."

"You'll have to wait just a bit more, I'm afraid." Mrs. Jeffries smiled sympathetically. "The little one's not feeling well so Betsy took her home. But she'll be here for morning tea tomorrow."

"What's wrong with her?" Smythe's eyebrows drew together in a worried frown.

"The same thing that was wrong with her yesterday." The cook pushed the cup of tea she'd just poured toward him. "Our Miss Belle is still teething and that's makin' her miserable. Betsy thought it would be easier on the both of them if they were at home."

Visibly relieved, he picked up his mug. "That's good. I'm glad it's just the baby's teeth that's botherin' her. There's rumors of another outbreak of measles over in Fulham and that's a bit worryin'."

"We all worry." Luty took her seat. "Every

time you turn around, there's another case of some miserable disease or another. Now I don't believe in coddlin' youngsters, but I'm awful glad our Betsy is a modern mother and keeps the baby away from infected areas and people. You just be sure to tell her to stay away from Fulham."

Mrs. Jeffries caught Ruth's eye and they both ducked their heads to hide their smiles. Luty coddled, fussed, and bragged about her goddaughter to anyone who would stand still for thirty seconds.

"Who'd like to go first?" Mrs. Jeffries glanced at the clock and noted they weren't pressed for time. The inspector shouldn't be home for at least another hour.

"I might as well tell you my bit," the cook offered. "I'll need to get up and baste that chicken in a few minutes. I had an old acquaintance here today and she jogged my memory as to where I'd heard the name of Lucius Montague." She told them about her conversation with Winnie Roberts. "Apparently, Abigail Pargeter chased Montague out of the house with an umbrella and then had his trunk tossed out of the upstairs bedroom window. Winnie said that Montague was going to sue for damages to his luggage but decided not to when someone pointed out to him that kicking a helpless dog down a flight of stairs wouldn't go over well with either a judge or a jury," she concluded.

"Cor blimey, and it wasn't even the family pet." Wiggins chuckled. "Good for this Miss Pargeter. People that are cruel to 'elpless animals ought to be given a dose of their own medicine." He glanced at Fred, who was curled up on his rug by the cooker.

"He sounds a terrible man," Ruth agreed. Personally, she was fond of cats and owned two of them. But she'd grown up with dogs and loved them as well.

"He is a terrible man," Phyllis blurted out. "He tries to get people sacked for the least little thing. Oh, sorry, I know it's not my turn."

"I'm done." Mrs. Goodge got up. "I'll just check that chicken. Carry on, I can listen while I work."

"Go on," Mrs. Jeffries told the maid. "You've obviously heard something as well."

Phyllis told them what she'd heard about Montague from the clerk at the greengrocers. "So you can see why the shopkeepers and all the clerks along the high street don't like him," she finished.

"I don't blame them," Hatchet murmured. "He doesn't pay his bills on time, he complains about the service, he tries to get people sacked, and he tortures poor animals.

Not only is he not a gentleman, but he seems a thoroughly bad lot to boot. One doesn't like to speculate; however, his actions do illustrate the kind of character the man has and, well, I wouldn't be surprised if he turns out to be the killer."

"I think 'e is the killer," Wiggins blurted out. "Anyone who'd kick a little spaniel puppy down the stairs hard enough to ruin its leg is capable of anything."

"We mustn't jump to conclusions simply because we don't approve of the man's character," Mrs. Jeffries warned. "There are other people in Mrs. Langston-Jones' circle and one of them might well be the murderer."

"Wait till you hear what I found out today," Wiggins said. "Then you'll see, 'e's a right bad one." He told them about his meeting with Lucius Montague's housemaid. He made sure he described everything, including the fact that the poor girl had been in tears. "Not only are their wages goin' to be late," he said, "but Shirley, that's her name, told me that once they get 'em, she's goin' to be charged for a pillow that's disappeared from his study. Poor Shirley doesn't know what's happened to the ruddy thing."

But Mrs. Jeffries had focused on something else he'd mentioned. "This case that Montague had kicked into the corner, did she know what had been in it?"

"She said she'd never seen it before. She said he was always cold and formal, but yesterday afternoon, they thought he'd gone mad. Then when he told them they'd not be paid this morning, they were really upset. Shirley gave me an earful. She went on and on about what a miserable place it was to work and now she thinks it's goin' to get worse. The housekeeper has handed in her notice, and the cook, who just started a day or so ago, has sent off a note to the domestic agency that sent her to Montague's house and told them she wasn't goin' to stay on. But poor Shirley is stuck there. She can't leave till she finds another position, but she's goin' to go as soon as she finds one. I tell ya, she did go on about the man, but I don't much blame her, this Mr. Montague is a real blackguard if there ever was one." He sat back in his chair. "That's it for me."

Mrs. Jeffries glanced at Ruth. "Did you learn anything at your women's group meeting?"

"Yes, I have two items to report." She grinned broadly. "One of which I heard at the luncheon and one of which I found out because I took a short walk to satisfy my

171

curiosity." She told them about her stroll past Ellen Langston-Jones' lodgings and the argument she'd witnessed.

"Now that's very interesting," Mrs. Jeffries murmured. "The poor woman isn't even buried, yet her brother-in-law turns up with a large removal wagon."

"Wonder what she had that he's so keen to get 'is 'ands on." Smythe took a sip of tea.

"Perhaps she had some nice furniture," Phyllis suggested. "You know, from her home in France."

"That's certainly possible," Ruth said. "But she and her son had rooms in a lodging house, not an unfurnished flat."

"Which means the rooms would have had their own furniture." Mrs. Jeffries nodded in understanding. "So if Jonathan Langston-Jones showed up with an empty removals wagon, he obviously thought there was something other than clothing, personal items, and the victim's papers to haul away."

"Now who is speculating?" Hatchet warned them with a smile. "For all we know, Langston-Jones showed up with a wagon because he knew she had half a dozen trunks stored in her landlady's attic, or perhaps that was the only vehicle available to him."

"True," Ruth said. "But I did find it curious that he was so insistent on getting inside her rooms. That struck me as very suspicious."

"Not as suspicious as Montague's kickin' poor innocent animals and tryin' to cheat servants out of their wages," Wiggins charged. "If you ask me, anyone who acts like that is capable of shootin' someone without so much as blinkin' an eye."

Mrs. Jeffries didn't want them to waste any more time arguing about Montague's character. But then something her husband used to say suddenly flew into her mind. "It's not good to jump to conclusions too early in an investigation, but evidence is evidence, and most of the time, the obvious person is the guilty person." She pushed the thought away and concentrated on the matter at hand. "Go on, Ruth, tell us the rest."

She smiled ruefully. "I'm afraid it isn't near as exciting as the argument. But at the luncheon, I heard a bit of gossip about a friend of Sir Donovan's late wife."

The cook shoved the chicken back into the oven and closed the door. "More than once it's been a bit of gossip that caught the killer. What did you hear?"

Ruth tapped her finger against the side of her mug. "Well, there's quite a number of women on the Executive Committee so we got through the business portion of the meeting first and then went into luncheon. Instead of using her dining room, Judith Seabourne had set up small tables in one of the reception rooms. They were crowded quite close together and everyone was chatting and it was very loud. I had to raise my voice in order to be heard, and I'd just asked if anyone knew anything about the poor murdered woman when we had one of those odd lulls in the noise and my voice carried quite clearly around the room." She gave an embarrassed shrug. "It was awkward, but as no one at my table knew anything, the conversational noise level moved back to where it had been. But just as I was leaving, Diana Osmond stopped me and said she'd seen Mrs. Langston-Jones and Sir Donovan Gaines in front of a building on the Strand last week."

"They were together?" Mrs. Jeffries asked.

"I asked her that specifically and she admitted she wasn't sure," Ruth said. "She said she saw Sir Donovan first, he was just standing on the pavement. Then a hansom pulled up and Mrs. Langston-Jones got out of it. But she couldn't tell if it was a prearranged meeting or accidental. She claimed she normally isn't one to stand and gawk on a public street, but when the lady had first stepped down from the cab, Diana had been sure it was her friend Mrs. Linthorpe and she wanted to say 'hello.' But it wasn't Mrs. Linthorpe, it was Mrs. Langston-Jones, and when Diana realized her mistake, she went on her way." She stopped and looked around the table. "Though I am loath to be a party to fostering society's negative views about females and gossip, once Diana started talking, she spoke very freely."

"I hope it was somethin' good and juicy." Luty helped herself to a slice of bread. "The gossip I heard today ain't hardly worth repeatin'."

"We're aware that your Women's Suffrage Group is dedicated not only to getting females the right to vote, but also to eliminating the unhelpful attitudes so many people believe about women in our society," Mrs. Jeffries said. "But what did she say?"

"Oh dear, I did sound pompous, didn't I." She laughed. "Diana told me that Hester Linthorp and Sir Donovan's late wife were good friends and that, since Christmas, Mrs. Linthorp had become a regular guest at the Gaines house. Martha Barclay invites her to dine with them at least once a week. The mourning period for the late Lady

Gaines is now past, and Diana thinks there might be a discreet announcement coming from that quarter."

"Mrs. Linthorp's going to become the second Lady Gaines?" Mrs. Jeffries clarified.

"Diana hadn't spoken to her recently, but when she saw her after the holidays, Mrs. Linthorp hinted that might be the case." Ruth shrugged. "I know it's just a bit of gossip and probably has nothing to do with the murder, but I did want to pass it along."

"At this point none of us know what information might end up being pertinent." Mrs. Jeffries looked at Smythe and then Hatchet.

"I'm afraid today wasn't very successful," Hatchet said. "Like Ruth, all I found out was a bit of gossip, and frankly, my source was in his cups."

"Buttonholed a drunk, did ya." Luty cackled. "That's sad, Hatchet, real sad."

"I most certainly did not 'buttonhole a drunk,' " he shot back. "I availed myself of the opportunity to have a word with Andrew Glassock, who is supposedly a friend of one of our leading suspects. Unfortunately, Glassock is also inordinately fond of whiskey."

"Which friend?" Phyllis took a sip of tea.

176

"Lucius Montague, but as I said, I learned nothing new."

"What did he tell you?" Mrs. Jeffries interjected.

"Nothing we didn't already suspect." He sighed. "During a conversation at a dinner party a few weeks ago, the subject of firearms came up and Lucius Montague took the opportunity to brag that he owned a Beaumont Adams and that it was inscribed with his initials. But I've other sources I'm seeing tomorrow and it's sure to be a better day."

"That's the spirit!" Luty cried.

Hatchet gave her a sour smile.

"If no one else 'as anything to say, I'll tell ya what I found out." Smythe paused and waited a moment. When no one spoke, he continued, "You're goin' to be shocked by what I tell ya. I was."

"Cor blimey, that doesn't sound good," Wiggins muttered.

"Accordin' to my source, Lucius Montague is goin' to be taken into custody soon. The evidence is piling up against the fellow and there's someone in the Home Office that's putting pressure on the police to arrest him."

"Arrested! But it's far too early in the investigation for that," Mrs. Jeffries protested. "The inspector won't do it. Not unless he's absolutely sure the man is guilty."

"I know." Smythe sighed heavily. "But if he doesn't, our inspector will be pulled off the case."

"But why?" Ruth asked.

"The only thing my source could tell me was that Montague might have some powerful friends, but he's also made some powerful enemies."

"That's not right." Wiggins frowned. "No one should be drug into the dock because some toff at the Home Office don't like you."

"Was your source absolutely sure of this?" Mrs. Jeffries pressed.

"He was," Smythe said. "For the life of me, I don't know how he found out his facts, but he was dead certain." That was a bald-faced lie, as Smythe had insisted the reporter tell him how he'd obtained his information and Henry cheerfully admitted he'd bribed two clerks at the Home Office. "What's more, there's worse news, and it affects our inspector as well. In tonight's papers, there's going to be hints made that the police aren't doin' a proper job because the chief suspect is related to European royalty."

"Cor blimey, it'll be just like them Ripper

178

murders. Remember what 'appened to the men in charge of that case once the newspapers went after 'em," Wiggins muttered. "It's not fair."

"And it's not going to happen," Mrs. Jeffries declared. "For goodness' sake, she was only murdered two days ago, and what's more, the circumstances were nothing like when the Ripper was terrorizing London. We're not going to let this stop us from doing what we always do. Nothing has happened yet. So let's get on with this meeting. It is getting late and sometimes, even when he's on a case, the inspector comes home early. Luty, do you have anything to report?"

"Nothin' as good as what Smythe just told us," Luty admitted. "But I did find out a little something. I found a source that told me Sir Donovan was fixin' to sell off most of his property here in London and he was liquidatin' all his stocks and bonds."

"Was your source reliable?" Hatchet asked archly.

"He's as reliable as yours was and mine wasn't drunk," she snapped.

"Just because mine was inebriated doesn't . . ." He broke off as they heard a knock on the back door.

Wiggins got up first. "I'll get it."

They waited in silence while he went

down the hall. Then they heard the door open, followed by the soft murmur of a well-bred female voice and the sounds of footsteps.

"We've got a visitor," he announced as he led their guest into the kitchen.

Uncertain of her welcome, Fiona Sutcliffe stood beneath the arched doorway of the kitchen and smiled nervously. She was smartly dressed in a pale blue jacket with a matching hat and veil. An oval garnet broach was pinned to the center of her high-collared white blouse, and matching earrings hung from her lobes. "Hello, everyone, do forgive me for barging in without so much as a by-your-leave, but my business is rather urgent."

Mrs. Jeffries got up. She wasn't sure how to react. Her sister-in-law was the last person she'd ever expect to come knocking on the back door. If asked, Mrs. Jeffries would have sworn on a stack of Bibles that using the servants or tradesman entrance was simply out of the realm of possibility for the woman, but nonetheless, that's the way she'd come. "Hello, Fiona. Do come in."

They'd renewed their acquaintance recently as she'd helped prove Fiona hadn't committed murder, but despite this, the dif-

180

ferences in both their characters and their social status ensured they'd have very little to do with each other. She gestured at the empty chair next to Smythe. "Have a seat."

"Thank you." She started toward the table and then stopped as Fred got to his feet.

"Don't worry, 'e won't 'urt you," Wiggins assured her. "Lie down, boy. It's fine, she's a friend."

"I certainly hope I'm considered a friend." She smiled at Wiggins as she went to her seat. "You've all done me a great service in the past and I shall never forget it."

Mrs. Jeffries kept her expression serene as she waited for Fiona to sit down. Inside, she was seething as all manner of thoughts raced through her head. What was she doing here? What did she want? She didn't think for one minute that she was here to renew either their kinship bonds or their friendship. "What kind of urgent business?"

"The kind all of you are very much familiar with." Fiona's smile faded as she pulled out her chair. "It's quite literally a matter of life and death."

CHAPTER 6

The traffic was so bad that it took the better part of an hour to reach the solicitor's office on the Strand. "We're sorry to come so late," Witherspoon apologized to Hamish Todd as they shook hands, "but there was an accident on Charing Cross Road that held us up. This is my colleague, Constable Barnes."

Todd, a small man with a ready smile, a ruddy complexion, and wispy gray hair sticking up in tufts, motioned toward two straight-backed chairs in front of his desk. "Not to worry, Inspector, my clerk and I work until six. I've been expecting you. You're here about Mrs. Langston-Jones, aren't you?"

"I'm afraid so." Witherspoon settled into his seat.

Todd sat down. "Dreadful business, absolutely dreadful. She was a lovely woman and I was very upset when I learned the manner of her death."

"You knew her in a professional capacity, sir?" Barnes asked as he took out his little brown notebook.

"That's correct. She came to see me soon after she arrived in London." There was a box file on his desk and he pulled it in front of him, unwrapped the string, and opened it up. Reaching inside, he drew out a thick sheaf of papers and put them on the desktop. "Let me see." He scanned the top page. "Yes, that's right, she came to see me on December twenty-eighth."

"December twenty-eighth?" Witherspoon interrupted. "Are you certain?"

Todd raised an eyebrow. "Of course, Inspector. I keep meticulous records and her first visit was the twenty-eighth."

"What address did she give?" Barnes asked.

Todd glanced down at the paper again. "The Lewiston Hotel. It's a residential hotel near Hyde Park. She and her son had been staying there since they'd come from France. As a matter of fact, my clerk had booked the rooms for her. She'd written that she needed someplace near the park so her son could have a place to play."

"You'd been in contact with her before she arrived?" the inspector asked.

"That's right, she'd written that she had several legal matters and asked for my assistance."

"What were they, sir?"

Todd leaned back in his chair and steepled his fingers together. "Now that she's dead, I suppose there's no longer a confidentiality problem. The first thing she wanted done was a will. She wanted to make certain that in the event of her death, her son was taken care of and that he would inherit her estate."

"What was pressing about that?" the inspector asked. "Surely he was her sole heir."

"It wasn't so much her property that she was concerned with." Todd smiled. "It was the guardianship of her son." He broke off and looked down at the paper again. "Oh dear, this is awkward. I haven't even informed all the interested parties, but as none of the proper procedures had been followed, I suppose it doesn't matter."

"I'm sorry, sir, but what do you mean?" Witherspoon asked. "What proper procedures?"

"Mrs. Langston-Jones has a brother-in-law, her late husband's brother, Jonathan. He lives in Weymouth, Dorset, and in the event of her death, would naturally be the one to take custody of a minor child. But she was adamant that her son was to be kept away from him. She gave me instructions that another person would be appointed Alexander's guardian and that person is indeed named as such in her will. But when it's a nonrelative, even with the parent's permission, there are a number of legal procedures that must be taken into account before a guardianship is awarded outside the family. Now I'm not certain what to do. Mr. Jonathan Langston-Jones has already sent me a telegram informing me that he intends to take custody of her son and her property. However, her will specifically states that all of her property is to go to Alex and, more importantly, that she wishes for Sir Donovan Gaines to be appointed his guardian."

"Had Sir Donovan agreed to this arrangement?" Barnes asked.

"Indeed he had." Todd shuffled through the papers again. "I've a letter from him agreeing to her wishes and stating that he'll be pleased to sign any legal documents assuring him of guardianship. Unfortunately, no such documents have been executed as yet, and if Mr. Langston-Jones presses the issue, I'm not sure where we'd stand legally."

"The legal issues aside, sir," Witherspoon

said. "Did Mrs. Langston-Jones say why she wanted her employer to act as guardian and not her brother-in-law?"

"She wasn't specific as to her reasons, but I had the general impression that she neither liked nor trusted the man. Apparently, they'd been estranged from the time Mrs. Langston-Jones married into the family. She did confide that at the wedding reception, Mr. Jonathan Langston-Jones made some rather awful comments about the marriage. She told me that she's known Sir Donovan for many years. She described him as a good person and a very decent man. That's why she wanted him to oversee her son's up-bringing." He sighed again. "Now I'm not sure what's going to happen. Hopefully, Sir Donovan will be prepared to go to court to ensure her wishes are respected if Mr. Langston-Jones presses the matter."

"How much of an estate is there?" Barnes asked. He was beginning to suspect there was more to the late Mrs. Langston-Jones than they'd suspected.

"Quite a substantial one." Todd smiled. "Her late husband's paintings have increased in value. Add to that the property in Dorset that had belonged to her husband and that she inherited and we're looking at something close to ten thousand pounds."

"No wonder she's got relations crawling out of the woodwork," Barnes muttered.

Witherspoon frowned. "I don't quite understand, Mr. Todd. If she had so much money, why was she tutoring in the Gaines household? Why not just buy a home and raise her child?"

"She didn't discuss her finances as such with me, but I imagine it was because a good portion of her net worth was tied up in assets rather than cash," Todd explained. "What happened to her late husband was rather tragic, you see. His paintings had begun selling for quite large sums right before he passed away, and since then, of course, his work has increased enormously in value. But over half of them are still in France waiting to be shipped. The ones that she had in her possession only arrived a few weeks ago and she'd only just recently sold some of them. She put that money in the bank for Alexander. The property in Dorset was a bone of contention. Her brother-in-law wanted to sell it years ago and she refused to sell her half. The place is rented to tenants but she only receives half that income. You raise an interesting point, Constable. She might not have had the cash to purchase a house, but she certainly had enough to support herself and her child. I expect she tutored so she could buy all those little 'extras' that are so dear to a woman's heart." He shook his head in disbelief. "It's still hard to believe she's dead. She was such a vibrant, intelligent woman. I saw her only last week."

"What did she come to see you about?" Witherspoon unbuttoned his jacket. The room was very warm.

"She wanted me to file a lawsuit. I'd cautioned her against taking any action in the matter, especially as the person in question had agreed to pay what he owed her."

"Someone owed her money?" Barnes pressed.

"Oh yes, he'd purchased several of her husband's paintings and not paid for them. She was trying to collect. But I told her it would be difficult. The sale was in a foreign country and it would be difficult to establish the facts of the case. I thought I'd convinced her to drop the matter, but on Friday afternoon, she popped into my office without an appointment and insisted I go ahead with it. She said she had a letter from the gallery owners in Paris confirming they'd never received payment for the paintings and that she also had a copy of the original agreement between her husband and the gallery that all monies, save for the gallery's commission, belonged to the artist when a painting was sold. I tried to reason with her, tried to tell her that it was really the Paris gallery that had cause to file the suit, but she was very, very angry." He smiled sadly. "She tried to hide her feelings, of course. She was nothing if not a lady. But something had happened to upset her and she wasn't in the mood to listen to my advice."

Witherspoon flicked a quick glance at Barnes and then looked at Todd. "Who was she going to sue?" he asked.

"Lucius Montague."

"A matter of life and death?" Mrs. Jeffries eased back into her chair.

"Oh dear, put like that, it does sound overly dramatic." Fiona took her seat. "What I should have said was that it could be a matter of life and death if the wrong person gets arrested for murder." She glanced at the clock. "I know it's getting late and I'm intruding, but please hear me out. I'll be as quick as possible."

"Go ahead." Mrs. Jeffries nodded.

"As you all know, I was very, very grateful for the help you extended to me recently. If you'd not come to my aid, there was a very good chance I'd have been arrested, tried,

189

and probably hung for a crime I didn't commit."

"We know that, Fiona," Mrs. Jeffries said. "Now tell us why you've come here today. Surely you're not in danger of being arrested again."

Fiona smiled faintly. "No, but a friend of mine might be and that's why I've come. I understand Inspector Witherspoon is investigating the case of that young woman that was murdered, Mrs. Langston-Jones. The lady who was shot on Sir Donovan Gaines' back stairs."

"Is 'e your friend, then?" Wiggins asked curiously.

"I know Sir Donovan," she replied. "But I'm not here because of him." She took a deep breath. "And knowing all of you as I do, I'm sure you're already out gathering information about everyone that was part of that poor woman's circle of acquaintances. Don't worry, I haven't told anyone about how you helped me or about what you do, I'm only here because my friend thought that I had some influence with the police. I suspect he found out that you" — she looked at Mrs. Jeffries — "and I were related. I disabused him of that notion immediately and made it quite clear I had no more influence than any other citizen."

"I believe you. Go on and finish telling us. Time's moving on and it's not unheard of for the inspector to come home early," Mrs. Jeffries said. She and Fiona Sutcliffe weren't close — there was too much history between them for all to be forgiven because she'd kept her from facing the hangman — but she did know that once Fiona gave her word, she'd keep it. Her sister-in-law had promised she'd never tell another soul about how Mrs. Jeffries and the others had helped in the inspector's case.

"Lucius Montague came to me and told me he's afraid he's going to be arrested for her murder," she blurted out. "Unfortunately, there is some evidence against him but he insists he is innocent. I've come to ask for your help."

It was Mrs. Goodge who spoke first. "You know he's a dreadful man, don't you. He's a bully and brute. He kicked a poor half-starved dog down a staircase just because it was in his way. Why would you want someone like that for a friend? Anyone capable of torturing a defenseless animal is more than capable of murder."

"And he don't pay people their wages on time," Phyllis added. She, more than the others, had been outraged when Wiggins told them what he'd heard from the Montague housemaid. She knew what it was like to be desperately poor and dependent on less than honorable people. "That's terrible. People have a right to be paid their wages when they're due."

"The gun used to kill that woman was 'is as well." Smythe eyed Fiona carefully as he spoke; he wanted to gauge her reaction. She might be Mrs. Jeffries' relative by marriage, but he didn't trust her. "And a pillow from his house was used to muffle the sound of the shot."

"Yes, I know it looks very, very bad," Fiona began. "But circumstances can be very deceiving."

"A few days before she was killed, he had two arguments that we know of with the victim," Mrs. Jeffries observed. "Are you sure you're not defending him because he's someone important and not because you think he's innocent?"

"What do you mean by that?" Fiona frowned in confusion.

"We're aware that he's got friends and relatives in high places." Mrs. Jeffries knew that Fiona was socially a very ambitious woman and that, even though she'd married up, she and her husband weren't accepted into the highest social circles.

Fiona drew back and stared at Mrs. Jeffries. "My God, you really think I'm that shallow? That I'd only want to help someone because they might in turn improve my position in society?"

By the expression of hurt that flashed across Fiona's face, Mrs. Jeffries knew she'd been wrong. "Forgive me, Fiona, I didn't mean what I said. Sometimes my tongue runs away with me. After what you went through, I imagine you'd help any human being you thought was in danger of arrest for a crime he or she didn't commit."

Fiona said nothing for a moment. "I should hope so, Hepzibah. We've never been close but I thought your opinion of me had improved somewhat. I assure you, I'm only here because I'm certain Lucius is innocent." She glanced at the skeptical faces around the table. "Everything all of you have said about him is true. He can be a terrible, terrible person, but just because he's selfish, stupid, and occasionally nasty to small animals doesn't mean he's a killer."

"Do you have any evidence that he is innocent?" Ruth asked. "He has no alibi for the time of the murder, he threatened the victim shortly before she was killed, the weapon used to shoot her belonged to him, and we know he's capable of cruelty, so why, Mrs. Sutcliffe, are you so certain he didn't do it?"

She asked the question in such a reasonable tone that Fiona was taken aback. She frowned slightly and thought for a minute. Finally, she said, "I'm not sure. I just know that, despite his flaws and they are legion, he's not a murderer."

"We often want to believe things that aren't true," Mrs. Jeffries began gently, "especially about people we like —"

"No, that's not it," Fiona interrupted. "The truth of the matter is that I don't particularly like Lucius, I never have. I find him stupid, arrogant, petty, and decidedly mean-spirited. I avoid him at parties. When he first came to me, I told him the same thing you told me when I came to see you when Ronald Dearman was murdered. Do you remember?"

"I advised you to seek legal advice," she murmured.

"That's right, but then you saw how terrified I was and you realized that you had to help me because it was the decent thing to do. My first reaction was the same as yours — I told him to find a good solicitor, but then he came back, and despite my dislike of him, I realized that he was in the same position as I'd been in, innocent but helpless to prove it."

194

The inspector arrived home late, but nonetheless, he insisted on having a sherry with Mrs. Jeffries. "Our little ritual relaxes me greatly," he explained as he settled back into his chair. "So much so that I do believe it helps me to think clearly."

"I'm so glad you feel that way, sir." She went to the liquor cabinet. In truth, she wasn't in a very chatty mood. The visit from her sister-in-law had upset her more than she'd let on to the others, and what she really wanted to do was go off and have a nice long think on her own. Furthermore, her spirits were a bit dampened by the fact that she couldn't for the life of her think of a way to communicate what they'd learned to the inspector and that meant she'd have to tell all of it to Barnes tomorrow morning.

She stifled a sigh as she poured out two glasses of sherry. She didn't want to put the constable in more of an awkward position than necessary. She knew it was difficult for him to constantly come up with explanations for all the information he learned from them, and now she had to tell him about the possible interference in the case by the

Home Office. There was no help for it; she had neither the time nor the mental agility right now to think very clearly, and the person to blame for it was Fiona. But her chats with the inspector were important so she took a long, quiet breath and forced herself to relax. "You know how much I enjoy hearing about your cases."

Witherspoon chuckled. "Indeed I do and I hope you won't be disappointed because it appears this one is going to come to a close much sooner than my usual cases. For once, we've got a murder that seems very straightforward."

She stared at him over the rim of the glass. "You're going to make an arrest?"

"I think so," he mused. "We've some very, very strong evidence against Lucius Montague. Thus far, he appears to be the only person who had a reason to want to murder Mrs. Langston-Jones. Well, of course, she was somewhat estranged from her late husband's family, but as far as we know, her brother-in-law was in Dorset. I hardly think he could have murdered the woman."

"It sounds as if you had a very productive day, sir," Mrs. Jeffries murmured.

"Indeed I did," he said. "For once, everyone we interviewed was more than willing to tell us everything they knew — even

Montague's own household, and you know how that sort of situation can go. Oftentimes servants are afraid to tell us the truth because they fear losing their jobs. That most certainly wasn't the situation today." He told her about the visit to Montague's house and his interview with the housekeeper.

Mrs. Jeffries listened carefully, occasionally interrupting with a comment designed to get further clarification or a question.

"Mrs. Redman was not in the least reticent to speak about Montague's movements on the day of the murder or his behavior since," he finished. "And I must say, the way the fellow has been acting is most suspicious."

"But surely you're not going to arrest him just because his servants don't like him and he behaved like a brute," she said. Despite her doubts about Montague's innocence, Fiona's words had hit home.

"No, of course not." Witherspoon took a sip, his expression thoughtful. "But there is substantial evidence against him. However, he wasn't the only person the victim had recently quarreled with. We had a very interesting chat with the landlady at Mrs. Langston-Jones' lodging house. Apparently, she'd had an argument with her brother-in-law last week." He repeated everything Cora

Otis had told them and then continued on with what they'd found when they searched the victim's flat.

"So Montague wasn't the only person she'd been fighting with recently," Mrs. Jeffries mused.

"True, but families have spats amongst themselves all the time," he replied. "And from what her solicitor told us, she had been estranged from her brother-in-law for years whereas the dispute with Montague seemed to have increased in animosity recently."

Mrs. Jeffries couldn't make sense out of any of it. There was simply far too much information and she needed to think about what it might or might not mean. "On the face of it, the letter Montague sent to her does seem to be a threat," she agreed. "But then again, his words could be interpreted to mean he was simply going to fight her in court and that, as we both know, is a very expensive process."

"True, but she had more than enough money to fight him in the courts."

Witherspoon drained his glass and set it on the table next to him.

"What do you mean, sir? She was a French tutor. Where would she get enough money for a prolonged legal battle?"

"From what we heard from her solicitor

today, she had plenty of resources. Those paintings that I told you were in her rooms, well, according to Mr. Todd, they're worth quite a bit of money. As a matter of fact, her estate will be worth well over ten thousand pounds." He repeated what Hamish Todd had told him. When he'd finished, he got to his feet. "Gracious, I'm famished. I do hope Mrs. Goodge has something wonderful for tonight. I could eat a horse."

It was past ten o'clock before Mrs. Jeffries had a free moment to think about the events of the day. The doors were locked, the curtains closed, and the house quiet save for the ticking of the clock in the hall. She sat in the dimly lighted drawing room and listened to the house settle about her. Outside, a harness jingled as a carriage trundled past. She tried to keep everything straight in her mind, but it was difficult. There were now so many facts that didn't make sense. Why was the victim tutoring French when she apparently needn't have worked at all? Her lawyer had said the money wasn't coming in all that quickly, yet she'd already sold a number of her late husband's paintings. And why was it so important to her to do a will? Did Ellen

Langston-Jones have a sense that someone was a threat and that her life was at stake?

But how could she? She'd only recently returned to England from living for years in France. She'd only been here six months or so before she was killed; that hardly seemed to have been enough time to make such a dangerous enemy. Yet someone had murdered her, quite deliberately and most definitely with premeditation. But who?

She hadn't liked her brother-in-law, but that estrangement had taken place years earlier, so why would she be worried about him killing her now? Supposedly, there was family property involved in the quarrel, but even with her dead, it would be her son who would inherit her late husband's share, not Jonathan Langston-Jones. But perhaps he hadn't realized she was going to appoint someone else as legal guardian of her son; perhaps he'd merely assumed he'd be the boy's guardian and he could do what he liked. She sighed heavily. None of this made sense to her, and she didn't know what to do next. Tomorrow morning she'd have to warn Constable Barnes about the interference from the Home Office, and if she were truly honest, there was one part of her that hoped Witherspoon would lose the case. At least then she could tell Fiona there was nothing she could do to help Lucius Montague. She got up from the settee and began to pace the room, her footsteps quieted by the thick rug.

She moved slowly and let her mind wander where it would. Those timetables and pamphlets from Thomas Cook found in the victim's rooms, did they mean anything at all? Why on earth was Sir Donovan Gaines paying the woman's rent until the middle of next month? What, if anything, did that mean? Had they become more than employer and employee? They were seen together on the Strand. Could Sir Donovan have been courting her? But if that was the case, why hide the fact? They were both free to see whom they pleased.

She found herself in the hall, her gaze on the front door. Lucius Montague couldn't pay his servants their quarterly wages; perhaps he was terrified of losing a lawsuit, especially if he knew that Mrs. Langston-Jones wasn't a pauper and that she could afford to fight him in court over what was owed her. Even in a court of law, he'd have hated being bested by someone from the "lower" classes. But would he have been willing to murder to stop it? Fiona didn't seem to think so, but Mrs. Jeffries wasn't so sure. Montague was the worst kind of aristocrat, a bully and a brute, and from what she'd observed, it was often men of that kind of character who felt they had a God-given right to do as they pleased. What's more, the evidence was mounting against him, and as her late husband often said, "Sometimes the bits and pieces point in the right direction."

She turned and started up the steps to her room. Just then, she thought of Fiona's parting words. *"I'm disappointed in you, Hepzibah. You seem to think that justice only applies to the sort of people you approve of, but just because someone is a fool and a ridiculous snob doesn't mean that they don't deserve the benefit of the doubt. On the face of it, things look bad for Lucius, but if you'll remember, they looked bad for me as well. If you'd not put your prejudices aside and helped me, I'd have been hung."*

Mrs. Jeffries paused on the landing. No, her sister-in-law was wrong. She wasn't letting her dislike of Montague color her judgment. Was she?

Luty stared glumly at the well-dressed gentleman sitting on her left. He was a tall, skeletal man with deep-set eyes, a face full of wrinkles, and a bald head. "How can you not be aware of the murder?" she asked plaintively. "It was practically right on your doorstep."

"Hardly, madam." Sir Adam Trent sniffed disapprovingly. "I live on the same street and we share the communal garden, but I've no idea about anything to do with this murder you speak of, though I will admit that Reading, my butler, mentioned the police had been around asking questions about someone who'd been shot."

"What in blazes is wrong with you? Weren't you even curious?" she snapped.

"Why should I be? It's nothing to do with me," Sir Adam muttered. "Furthermore, it is not the kind of subject that ought to be discussed in polite society."

Luty's eyes narrowed angrily yet she kept control of her temper. She'd like nothing better than to make a scene, but it wouldn't get her any information. But it would sure make her feel good to tell this old snob what she thought of him.

As she turned away, her gaze caught the place card next to her wineglass. Her name was beautifully written in elegant black script. That was sure a wasted effort, she thought in disgust. She'd snuck in when no one was looking and switched her card so she'd be sitting next to Sir Adam Trent after she'd learned he lived three houses down from Sir Donovan. She surveyed the other people busily eating and drinking around the long table. But among the brilliantly garbed, coiffed, and bejeweled women, she saw no one who might be a likely candidate for information and the men were no better. Blast and drat, she thought, what a miserable evening this was turning out to be.

Downstairs in the butler's pantry, Hatchet was having a much better time of it. The Eagletons were a generous household, and they had set out platters of cold meats, chicken, bread, and jugs of ale for the coachmen and butlers who had accompanied elderly or female guests to the dinner party. There were six of them around the table. Two butlers talked quietly at the far end of the table while casting curious glances at Hatchet, who'd chosen to sit with the coachmen. Another coachman, a thin man with red hair, sat reading a newspaper and sipping a mug of ale.

Hatchet speared a slice of ham and put it on his plate. "So you knew the Langston-Jones family?" he said to the burly fellow opposite. His name was Joseph Clifton and he was a coachman to the elderly Lady Mingle.

"Can't say that I knew 'em," he replied.

"But I lived in Weymouth and heard of 'em when my sister got a position as house-keeper to the village vicar. The Langston-Jones family was the local gentry. Why, they friends of your mistress?"

Hatchet nodded assent. Upon arriving, he'd casually mentioned the murder and Clifton had muttered that it was such a shame, that the Langston-Joneses were a decent enough family. As no one else had made much of a comment, Hatchet decided to sit close to Clifton and see if he really knew anything or if he just liked to talk.

The coachman poured himself a second glass of ale. "The only one left in that part of the country is the youngest son, Jona-than. The eldest son moved to France and died then his poor widow up and is mur-dered." He shook his head. "It's sad how some families just seem to have the worst luck."

"The family had a history of bad luck?"

He shrugged. "Probably no worse than any family exceptin' that theirs seemed to come all at once. Right after the eldest one married, that was young Mr. Brandon, he up and left for France with his new bride, and believe me that set tongues to waggin', but that's by the by. Right after they left, old Mr. Langston-Jones died of a septic toe, and two months later, his missus got struck by lightning and died two days later. The only one left was young Mr. Jonathan and everyone, my sister included, thought he'd be left the farm, it's quite a large one, too, but turns out they'd left the property to both boys." He grinned broadly. "There's some that say that's the only reason Mr. Brandon married Miss Ellen. The gossip was that was how the old man got him to settle down. Mind you, there's always those that will think the worst of their fellow men, isn't there."

"Indeed there is," Hatchet said. "Is that the only reason tongues were wagging?" he asked.

Clifton laughed loudly. "Oh no, the gossips were just surprised because the weddin' was so sudden like. Miss Ellen was well liked in the village, she'd given up her youth to take care of her ailin' mother, and when the lady passed on, she'd gone to London to be a governess. The Ardens and the Langston-Joneses were neighbors, but when she suddenly showed back up and they got married three weeks later, well, you know how people are. Then when we got word the child was born just seven months after the weddin', you can imagine what people thought."

"That she'd been pregnant before the nuptials," Hatchet guessed.

Clifton nodded, glanced over his shoulder to see if anyone was listening, and then leaned toward Hatchet. "Mind you, the gossip wouldn't have been so bad if it'd not been for Jonathan. He's the one that kept sayin' the child was nothin' more than a little bastard."

Mrs. Jeffries came into the kitchen and stopped in the doorway. "What are you doing up so early? It's barely half past five."

The cook put the kettle onto the top of the cooker. "I couldn't sleep. I expect that's why you're down as well. That visit from your sister-in-law got me to thinking and I tossed and turned all night."

"That is precisely what happened to me." She went to the sideboard. Reaching in, she got down the big brown teapot, put it on the table, and then grabbed two mugs. "I simply couldn't settle down and sleep but I'm not sure whether it was because of Fiona or because of the idea that the Home Office is getting ready to interfere in the case."

Samson trotted into the kitchen, hopped up on the stool, and gave a plaintive cry.

"Does my baby want his breakfast?" Mrs.

Goodge ran her hand down Samson's broad back and gave him a little nudge onto the floor. He landed with a loud thud. "Come along then, I've got a nice piece of fish left from last night's dinner for you in the wet larder. Pour the water when the kettle boils," she called as she and the cat disappeared down the dim hallway.

Mrs. Jeffries put the tea in the pot, got the sugar down from the cupboard, and yanked two spoons out of the drawer as she waited. She wasn't being truthful with her friend; she hadn't lost sleep just because Fiona's words had pricked her conscience — it was far worse than that, and to her mind, the demons that had kept her awake didn't do her character any credit.

The kettle whistled and she grabbed a tea towel, picked it up by the handle, and poured the boiling water into the waiting pot. Perhaps she ought to discuss it with Mrs. Goodge; perhaps that would make her feel better.

By the time the cook returned carrying a jug of fresh milk, the tea had steeped properly and Mrs. Jeffries had made up her mind. Confession, it was said, was good for the soul. "Sit down and I'll pour us tea," she offered.

Mrs. Goodge put the jug on the table and

eased her bulk into a chair. "Consciences, I've discovered, are very inconvenient things. Mine kept me awake half the night and I shall pay for it today. Perhaps I'll have time to take a short nap this afternoon."

"Was it just what Fiona said?" Mrs. Jeffries poured milk into both mugs. "Or was something else bothering you?" There was no need to confess her failings quite so quickly and it was important to be a good listener.

Mrs. Goodge yawned. "Mostly it was your sister-in-law. But I will admit, I'm troubled about this Home Office nonsense. I don't understand. There have been lots of times in the past when the inspector has refused to rush an arrest. Why are the politicians poking their nose in on this one?"

"Perhaps it is as Smythe's source said and Lucius Montague has a powerful enemy."

The cook added a teaspoon of sugar to her mug. "That's possible, he is an awful person, but as Fiona said, just because he's horrid doesn't mean he killed that woman. The truth of the matter is that last night I realized we've all focused so much on him we've not properly looked elsewhere, if you see what I mean."

"I'm afraid I do," Mrs. Jeffries agreed. "Like you, I was very troubled by Fiona's visit. But at the same time, I kept thinking of something my late husband used to say, namely, that evidence is evidence and the person it points to is usually the guilty party."

"But we know from our own experience that's often not the case," Mrs. Goodge argued. "And once I started thinking about the evidence, it seemed to me that it would be dead easy for someone to frame Montague."

"How so?"

"First of all, we know that only weeks before the murder, Montague was at a dinner party bragging that he had a Beaumont Adams inscribed with his initials. Lots of people heard him, and to my mind, one of them could have decided right there and then to steal the weapon and frame him."

"You mean some other person might have been present who wanted Ellen Langston-Jones dead?"

"That's right. Add to that, the inspector told you that the housekeeper said no one went into Montague's study except on Thursdays to clean and it would be dead easy for someone to have stolen that pillow off his settee and then hidden it under a bush just outside his house."

The same ideas had occurred to Mrs.

Jeffries as well but she wanted to play the Devil's advocate, to hear another point of view and see if it matched her own. "How would the killer have gained entrance to his house? His servants are on the premises constantly."

"Please, Mrs. Jeffries, you know exactly how he or she got in." Mrs. Goodge frowned skeptically. "Through the kitchen, of course. Montague can't even hang on to a cook, so you know as well as I do that if there isn't someone in charge, the minute breakfast is over, that part of the house is probably empty. The housekeeper certainly isn't going to hang about, she'll have other duties and won't want to be saddled with that chore as well, and the maids will have scarpered off as soon as the last dish was washed. You wouldn't have to be that clever to nip into an empty kitchen, slip up the back stairs, and into the man's study to get the gun."

"That presupposes the killer knew where the gun was kept."

"True, but again, finding out bits and pieces about people isn't hard." She grinned. "We do it all the time."

Mrs. Jeffries nodded. "I've come to the same conclusion myself. Oh, I don't agree with Fiona that the man is innocent; that's yet to be seen. But I will admit that despite all my nagging and carping about the dangers of jumping to conclusions too early in the case, that's exactly what I've done."

"That's what we all did. Once the stories about what a terrible person Montague is began rolling in, we all decided he was guilty and shut our eyes and our ears to anything that might prove otherwise."

"We allowed our prejudices to color our thinking about this case." Mrs. Jeffries closed her eyes for a moment. "Oh dear, I suppose I'm going to have to go see her now."

"Why?"

"It's only fair to let her know that her visit had the desired effect upon us." She sighed. "When she left here yesterday, it was with the distinct impression that we all thought Montague was guilty. Now I'm going to have to go tell her that she was right and that I was wrong. I don't mind saying that I'm not looking forward to it."

Mrs. Goodge angled her head to one side and stared at her friend. "You've never had a problem in saying you were wrong."

"Generally, no, I don't. But I'm going to hate admitting it to her. You see, for all these years, when it came to Fiona, I always felt that I held the moral high ground, that my character was somehow better than hers, that she'd valued money and social position more than family or integrity. When she married, she did turn her back on David and it hurt him deeply. When she showed up for his funeral, I barely spoke to her." She looked away. "My behavior did me very little credit. In my own way, I was as much of a snob as I thought her to be. I was judgmental, angry, and if I'm totally honest, just a little envious. When David died, I was furious that she who'd hurt him so badly ended up with money, position, and influence while all he had before he died was a small cottage and his pension."

"You're forgetting he had a happy marriage and peace of mind," Mrs. Goodge said gently. "You can't put a price on that, Hepzibah."

"Thank you for reminding me." She smiled at her friend. "David and I were wonderfully suited to one another, which is rare in this old world. Nonetheless, it's time to face the here and now. Either Fiona has changed or all these years I've been wrong about her character. Now it seems she's more concerned with justice than I am. It was foolish of me to focus on one suspect because he's an odious person."

"Don't be so hard on yourself. We were

all thinkin' the same thing, that Montague's guilty as sin. Now it may turn out he is, but as your sister-in-law pointed out, we're duty bound to find the truth, and if he's not guilty, we've got to help the inspector find the real killer."

"But how can we do that if the inspector is taken off the case?" She'd grappled with that problem half the night and still hadn't come up with a reasonable solution.

"I've thought about that." The cook took another sip. "And I've come to the conclusion there's only one thing we can do. We've got to see if there's any evidence that points to someone else, and if there is, we've got to find a way to make sure that fact gets printed in the newspapers. That's the only way you'll be able to turn the tide on this one."

They discussed the case, going over every bit of information they had thus far, and it was soon apparent to both women that there were other avenues that needed to be explored. The evidence still pointed to Montague, but he wasn't the only one who might have wanted the victim dead.

"We've not sent anyone around to find out a few bits and pieces about Neville Gaines." The cook shook her head in disgust. "And he obviously was lying when he told the inspector he barely knew Ellen Langston-Jones. He knew her well enough to know that she had a brother-in-law that might object to Sir Donovan taking custody of young Alex."

"And what about Mrs. Linthorp?" Mrs. Jeffries said. "If the gossip Ruth heard is true and she was setting her sights on becoming the second Lady Gaines, how must she have felt when a young, well-educated, and rather lovely woman began working in his house every day? The key strikes me as odd as well."

"What key?"

"The one to the communal garden," Mrs. Jeffries replied. "Ellen Langston-Jones was only at the Gaines house two hours a day, so why did she have a key to get into the garden, and most importantly, how did the killer get into the garden? He or she must have had a key as well."

"That's what I mean about this case. There's a lot of things we've not looked at properly," the cook agreed.

They drank a whole pot of tea and were working on a second when there was a soft knock on the back door. "That must be Constable Barnes." Mrs. Jeffries got up to let him in as the cook grabbed another mug from the sideboard.

"You're here early." Mrs. Goodge gave him a smile as he trailed the housekeeper into the kitchen.

"I had a bad night and I was up before daylight."

"That's what comes of gettin' older." Mrs. Goodge poured his drink. "Lucky for you, Mrs. Jeffries and I are gettin' older as well and we're up bright and early."

"It wasn't just that keepin' me awake." He grinned. "Mrs. Barnes has a bad cold and her snufflin' and snorin' kept me awake all night. It was impossible to get any sleep so I finally just gave up."

"Sit down and have your tea." The cook put his mug in front of him. "It's just as well you're a bit early. We've a lot to tell you."

"I've a bit to tell you as well." Barnes picked up his cup and took a long sip. "Go on, then, what have your lot learned?"

"I'm afraid we've some bad news," Mrs. Jeffries said. She wanted to get the worst over with right away. "Supposedly in yesterday's evening papers, there were going to be hints that the police weren't arresting their chief suspect, Lucius Montague, because he had aristocratic and powerful connections."

"I know, Mrs. Barnes had my evening paper sitting next to my dinner when I got

216

home. But whoever wrote the article was clever and they didn't come right out and call us incompetent. It's a bit too early in the game for that."

"That's a relief," Mrs. Jeffries said. "But I'm afraid the newspaper article isn't the worst of it. We have it on good authority that someone in the Home Office is going to interfere in this case. If the inspector doesn't arrest Montague soon, he's going to be pulled off the case."

Barnes listened without further comment until she'd finished. Then he smiled cynically. "I know."

CHAPTER 7

"Last night an old friend from Scotland Yard stopped in to see me," Barnes said. "Eddie Harwood's an old mate of mine and he said he'd heard something I ought to know about. He tends to keep his ears open for anything concerning Inspector Witherspoon or me. Eddie used to walk patrol but his knees started givin' him trouble well before he could get a pension. He's a good man so I had a word with the inspector and he recommended him for the post at the Yard and Eddie ended up with the day shift behind reception."

"That was kind of you, Constable," Mrs. Jeffries murmured. "I take it your friend heard something about this case?"

Barnes nodded. "My wife had gone to bed because of her cold, and I didn't want to disturb her so Eddie and I went to the pub and had a pint. At Scotland Yard, everyone other than policemen have to report to him when they come into the building, and yesterday afternoon, two gents from the Home Office showed up. They were talking as they crossed the room. Eddie distinctly heard one of them say that there was nothing to worry about, that Inspector Witherspoon didn't have any political power so there was nothing he could do. When they got to Eddie, one of them said they were there to see two people, Chief Inspector Barrows and Inspector Nigel Nivens."

"I don't like the sound of that," Mrs. Goodge muttered. "It's never good news when someone mentions Nivens in the same conversation as our inspector."

Mrs. Jeffries didn't like it, either, but she held her peace. Nivens was an old enemy of the household. He'd spent years trying to prove that Witherspoon had help with his cases, and of course, he was correct. But he was an odious toad of a man who'd obtained his position because of his family's wealth and political connections. Even worse, he wasn't a good policeman. He bullied his subordinates and there were some that claimed he wasn't above beating a suspect to gain a confession.

Barnes took a sip of his tea. "It's not good news now. Nivens is back to his old tricks. It was bound to happen — men like him

219

don't stay grateful for long."

"Political connections or not, if it hadn't of been for Inspector Witherspoon, he'd have been tossed off the Force without so much as a by-your-leave," Mrs. Goodge exclaimed.

She was referring to an earlier case where Inspector Nivens had withheld evidence, probably in an attempt to make Witherspoon look incompetent. When Nivens had finally done the right thing and turned over the material, Inspector Witherspoon had been decent about the whole matter. Nivens had been so thankful, he'd given up trying to prove their inspector was able to solve so many homicides only because he had a small army of helpers.

"As time passes, men like Nivens forget what they owe and he's back to his true self. It looks like he's using his political connections to get Inspector Witherspoon pulled off the case," Barnes said.

"But he's done that lots of times and it's never worked," Mrs. Jeffries pointed out. "Chief Inspector Barrows has always stood up to the politicians when they've tried to interfere. What's more, this case is only three days old."

"From the gossip Eddie heard, it's not just Nivens that is applyin' pressure. Montague has made some powerful enemies and one of them has the Home Secretary's ear. When we get to the station, I've no doubt there'll be a message ordering the inspector to report to the Yard."

"What are we goin' to do?" The cook tapped her fingers on the tabletop. "Mrs. Jeffries and I have already had a good natter about this case, and we're both of the opinion that despite all the evidence pointin' to Montague, there's others that could be guilty as well." She didn't think it was her place to mention Fiona Sutcliffe's visit.

Barnes stared at her skeptically. "Do you really think so?"

"We do," Mrs. Jeffries answered. "Montague is a horrid man and I think that's colored our opinion of him. If you consider all the bits and pieces we've learned, it's quite possible that the victim had other enemies."

The constable didn't look convinced. "Like who?"

"Well, her brother-in-law for one. Have you actually confirmed he wasn't in London on the day of the murder?"

"No, but —"

The cook interrupted. "And what about Mrs. Linthorp? We've found out she was lookin' to be the second Lady Gaines. She'd not like a pretty young woman working in Sir Donovan's house every day. Maybe she felt her position was threatened? Gaines is a rich man and she'd not be the first to murder a rival. Has anyone asked her what she was doing at the time of the murder?"

"No, but we've no reason to interview her," he protested. "We had no idea she and Sir Donovan were courting."

"Of course you didn't," Mrs. Jeffries said. "That's our fault. We've found out a number of things we need to tell you but we've been terribly distracted by this news about the Home Office."

"Tell me what you've found out and then I'll see to it that it reaches the inspector's ears. If it looks like there's real evidence against anyone else, I'll make sure that it is trotted out and put on the chief inspector's desk. Once that happens, he won't pull Witherspoon and I off the case. Barrows is too good a copper for that."

They took turns telling him everything the others had reported at their afternoon meeting. The only item that was omitted was Fiona's visit to the kitchen. Mrs. Jeffries wasn't sure how Barnes would feel about that, and as they'd not heard any new facts from her sister-in-law, in all good conscience, she needn't mention it.

When they'd finished, Barnes said, "That's all very interesting. But nothin' you've told me points to anyone else as a suspect."

"We're not through," Mrs. Goodge declared. "There's two or three bits that don't add up. I'm not sayin' it's real evidence, but I am sayin' they kept me awake most of last night. According to the housemaid you spoke to, Neville Gaines and Martha Barclay disliked Mrs. Langston-Jones from the moment she set foot in the house. They didn't bother tattling to the master about any of the other staff. So why did they hate her so much? That makes no sense at all."

"Some people just don't get along." He took a quick sip of tea.

"That's not all that's bothering us," Mrs. Jeffries interjected. "You might want to find out why the victim had a key to the communal garden. She was only at the Gaines house for a few hours a day, and it isn't the sort of household to hand out keys willynilly. But someone gave her one."

"And you'll need to find out if she was in the habit of using the garden gate all the time," the cook added. "If she was, find out who knew about it. I'm certain that the killer followed her in that day."

"Montague lives just across from the Gaines house. He could easily have already been in the garden waiting for her."

"In which case that would mean he knew there was going to be such a thick fog that the garden would be empty, that Mrs. Langston-Jones was not going to the Gaines house at her usual time." Mrs. Jeffries glanced at the clock.

"He did know all those things," Barnes said. "He was at the Gaines house having breakfast when Sir Donovan told Mrs. Barclay that Mrs. Langston-Jones would be late that day, and as to the fog, all he had to do was look out his window."

"Then tell me, Constable, if he planned on killing her, why did he leave a gun that was easily identified as belonging to him next to her body?"

"Because he's an arrogant sod." The constable realized how weak that sounded as soon as the words left his mouth.

"Not only arrogant, but stupid as well." The cook looked him straight in the eye and folded her arms over her chest. "He didn't just leave the gun there, he left the pillow from his own settee right under a bush outside his window. Then, just to make sure the police would know for certain that it belonged to him, he accused his maid of losing it and said he was taken' the cost of it out of her wages. That's one way of makin' sure it reaches the ears of the police."

"Put like that, it does sound unlikely," he muttered.

"Constable, we're not havin' a go at you." Mrs. Goodge reached over and patted his arm. "But you can see why we're bothered by some of these bits and pieces. It just doesn't make sense to us."

Barnes said nothing for a long moment. "Even with all you've told me, I still think Montague's our killer, but you're both right, there's enough here to sow doubts. Another day or so won't matter one way or the other."

"But what if the case gets given to Nivens?" the cook asked. Samson trotted over and jumped on her lap. She reached down and absently petted him.

"That won't happen."

"How can you be so certain?" Mrs. Jeffries asked.

He grinned. "Let's just say that Nivens isn't the only one with friends in influential places. There's a couple of newsmen that owe me a favor and an article appearing in tomorrow's papers implying that evidence in the case was bein' overlooked because some politician had a grudge against Montague would set the cat amongst the pigeons."

Mrs. Jeffries gave him an admiring smile. "Indeed it would."

"Then let's hope you're wrong about there being a message already waiting for the inspector when he gets to the station this morning." Mrs. Goodge rose to her feet and began clearing up.

"The answer is simple." Mrs. Jeffries looked at Barnes. "Don't go to the station."

They continued talking as Wiggins and Phyllis came down and began their morning routine. Barnes waited until the inspector had time enough to eat his breakfast before going to the dining room and joining him.

As soon as the two policemen had left, the others arrived for their morning meeting. "My evening was a complete waste of time," Luty announced as she took her chair. "I jumped through more hoops than a circus bear makin' sure I sat next to one of Sir Donovan's neighbors, but Sir Adam didn't know a danged thing."

"I, on the other hand, found out something that may be useful," Hatchet announced with a cheery smile. He told them what he'd heard from Joseph Clifton.

"So the farm the Langston-Joneses own is a large one," Ruth murmured. "And she wouldn't sell her half to her brother-in-law.

That alone could be a motive for murder."

"Constable Barnes is going to try and find out if Langston-Jones was in Dorset on the day of the murder," Mrs. Goodge told them.

"If he wasn't, then I suggest we include him on our list of suspects." Mrs. Jeffries glanced at Hatchet. "Have you anything else to tell us?" When he shook his head, she continued. She gave everyone a quick, concise report of recent events, taking care to leave nothing out. She wasn't surprised to find that the others had all come to the same conclusion that had kept her and the cook awake for most of the night. Namely, that they'd let their dislike of the main suspect blind them to any other possibility. "So, to use Mrs. Goodge's words, the only way to turn the tide on this case is to find evidence that someone other than Montague is the murderer," she finished. "Or to find proof that he did do it."

"Cor blimey, I'm glad everyone else feels the same," Wiggins said. "I was awake 'alf the night thinkin' about this case and knowin' there was somethin' wrong. But I couldn't put my finger on it. I think I'll 'ave a go at findin' out if Neville Gaines really was lookin' at property when she was killed."

"Mrs. Sutcliffe's visit prodded my conscience as well." Hatchet pursed his lips. "I've an excellent source in the art world and as both dead artists and valuable paintings seem to have played a part in this drama, perhaps I'll learn something useful." He looked at Luty. "Have you plans for today, madam?"

"Wouldn't you like to know." Luty chuckled. "Just teasin' ya. Mine might end up bein' a wild-goose chase so I'd like to keep it to myself."

"I'm having morning coffee with a friend." Ruth pushed back in her chair and got up. "I'm hoping she'll know something useful."

"I'm not sure what I ought to do." Phyllis's face crinkled into a worried frown.

"Try the shops in Bayswater," Smythe suggested as he got to his feet. "That's Hester Linthorp's neighborhood, and on my way out this mornin', Betsy reminded me that she was anglin' to become the next Lady Gaines."

"Thank you, Smythe." Phyllis grinned in relief and leapt up. "What'll you be doing?"

"Like Luty, mine might be a wild-goose chase so I'd just as soon keep it to myself."

"Good, I'm glad we're all roused to action." Mrs. Jeffries began to gather the cups and mugs by the handles. "I, for one, am going to have a good, long think about the case."

"Of course, Neville Gaines hated Lucius Montague." Catherine Winchester looked at Ruth as she spoke. She picked up the silver coffeepot and poured the fragrant brew into exquisite blue Wedgewood cups. "But then again, a number of people in London loathe the man, myself included. He's one of the most obnoxious human beings I've ever met."

Ruth smiled uncertainly. She was in Catherine's lavish drawing room. A pale rose-colored paper hung on the walls, pink satin curtains graced the two long windows overlooking a view of Regents Park, and the polished wood parquet floors were covered with an exquisite red and gold carpet.

She quite agreed with Mrs. Jeffries that the only ethical course of action was to continue investigating instead of just assuming that Montague was guilty, but then again, thus far, she'd found no one who had a good word to say about him. After she'd left the morning meeting, she'd spoken to several members of her women's group, and of those who knew Montague, there was universal agreement the fellow was both a snob and a misogynist. But luckily, she'd accepted an invitation for morning coffee with Mrs. Winchester two weeks ago, and now that she was here, she'd found the woman was a veritable font of information. She and Catherine weren't close friends, and she felt a bit guilty as she'd originally accepted the invitation to see if she could persuade the woman to stand for corresponding secretary in the next round of elections at the British Society for Women's Suffrage.

Catherine Winchester was a tall, red-haired, middle-aged woman with blue eyes and the kind of bone structure that meant she'd still turn heads when she was eighty. She'd joined the London branch of the Society a year earlier. She was lovely, well dressed, and rich. Even better, she'd open her bank account if one of their own needed a solicitor or if they were falling short of money to pay the printers. Catherine was the first to declare that good lawyers and educational pamphlets were of paramount importance to their cause.

Some of the group didn't trust her as she was somewhat vague about her background, but Ruth instinctively felt this was a woman whose heart was in the right place. Better yet, she wasn't afraid to speak her mind or share her opinions. "I've heard that Montague wasn't a popular man, but I had no idea he was so disliked."

"Disliked is putting it mildly." Catherine laughed. "You're so very kind, Lady Cannonberry."

"Please, call me Ruth," she interrupted.

"And you must call me Catherine," the other woman exclaimed. "I've so admired you and I was so pleased you accepted my invitation for coffee."

Ruth blinked in surprise. "You admire me? Gracious, that's most flattering, but I can't imagine why."

"Don't be so modest. Surely you must know that everyone thinks highly of you — you actually practice what most people merely preach." She cocked her head, her expression thoughtful. "But let's get back to Mr. Lucius Montague. That's really why you've come, isn't it?"

Ruth grimaced slightly. "I didn't realize I was so obvious."

Catherine laughed. "Don't worry, you're not in the least obvious. Most of the women in our group have no idea that you occasionally seek information to help your lover, the great detective, Gerald Witherspoon."

"He's not my lover," Ruth protested and then immediately wished she hadn't. The truth was, she did love Gerald Witherspoon, but she'd never spoken of her feelings to another living soul. "Oh dear, that's not what I meant."

"I'm sorry, I'm generally more discreet. I didn't mean to be so bold, but you've the sort of countenance that makes one feel safe enough and secure enough to speak one's mind. That's a very rare gift, but perhaps not one you wish to acknowledge. I do apologize."

Ruth laughed helplessly. She couldn't stop herself; it was simply too funny. On the one hand, she ought to be offended by the woman's honesty, but on the other, she was extremely flattered. Perhaps that was part of Catherine's charm. "I'm not sure whether to be pleased or offended, so I shall choose to be flattered. Now, as you've been so forthright with me, I shall do you the same courtesy. Please tell me what you know about Lucius Montague and any other members of the Gaines household."

Catherine laughed. "Well, as I said, Montague is universally disliked, despite the fact that he's got aristocratic relatives on both sides of his family. As to the other members of that unlucky family, the one I know the most about is Neville Gaines."

"You said he hated Lucius Montague." Ruth took a sip of her coffee. "How so?"

Catherine raised her eyebrows. "What usually engenders hatred between people?"

"Money or love?"

"Correct. In this case, it was money. A few years ago, Montague advised Neville to invest in some sort of mining enterprise in the Far East. I don't recall all the details, but I do remember that the gossip was that Montague had vouched for the company and used his friendship with Sir Donovan to convince Neville to invest." Catherine smiled wryly. "I'm sure you can guess the rest of it. The company ended up in bankruptcy, and Neville Gaines lost everything he'd invested."

Ruth took a sip of her coffee. "Was it a lot of money?"

Catherine sipped her coffee. "I don't know the exact amount, but the gossip I heard was that he lost everything, including his home. That's the reason he moved in with his uncle."

"But I thought he moved in to keep Sir Donovan company after his wife passed away," Ruth said.

Catherine smiled cynically. "That's what Neville Gaines told everyone, but except for his salary, he had nothing. It was fortunate for him that by the time the dust settled on the bankruptcy and he was broke, Lady

Gaines had died and Sir Donovan was rattling around in that big empty house."

"Wasn't Sir Donovan upset with Montague?" Ruth asked. "He'd bankrupted his nephew? My understanding is the two men are still friends. As a matter of fact, Montague was on his way to the Gaines house when he discovered that poor woman's body."

"One would think so." She gave a delicate shrug to her shoulders. "But apparently, he didn't let his nephew's financial disaster influence his friendship with Montague. Of course, as I said, the entire matter became public close to the time Lady Gaines was dying. She'd been ill for many, many years but they were a devoted couple so I imagine Sir Donovan simply didn't take much notice of anything except the fact that she was dying. But then again, he's supposedly made it up to Neville."

"Made it up?" Ruth repeated. "How?"

"When Lady Gaines finally passed away, Sir Donovan changed his will. Neville Gaines and his sister, Mrs. Barclay, will get the entire estate. They are his only heirs."

Witherspoon grabbed on to the handhold as the hansom lurched forward and swung around the corner. "We've a very full day,

234

Constable, but at least we know that the letter we found at the victim's home was nothing more than a shipping advice. That's one thing off our plate."

"True, sir," he agreed as the cab pulled up in front of the Montague home. Barnes had done some very smooth talking to keep the inspector from going to the station. As they'd reached the cabstand on Holland Park Road, he'd been congratulating himself on his cleverness when he'd seen Constable Deloffre racing toward them. Thinking it was the dreaded summons to Scotland Yard, Barnes almost had heart failure. Grinning like a madman, Constable Deloffre had skidded to a halt. "It's a shipping advice, sir," he'd said. It took a moment before Barnes realized that the paper he was gleefully waving under their noses was the one they'd dropped at the station yesterday to get translated. Deloffre's mother was French. "That's all. It says that the goods shipped by Mrs. Langston-Jones will be arriving on July fifth at Southampton."

"Why, thank you, Constable," Witherspoon said as he took the letter. "You didn't have to bring this to me. We were going into the station later today."

"My shift is over, sir." Deloffre grinned broadly. "I live nearby, and when I saw the

235

two of you coming up the road, I thought it best to tell you what was written on the document. The translation is written underneath each line, sir. As it's a murder case, I knew you'd need it right away." He nodded respectfully, left, and the two policemen climbed into a cab.

The inspector had read the translated document on the short ride here while Barnes had stared out the side of the cab in an effort to calm down. He felt as if he'd dodged not only a bullet, but a ruddy firing squad. He dug coins out of his pocket while he waited for the inspector to finish reading.

"Gracious, it appears that the late Mr. Langston-Jones must have painted enough pictures to fill a hay wagon." He folded the letter and tucked it into his jacket pocket. "That's all to the good, wouldn't you say, Constable? From what the solicitor told us, it's going to be a big part of his son's inheritance." Witherspoon grabbed on to the side of the cab and swung out onto the pavement.

"Maybe he had a feeling there was something wrong with him." Barnes climbed out. "Painting all those pictures might have been his way of making certain his family was taken care of properly."

"That's possible. Todd did mention that Langston-Jones' work increased in value the year before he died. I'm not looking forward to interviewing young Alex," he said as Barnes paid the driver. "He's just lost his last parent, and now we'll be badgering the poor lad about who might have hated his mother enough to murder her."

"Not to worry, sir. You'll be gentle with him."

"I'll do my best, but I'm not very experienced with children. I'm glad he's at Sir Donovan's house. That will save us some time. After we finish here, we can cut across the garden to the Montague house."

The constable started up the walkway. Despite his conversation with the ladies of Upper Edmonton Gardens, he was still convinced Montague was guilty. "We don't have to be gentle with this one. I'll bet you a month of Sundays he's been deliberately avoiding us. Let's hope we're early enough to catch him in, sir."

"If we're not, then despite where he's gone, we'll track him down." Witherspoon fell into step behind the constable. "It's only eight o'clock so perhaps we'll be in luck."

The door opened before they knocked. Jane Redman grinned slyly. "Good day, gentlemen. Mr. Montague is in the drawing room having his morning coffee." She motioned for them to come inside.

"Thank you, Mrs. Redman," Barnes said as they stepped over the threshold.

"He's not in a nice mood. The housemaids gave their notice this morning." She snickered as she led them down the short hall to a set of open double doors.

"What is it?" Lucius Montague snapped irritably. He was reading the newspaper and didn't bother to look up as they entered the room.

"The police are here," she said bluntly. "They want to speak to you." She caught Witherspoon's eye and gave him an impish grin as she withdrew, closing the doors firmly.

That got Montague's attention. His head whipped around and his mouth gaped open in alarm. "I've already given my statement," he blurted out.

"I'm afraid there were a number of matters you neglected to mention when we spoke to you last," the inspector said. He looked pointedly at two empty chairs across from where Montague was still sitting. "May we sit down? This might take some time."

Montague nodded reluctantly. "Go ahead. But I've an appointment this morning so I can't spare you more than a few minutes."

Barnes looked him straight in the eye, holding his gaze as he took one of the chairs. "Then perhaps, sir, you'd like to accompany us to the station," he said.

"There's no need for that, surely." Montague gulped in air. "I only meant that there's nothing really more than I've already told you so this shouldn't take very much time."

"There's a great deal you didn't mention." Witherspoon sat down and glanced at Barnes, who was taking out his notebook. He waited till the constable had fished out his pencil before he turned his attention back to Montague. "Why didn't you tell us the gun used to murder Mrs. Langston-Jones belonged to you?"

"I, uh . . . well, you see, I never even noticed the gun. For goodness' sake, the moment I saw all the blood and realized she was dead, I ran to the kitchen for help. Once your lot arrived, I stayed well away from the body. IIow could I have known it was my gun?"

Barnes looked up. "Because it was lying in plain sight right beside her body. You got close enough to see that she'd been shot, so you must have seen the gun."

"But I didn't." He bit his lip. "I told you, once I saw the bullet hole and blood, I ran

239

for help. You must believe me."

"Why didn't you tell us Mrs. Langston-Jones was going to sue you?" The inspector deliberately changed the topic, as this method had proved successful in other cases. He'd trust his "inner voice" to help him make sense of everything later.

Montague stared at them for a long moment. Finally he said, "Because I didn't think it was pertinent."

"You didn't think the fact that someone who was going to take you to court and publicly expose that you were no better than a thief was pertinent to a murder investigation?" Barnes said.

"How dare you speak to me like that?" He sucked in air. "Do you know who I am?"

"We know exactly who you are, sir," Witherspoon said. "And we're not trying to insult you, we're merely trying to establish the facts of this murder. Thus far, sir, you're the only person who had a reason to want Mrs. Langston-Jones dead."

Montague gaped at them. "You've no right to do this to me. I didn't kill that woman, and if you try to imply that I did, I'll have a word with some of my friends at the Home Office."

"You may have a word with anyone you like," Witherspoon said softly. "But we will

240

continue our investigation into this murder and that will include asking you questions."

"You had an argument with the victim shortly before she was murdered," Barnes pressed.

"Who told you that?"

"Don't deny it, Mr. Montague, we have witnesses," the constable said. "As a matter of fact, you had more than one quarrel with the victim."

"Alright, so what if I did have words with her? I wasn't the only one. That woman had plenty of enemies. She didn't go out of her way to endear herself to anyone except Sir Donovan, and that was just because he paid her wages."

Witherspoon leaned forward in his seat. "Who else did she quarrel with?"

"Mrs. Linthorp. They had words two or three days before the murder," he said. "I overheard them. It was a loud and rather vicious row."

Barnes stared at him, his expression skeptical. "Where did this argument take place and how did you happen to hear it?"

"I wasn't eavesdropping, if that's what you're implying, and it took place right out in the open where anyone walking past could have heard it." He flung up his hand and pointed toward the rear of the house.

"Last week, Mrs. Barclay invited me to luncheon with herself and Mrs. Linthorp. Mrs. Barclay asked to borrow my copy of Mr. Hardy's *The Mayor of Casterbridge*. After luncheon, I went home to get it for her. But those stupid housemaids never put things back in their proper place and it took some time to find it. As I came around the path to the Gaines house, Mrs. Linthorp and Mrs. Langston-Jones were standing by the big oak tree having a dreadful row. Naturally, I didn't wish to intrude so I stepped back behind a hedge and waited for them to finish."

Barnes stared at him. "Were you close enough to hear what they were quarreling about?"

"I didn't have to be particularly near them; they weren't bothering to keep their voices down. Mrs. Linthorp did most of the talking. She told Mrs. Langston-Jones that she knew the truth and that if she didn't give up her post and go back to Dorset with her brat, she'd make her sorry." He smiled triumphantly. "So you see, I wasn't the only one that quarreled with the woman. Why don't you ask Hester Linthorp where she was when the murder took place?"

"We intend to do just that," Witherspoon replied. "However, it was your gun that was

242

used to commit the murder."

"But anyone could have stolen it to make me look guilty."

Barnes smiled cynically. "Are you suggesting that Mrs. Linthorp or, for that matter, anyone else could simply waltz in here and steal whatever they liked? Don't you keep your doors locked?"

"Of course I do!" he cried. "But my servants are stupid and lazy. They're always leaving the servants' door unlocked so they can slip in and out whenever my back is turned."

"Mr. Montague, we shall most definitely interview Mrs. Linthorp and anyone else connected with this case, but I must warn you, the evidence against you is very strong," Witherspoon said. "In addition to everything we've mentioned thus far, we also have the letter you wrote to Mrs. Langston-Jones threatening her with dire consequences if she went ahead with the lawsuit."

Montague suddenly leapt up, the newspaper falling onto the floor. "I know what you're doing. You're trying to make it look as if I killed her, but I didn't, I didn't."

Barnes was relentless. "There's a green pillow missing from your study and I suspect it's exactly like the one we found just outside your back door stuffed under a bush. It's got a hole in the center which makes us think it was used to stifle the sound of the gun being fired."

Montague's eyes widened and his face paled. "Am I under arrest?" he finally asked.

Barnes glanced at the inspector, who gave a barely imperceptible nod. They weren't going to get anything further from him. "Not as yet." The constable closed his notebook and tucked his pencil into his jacket pocket. "But please don't leave the city. I'm sure we'll be speaking to you again."

Betsy pushed Amanda's black pram into the empty space between the table and the edge of the counter. She smiled at her companion, a dark-haired young woman wearing an old-fashioned straw bonnet and a threadbare green and gray plaid jacket over a gray skirt. She took the chair closest to her sleeping daughter and gestured at the empty seat. "Don't be shy now. It's good of you to keep me company. Sit down and I'll order us a pot of tea and some buns."

The girl hesitated. "If you think it's alright, ma'am, I will." She sat down and gave Betsy a shy smile. "It's ever so nice of you to treat me like this."

"Please, it's the least I can do. You've saved me a great deal of trouble," she replied. She was determined to find out something about this murder before the afternoon meeting. Betsy knew that she didn't really have to stir herself to help, but she'd been feeling a bit left out so she'd taken Amanda for her afternoon walk to Portland Villas. It wasn't far and it was a nice day, so she'd decided the fresh air would do both of them good.

As she'd come abreast of the Gaines house, she'd slowed her pace and stopped. She was pretending to adjust Amanda's blanket when she'd heard a door slam, and a second later, this young woman had come up the lower ground stairs of the house next to Sir Donovan's. Betsy didn't look a gift horse in the mouth. She moved fast, grabbed the pram, and pulled one of her gloves out of the waistband of her dress. She swept past the girl and then dropped the glove. When the girl had picked it up and come running after her, she'd been so grateful that she offered to buy the young lady a cup of tea.

"You saved me," she'd said. "My husband just bought me these gloves and he'd have had a fit if I'd lost one of them. He got them in Paris, you see, and I don't think I could have found another pair here." It hadn't taken much persuasion to get the girl here. Now Betsy hoped that Amanda wouldn't wake up and start howling her head off to nurse.

The girl glanced around the elegant tea shop. "I've never been in a place like this," she said. "I've passed by, of course, but I've never had the nerve to come inside. It's lovely, isn't it."

"It is and they do wonderful pastries as well." She broke off as a black-coated waiter appeared. "A pot of tea, please, and two raspberry tarts." She paused and looked inquiringly at her companion, who nodded eagerly. As soon as he'd gone, she said, "Do forgive me, I'm being very rude. My name is Eliza Canfield. What's yours?" She never gave out her real name when she was on the hunt, and she realized that she was tickled pink to be back doing this again.

"I'm Dorothy Edmonds. I'm a maid."

"And where do you work?"

"For the Bramptons," she said. "I'd just come out of the house when you passed by and I saw the glove drop. It's my afternoon out."

"I'm very pleased to meet you. What do you usually do on your afternoon off?"

Dorothy shrugged. "Sometimes I go for a

walk on the high street and look in the shop windows and sometimes I go to Holland Park. Once I went to Regents Street but that's a long way off and I got a bit muddled about which omnibus to take, so I'm not wantin' to do that again."

"Don't you ever go home to see your family?" She stopped as the waiter pushed a trolley toward them. While he put their order on the table, she stretched up and peeked over the side of the pram. Her little Miss Belle was still sound asleep.

"My family lives in Wortham," Dorothy explained as soon as they were alone again. "That's in Suffolk. It's a bit of a ways to go so I don't get to see them very often. I'm goin' home this summer for my sister's wedding, though. Mrs. Brompton has already said I could take two whole days off. Mind you, they'll be deducted from my wages, but that's fine. It'll be worth it to see Carolyn get married."

Betsy kept her smile firmly in place as she poured the tea and passed Dorothy her cup. But inside, the old resentment welled up as she realized that there but for the grace of God, Inspector Witherspoon, and her beloved Smythe, she might still be having to work her fingers to the bone and feel grateful to get two blooming days off in a row.

She pushed her anger aside and concentrated on the task at hand. "I'm sure it'll be lovely. Have you been in London long?"

"It's been about nine months. But I don't think I'm going to stay much longer. When I go home in June, I'm going to see if I can get a position. I'll have a reference by then and Mum says there's some hotels opening in Bury St. Edmonds." She leaned forward, her expression serious. "I don't want to stay here any longer than I have to. There was a murder at the house next door. I don't dare tell Mum about it — she'll have me on the next train home, and I can't do that. We need my wages so I can't go till I've got a reference, and Mrs. Brompton won't give a reference until you've been here a year. But come the end of May, I'll have been here that long and I think she'll give me one then."

"Gracious, who was murdered?" Betsy shook her head in disbelief.

"The French tutor from the house next door." Dorothy picked up her tart. "It's been in all the papers," she said as she took a big bite.

"Oh my goodness, no wonder you're terrified. Have they caught the killer yet?" She reached for her cup and took a quick sip.

"Not yet," Dorothy said around a mouthful of pastry. "Everyone says it is a maniac but Mrs. Minton, she's the cook, she reckons it was that Mrs. Barclay that did her in." She put the tart down and grabbed her teacup.

"Who is Mrs. Barclay and why on earth would she kill the poor French tutor?" Betsy knew perfectly well who Mrs. Barclay was, but of course, she had to pretend total ignorance.

"Mrs. Barclay is Sir Donovan Gaines' niece. He owns the house where the murder was done," she explained. "And she's the mother of the girls who were bein' taught French." She took a fast sip. "Cook reckons that Mrs. Barclay had one of her spells and went off her head and killed the poor teacher."

"You mean this Mrs. Barclay had no reason to want to murder someone, she simply went insane?" Betsy pressed. Ye Gods, this was turning into a waste of time. This girl knew nothing except some silly kitchen gossip she'd gotten from someone who didn't even work in the Gaines house.

Dorothy grabbed the remainder of her tart. "Cook claims she has spells. Mrs. Min is good friends with Mrs. Crawdon, Sir Donovan's cook, and she told her that Mrs. Barclay's husband went off to the East to work so he could get away from her. Mrs. Min says Mrs. Crawdon claimed that during one of Mrs. Barclay's spells, she clouted her husband with a brass doorstop and that's why he left her." She stuffed the last bite of pastry into her mouth.

To give herself a moment to think, Betsy stretched again and looked into the pram. Amanda was still asleep. She turned back to her guest. "Sometimes married people do get violent with one another. Perhaps this Mrs. Barclay's husband was trying to beat her. Perhaps she was only defending herself."

Dorothy shrugged. "I guess that's possible, but Mrs. Min has got no reason to make up such a tale. On the other hand, she does like to gossip, but then again, don't we all. Just last week she and the housekeeper were talking about how Mrs. Barclay and Mr. Neville Gaines had changed their tune about Mrs. Linthorp."

"Who is Mrs. Linthorp?"

Dorothy laughed. "She's a friend of the Gaines family, and until recently, Mrs. Barclay and Mr. Gaines didn't have a good word to say about her, but since Christmas, they've treated her like a long-lost cousin."

Sir Donovan Gaines stared at them stonily

as he stood by the massive drawing room fireplace. "Is it really necessary to pester the boy with your questions?" he asked. "He can know nothing about how his mother was murdered. He was at school when it happened."

"Yes, sir, but I'm afraid we must speak with him," Witherspoon replied. "We're aware he wasn't there when it happened, but he lived with her and he may know some fact that will help us catch her killer."

Gaines sighed and smiled sadly. "You're right, of course. I've just been trying to protect him. He's alone in the world now." He walked to the door and yanked on the bellpull.

"I understand that Mrs. Langston-Jones appointed you his guardian?" Witherspoon said.

"That's correct."

The door opened and the butler stepped inside. "You rang, sir?"

"Please ask Alexander to come in here," Gaines ordered.

As soon as the door closed behind him, Gaines turned back to the two policemen. "Mrs. Langston-Jones asked if I'd be Alex's guardian and I agreed. But how did you find out?"

"We've had a word with her solicitor, sir,"

Barnes said. "It's normal procedure when we're investigating a murder."

"How stupid of me, I should have realized." He sat down on the end of the couch and clasped his hands together.

"Mrs. Langston-Jones' landlady says you've paid the rent on her rooms until the middle of next month," Barnes asked. "Is that right?"

"That's correct," he said. "I didn't want anyone bothering her things, especially the paintings, until I have a chance to get them properly inventoried and stored. They're quite valuable and an important part of Alexander's inheritance."

"Had you met young Alexander before you agreed to become his guardian?" Witherspoon asked. He couldn't imagine where that question had come from, but as it had popped out of his mouth, he couldn't take it back.

He looked surprised and then shrugged. "Of course, we've met a number of times. Ellen wanted to ensure that if something happened, we knew one another."

"When was the first time, sir?" Barnes asked.

"I'm not certain of the exact date, but it was in the week between Christmas and New Year's Day. I saw them in Hyde Park and renewed my acquaintance with Mrs. Langston-Jones."

"She was employed next door as the governess," the constable said. "That would have been eight years ago, correct?"

"That's right. But I don't see what her former employment has to do with her murder." Gaines got up and began to pace the room. "She worked as a governess next door a number of years ago."

"Was there a specific reason she didn't want her husband's family to act as Alexander's guardian?" Witherspoon asked. "We know that the boy has an uncle, his father's brother."

"There was a very good reason." He smiled faintly. "She didn't trust her brother-in-law. She was afraid he'd rob the boy blind."

CHAPTER 8

Wiggins gave the footman a reassuring smile. "Thanks for taking the time to talk to me. If I go back without getting anything, my editor will 'ave my guts for garters. Now, will a pint do ya?" They were sitting in a pub a good quarter of a mile away from the murder house. It was a good working-class place, crowded now with shop clerks, cab drivers, and assorted laborers all hoping to have a quick one before going back for a long afternoon's work. Wiggins thanked his lucky stars he'd decided to walk down Portland Villas. If he'd not, he'd have missed this gangly young lad coming out the servants' door.

"A pint'll be fine. I don't usually drink in the daytime but today's my afternoon out," he replied.

Wiggins stood up and caught the barman's attention. "Two pints of bitter," he called. He slid back onto the stool and looked at his companion. Curly brown hair, blue eyes, and a pale face with a few spots on the chin; he wasn't quite a man, yet he was more than a lad. He sat awkwardly on the short stool with his knees touching the rim of the wobbly table.

His expression hardened as he noticed Wiggins studying him. "What did you say your name was?" he asked.

"Clarence Stevens," Wiggins said quickly. He'd used that name before and it made sense to keep on using it if he was going to continue to pretend to be a newspaper reporter. "What did you say yours was?" he asked.

"I didn't, but it's Tommy Wheaton." He jumped as the barman rapped on the top of the counter, signaling their drinks were ready. "Sorry." He smiled sheepishly. "That startled me."

Wiggins got their beer, brought it back to their table, and slid one of the glasses to Tommy. "Tell me about yourself, Tommy." Experience had taught him that you got more information out of someone who wasn't such a nervous Nellie and this lad was as jittery as a cat in a roomful of bulldogs. He wondered if maybe young Mr. Wheaton had seen or heard something that scared him.

"There's not much to tell, really." Tommy took a deep breath. "I've been a footman at the Gaines house for three years now. You did say you'd pay me for my trouble, right? I mean, I'm taking a risk here. I don't think Sir Donovan would like me telling tales about the household to a reporter."

"I keep my word, and I'll pay you like we agreed, five shillings."

"Thank you. I don't mean to sound greedy, but I've got to save every bit that I can now that I'm fixing to leave and that much money will help. But I don't know what it is that you're wanting to know."

Wiggins wasn't sure, either. "You knew Mrs. Langston-Jones, the lady who was murdered, right?"

"She's been coming to the household every afternoon since just after Christmas." He took a sip of beer. "She was a nice lady and I hope they hang that Mr. Montague."

"What makes you think Mr. Montague is guilty?"

"That's what everyone says," he replied. "And I overheard Mr. Neville telling Mrs. Barclay that it was Mr. Montague's gun that was used for the murder. Plus, everyone knows he didn't like her much. He was barely civil to her when he came to the house and she was there."

"Was there anyone else that didn't get along with Mrs. Langston-Jones?"

"Mrs. Linthorp wasn't very nice to her, but she'd gotten more polite lately." He snickered. "Mind you, I imagine that was because the master overheard her being rude to her last month, and when Mrs. Langston-Jones took the young misses up to the schoolroom for their lesson, he told Mrs. Linthorp she'd not be welcome in his house if he ever heard her speaking disrespectfully to Mrs. Langston-Jones again." He took another, longer drink. "That caused a right old row, I can tell you that! Mrs. Linthorp pretended she didn't know what the master was talking about and insisted she'd never be rude to the servants. Master said Mrs. Langston-Jones wasn't a servant and Mrs. Barclay jumped in and said yes, she was a servant. That was one of the few times I've seen Sir Donovan lose his temper."

"What happened then?" Wiggins asked.

"Mrs. Barclay and Mrs. Linthorp both realized he was really angry so they mumbled their apologies and then left. But they were furious. They kept their voices down, but I could still hear them complaining about how improper it was for the master to always be jumping to Mrs. Langston-Jones' defense." He sighed heavily. "Then again, I wasn't surprised that he took her part. He defends us when we get blamed for things, you know. Right after Christmas, one of the housemaids was accused of pilfering through Sir Donovan's private papers. The poor girl was terrified she was going to lose her job, but I had a quiet word with the master and he believed me when I told him it hadn't been Susan going through his papers, but Mr. Neville."

"What was Mr. Neville looking at?" Wiggins sipped his drink.

"I don't know exactly what it was, but it was something from the master's private box." Tommy made a face. "I'm a footman but nowadays Sir Donovan hardly ever uses his carriage and Mr. Totts, he was the butler, he retired a few months back and he's not been replaced, so I do whatever needs doing, all the heavy work and sometimes I act as valet to Sir Donovan."

"I know," Wiggins agreed quickly. "Things aren't like in the old days. Most footmen these days do everything from cartin' rugs out to polishing sconces. But go on, what did you see?"

"One of my jobs is to take Sir Donovan's boots to the cobbler when the soles need redoing, so I went up to his room, and just as I got there, I saw Mr. Neville with Sir Donovan's box. It's a big, old-fashioned box with brass handles and the master keeps old letters and mementos and such in it. I wondered what Mr. Neville was doing in the master's bedroom, but it wouldn't do to ask, so I closed the door and left. But he must have heard me, because he come out a few seconds later and stalked off. That evening, I was refilling the brandy snifters in the drawing room and I overheard Sir Donovan asking who had been snooping about in his room and I heard Mr. Neville and Mrs. Barclay both say it hadn't been either of them."

"How did Sir Donovan know someone had been there?"

"The silly fool had dropped an old drawing of Sir Donovan on the floor. It was a picture of him and his sister from years ago when they were children. It was one of them pen and ink likenesses, not valuable, but the sort of thing you'd keep. Then Mrs. Barclay said that the maid had cleaned in there that morning and it was probably her who'd done it." He snorted faintly. "But that's what they always do, isn't it, blame it on the servants. Mrs. Barclay said she'd have a word with the housekeeper about it, but Sir Donovan told her not to, that he'd take care of it. Susan, she's the maid, she'd overheard everything. She'd just brought up the coffee and was out in the hallway. She was in tears thinking she was going to be blamed for something she'd not done. I told her not to worry, and as soon as they went up to bed, I asked Sir Donovan if I could have a word and I told him what I'd seen, that it had been Mr. Neville in his room."

"He believed you?"

Tommy nodded. "He did. Like I said, he's a good master."

"It sounds like you like Sir Donovan," Wiggins said.

"I do. He treats us decently and pays proper wages."

"If that's the case, then why are you savin' your money so you can leave?"

"Because he's not going to be here much longer," Tommy explained. "And when he leaves, I want to have enough saved to buy a ticket to New Zealand. My brother's there and I want to go join him."

Wiggins wasn't sure he understood. "What do you mean? Are you sayin' that Sir Donovan Gaines is leaving London?"

Tommy gulped more of his beer and wiped his mouth with his hand. "Not just London, he's leaving England, and I don't think he's planning on coming back." His eyes widened as he realized what he'd just said. "You can't put that in your paper. You can't. I've not told another living soul about this and I'll lose my job if he finds out what I've done. Oh damn, I knew I shouldn't have had a pint. I'm just like my old dad — just the smell of liquor causes me to lose control of my tongue."

"I'll not write it in my newspaper," Wiggins assured him. "But you've got to tell me what you mean. Has Sir Donovan decided to leave the country since Mrs. Langston-Jones was murdered?"

"No, no, he decided to do it months ago. He's going to sell everything and not come back. He's going to start a new life in San Francisco."

Betsy wheeled the pram into the kitchen. She was the last one back for their afternoon meeting. "Where's Samson?" She scanned the room, making sure the big tabby was nowhere in sight. "I don't want him jumping in with the baby. She's asleep."

"Samson wouldn't do such a thing," the cook declared. "But if you're worried, let me take her into my room and put her in her cot." She adored her cat almost as much as she loved her goddaughter and felt obligated to defend his character.

"Let me." Smythe scooped the sleeping baby up, kissed her on the forehead, and then went past the stairs to Mrs. Goodge's quarters.

"I hope the baby wakes up before we have to leave." Luty glanced toward the hallway. "I hardly ever get to see her."

"That's a ridiculous assertion, madam, and you know it." Hatchet snorted faintly. "You see the little one frequently."

"I've got something to report," Betsy announced as she took her seat. "But I'll wait my turn."

Smythe returned and slipped into the chair next to his wife. He glanced at her curiously. "You look pleased with yourself, love." He grabbed her hand under the table and gave it a squeeze.

"I am." She laughed. "It felt so good to be back on the hunt."

"Why don't you go first, then," Mrs. Jeffries suggested.

"Alright, I will." Betsy's eyes sparkled with excitement. "I hadn't meant to do anything on the case, but out of curiosity, I walked by the Gaines house, and just as I was passing, I saw the maid from the house next door coming out of the servants' entrance. So of course, I couldn't pass up an opportunity like that."

"I take it you managed to speak to 'er," Wiggins said. "Cor blimey, you've still got the magic touch."

"I used the old dropped glove trick," Betsy said. "And bought her tea at Neffs Tea Shop. Her name is Dorothy Edmonds and she had quite a bit to say." She told them the gossip about Martha Barclay's bad temper sending her husband off to the Far East. When she'd finished, she helped herself to one of Mrs. Goodge's scones.

"So Martha Gaines Barclay has spells and gets violent," Ruth murmured. "How awful that must be for her children."

"Maybe that's why she's livin' with Sir Donovan," Luty suggested. "Maybe he wanted to keep an eye on her and make sure them nieces was safe."

"What I find more interesting is that it was right after Christmas that both Mrs. Barclay and Mr. Neville Gaines suddenly changed in their attitude to Mrs. Linthorp," Mrs. Jeffries said. There was a faint tug at the back of her mind, but it was gone before she could grab it.

"The bit I heard from Dorothy's information is just kitchen gossip, but it wouldn't be the first time a tidbit has pointed us toward the killer." Betsy spread butter on the top of her pastry. "I liked being out and on the hunt again."

"I'm not sure it was a good idea to take Amanda Belle into Neffs." Mrs. Goodge looked a bit disapproving. "The loud noises must have frightened her."

"She slept through it all and didn't wake up until I got her home this afternoon." Betsy glanced at Smythe, not sure of his reaction, but he simply smiled.

"Miss Belle's got grit," Luty declared. "She's not going to git scared by a few clankin' spoons."

"Who would like to go next?" Mrs. Jeffries asked.

Hatchet put down his tea. "I've nothing of importance to report. The source I wanted to speak with is out of town but is expected this evening." He glanced at Luty. "As a matter of fact, madam, if you don't need me, I'd like to try again tonight."

"I ain't goin' nowhere, so you do as you please," she replied. "And you ain't the only one who had a miserable day. No matter who I talked to, the only thing I heard was Sir Donovan Gaines had rented a small warehouse over near the East India Docks."

"Not to worry, some days are like that," Mrs. Goodge said cheerfully. "I didn't have much luck today, either, but I did hear that on the day of the murder, Sir Donovan was

264

lunching at Bailey's Hotel on the Gloucester Road with a woman."

"Did your source know who this person might be?" Mrs. Jeffries asked. Again, something brushed the back of her mind, but it was gone before she could grasp it properly.

The cook smiled ruefully. "Mavis had no idea who it was. She only knew about it because of the murder. Her nephew is a waiter at the restaurant there and happened to comment that Sir Donovan had been there that day. He had the poached filet of sole and the lady had the creamed chicken."

"If you're finished, I'll go next," Ruth volunteered. "I did find out something rather interesting today." She told them about her visit to Catherine Winchester, making sure she repeated everything she'd heard almost word for word.

"Now that's very interesting," Hatchet mused. "Apparently, our original information was incorrect. Neville Gaines moved into his uncle's household because he had no choice. He was bankrupt."

"And it sounds like his sister moved in because her husband had scarpered and she didn't 'ave anyplace else to go," Wiggins pointed out.

"But what does any of it have to do with

Mrs. Langston-Jones' murder?" Phyllis asked. "Both of them moved into the Gaines house before she was hired to work there, and besides, it's natural they'd have wanted to live in that big house. They were his only relatives and his heirs. I still think Lucius Montague is our killer. He seemed to really hate that poor woman."

Everyone stared at her in stunned surprise. Phyllis was always very shy about giving her opinions.

She swallowed and looked down at the tabletop. "I'm sorry, I shouldn't have said that." She glanced at the housekeeper. "I know what you said this morning, that we wasn't to convict the man in our minds based on what we knew so far, but I can't seem to help myself. I've known people like him before; they're mean and nasty and they take real pleasure in hurtin' them that can't defend themselves. My first master was like that." She broke off and looked away as her eyes filled with tears.

For once, even Mrs. Jeffries was at a loss for words. But Betsy said, "Phyllis, don't be embarrassed, we've all had nasty ones like your old master in our pasts, but that's over and done with. No one's ever going to hurt you again, I promise you."

Phyllis said nothing. She merely swiped at

her cheeks and kept her head down.

"Cor blimey, this is gettin' right complicated and the bit that I 'eard today is goin' to muddle it even more," Wiggins blurted out. He wanted to distract his friend; it was as plain as the nose on your face that she was reliving a bad moment in her life. He told them about his conversation with Tommy Wheaton. When he'd finished, Phyllis wasn't studying the floor anymore. She gave him a grateful smile. She was back with them in the kitchen of Upper Edmonton Gardens, where she was safe.

"Did Tommy tell you how he knew Sir Donovan was leaving the country?" Mrs. Jeffries asked.

"He overheard 'im talkin' to his solicitor," Wiggins said.

Smythe reached for a scone. "He was eavesdropping?"

"Not on purpose. The lad was just outside the study because the housekeeper had sent him to get the sconces on the gas lamps in the hall so they could be cleaned. There's a light on either side of the study door and he was workin' away at pryin' the ruddy things off when he heard the solicitor and Sir Donovan talkin' plain as day. He must 'ave made a noise because, all of sudden, Sir Donovan come chargin' out and asked Tommy what 'e was doin'. Tommy told 'im he was just doin' as he was told. When the solicitor left, Sir Donovan called him in and swore 'im to secrecy. He said Tommy mustn't tell anyone in the 'ousehold what 'e'd heard."

"But he told you," Ruth pointed out.

"I'm not in the 'ousehold." Wiggins grinned. "And I bought 'im a pint. Lad doesn't hold his liquor very well."

"You're right, Wiggins, this does complicate the case even further," Mrs. Jeffries admitted. "I wonder if that's the reason Neville Gaines was snooping in Sir Donovan's box." She looked at the footman. "When did Tommy overhear this conversation?"

Wiggins winced. "I didn't ask. I meant to, but once Tommy realized what he'd told me, 'e was out of there like a shot and I didn't get a chance."

Alexander Langston-Jones stared at the inspector solemnly. He was a nice-looking boy with black hair and brown eyes. Witherspoon was no expert when it came to children, but he thought the lad was tall for his age. When Sir Donovan had brought the child in and introduced him to the policemen, the inspector had the fleeting thought that there was something familiar about him and concluded the boy took after his mother in looks. "Alexander, I'm very sorry about what has happened," Inspector Witherspoon said.

"Sir Donovan said you're going to find the person who killed her." Alex's eyes filled with tears and he looked over his shoulder at his mother's employer. Sir Donovan gave the child a reassuring smile but said nothing.

"Indeed we are," Witherspoon declared. "Constable Barnes and myself and many others on the Metropolitan Police Force shall not rest until the murderer is brought to justice." Generally, the inspector tried to refrain from pompous speeches, but he felt, in this case, it might reassure the boy.

"Good, because I want the person who killed my mama to hang till they are dead," he replied. Tears threatened again, but this time, he managed to hold them back. "Sir Donovan said I was to assist you, to answer all your questions, and I want to do that, sir. I want to help you find who took my mama away from me."

"Excellent, I'm sure you'll do just fine." The inspector glanced over and made sure Barnes had his little brown notebook at the ready. Truth be told, he wouldn't have minded if the constable had wanted to start the questioning; he wasn't certain exactly how he ought to begin. "Uh, Alexander, you don't mind if I call you that, do you?"

"Not at all, sir, but please call me Alex."

"Right, then, Alex, uh, do you speak French?" Witherspoon asked. It wasn't what he'd intended to say; it had just sort of slipped out and he'd no idea why. But as Mrs. Jeffries always said, "His inner voice hadn't failed him yet."

"Of course, sir, I've lived in France for most of my life."

"Did you speak English when you lived in France?" Barnes asked. "I mean, when you were at home with your parents?"

Alex smiled and it transformed his face. "Oh yes, sir, Mama and Papa always spoke English. Papa's French wasn't very good and I used to go with him to buy all his paints. Mine was much better, but Papa didn't mind, he just laughed when I had to correct him, though Mrs. Barclay says one shouldn't ever correct an adult . . ."

"Mrs. Barclay is wrong," Sir Donovan interjected. "And I'm sure you were very polite when you corrected your papa."

Alex turned and looked over his shoulder. "I was, sir. Mama would never have let me be rude to Papa, though he wouldn't have minded." He turned back to Witherspoon.

270

"Papa loved to paint, to eat, and to laugh. Nothing made him happier than the three of us sitting down over one of Mama's wonderful dinners."

The inspector wanted to get the boy talking about his daily routine with his mother. "I'm sure your mother was a wonderful cook. Can you describe what the two of you did every day?"

Alex thought for a moment. "Well, most days I got up and washed while Mama sat at her dressing table and did her hair. Then we went down to breakfast and after that Mama walked me to school. After school, I met Mama at the corner and we usually went to the park so I could play. Then we'd come home and have dinner. After our meal, we'd read together or perhaps work a puzzle. Saturdays and Sundays we were always together, but sometimes we did different things."

"Did your mother ever leave you alone?" Barnes asked.

"Sometimes Mama would leave very early in the morning and then Miss Martin would take me to school."

Witherspoon glanced at the constable and then looked at Alex. "Did your Mama say where she went on those mornings when she left you alone?"

"No sir, she didn't. She just said she had to go and that Miss Martin would take me to school."

"Are you sure she didn't say where she was going?" Barnes pressed.

"I'm sure. She just said to mind Miss Martin," he insisted.

"Are you certain, Alex?" the inspector interjected. "This could be very important."

"But she never told me where she was going." His eyes filled with tears again. "I'd tell you if I knew."

"Don't browbeat the lad." Sir Donovan frowned at the two men. "Alex doesn't lie. If he says he doesn't know, then he doesn't know."

"I'm sorry, I didn't mean to frighten you." The inspector smiled kindly at the boy. "Was your mother frightened or upset about anything or anyone?" He tried to come up with a way to be subtle about the question, but honestly, there simply wasn't a nice way to ask who might have wanted to murder the poor woman.

"She didn't like my uncle Jonathan!" Alex cried. "And I didn't like him, either. He came to see Mama and they had an argument. He's a mean man, he yelled at Mama." He leapt up from the settee, his hands clenching into fists. "He called us

272

both names and said he was going to take us to court . . . and now he wants to take me away to his horrible farm in Dorset, but I won't go, I won't go . . ." His voice broke as tears streamed down his face.

"Alex, Alex, calm yourself." Sir Donovan jumped up and rushed to him, rounding the couch and pulling the lad into his arms. "You don't have to worry about your uncle. I'll never let you go to him. Never."

Witherspoon glanced at Barnes, who gave a barely perceptible shrug. Apparently he didn't know what to say next, either. "Alex, please, listen to Sir Donovan," Witherspoon said. "No one is going to make you do anything . . . uh . . . er . . ." Ye Gods, what to do now? He couldn't promise the boy they'd not let his uncle take him; that was the sort of thing the courts decided.

"Anything that's wrong," Barnes finished. "Now get hold of yourself, lad, you need to help us."

The constable's kind, calm tone seemed to do the trick and Alex pulled away from Sir Donovan's embrace, took a deep breath, and sat back down. "I'm sorry, I didn't mean to act like a baby, and Mama wouldn't be pleased."

"Don't be silly, Alex." Sir Donovan sat down next to him on the settee. "You were understandably upset." He shot the two policemen a cold, quick frown as he pulled a pristine white handkerchief out of his coat pocket and handed it to the child.

"Alex, can you answer more questions for me?" the inspector asked.

He nodded and rubbed his face with the kerchief. "Yes, Mama would expect me to do my duty."

It was Barnes who asked the next question. "Alex, in the week or so before your mama passed away, did she act differently in any way? Take your time now and think about it. We're in no hurry."

Alex took him at his word and sat silently, his gaze focused on the far wall as if in deep thought. The only sound was the ticking of the antique French clock on the mantelpiece and the faint noise of the traffic from the street. Finally, Alex blinked. "Mama was different. One moment, she'd be happy, I could tell because she'd sing in French, and then the next day, she'd be quiet, and when I asked her what was wrong, all she'd say was that no matter what happened, we were going to be where we belonged."

Witherspoon wanted to ask what that meant, but he didn't think the child could possibly know. "Was there any particular day she was happy?" he finally asked.

Alex grinned broadly. "A few days ago, after Mama had finished tutoring, she picked me up at St. Matthew's School and we went to a wonderful place where they had pictures of lovely places. Mama called it Thomas Cook's. We'd been there before, when we first came to London."

"Is that where she got the pamphlets we found in your rooms?" Witherspoon asked. "The ones with ships going to the Far East?"

"Yes, but she got those when we first came to London." He frowned and wrinkled his nose. "When we came here, she looked at them all the time, but then she stopped and put them away in her drawer. When I asked her why, she said it was because she didn't think we'd need them anymore."

"Why was that? Did she say?" the inspector asked.

"Mama said we might be going somewhere else. I asked if we were still going to see the cowboys, you know, those American ones, and she said we would."

"Inspector Witherspoon." Sir Donovan stood up. "Don't you think this is enough for right now? He's just lost his mother and he needs time to grieve. The funeral is tomorrow — can your questions wait until then?"

"The lad seems to be holding up well."

Barnes stood up, too. "What's more, he's a very smart young chap who appears to understand everything we've asked."

"I've just got one more question." Witherspoon looked at Alex. "When was the last time you saw your uncle Jonathan?" Again, he'd no idea why that question popped into his head, but it had.

"The day Mama died," Alex replied. "I saw him outside our rooms. He was getting out of a hansom cab. I told Mama and she said she didn't want her day ruined by seeing him. That was a day when she was singing, so we went out the back door and not the front."

Sir Donovan gasped. "Alex, why didn't you tell me that?"

"I forgot." His shoulders slumped. "I'm sorry. I didn't think of it until the inspector asked about him. I don't like thinking of him. He's a horrible man who called me a bad name."

"Are you certain it was your uncle?" the inspector pressed.

"It was him. I know what he looks like."

There were suddenly loud voices in the hallway. "You can't go in there, sir. I insist you leave immediately."

"I'm not going anywhere until I speak to my nephew!" a man's voice shouted.

"What is going on here?" Martha Barclay cried. "Mrs. Metcalf, please show this person the door. He's scaring my daughters."

"Oh dear, that doesn't sound good." Witherspoon and Barnes both charged toward the ruckus in the hallway. Sir Donovan clutched Alex's arm and pulled him toward the French doors leading to the balcony. Just then, the drawing room doors opened and a balding man in a blue suit burst into the room.

Mrs. Metcalf and Mrs. Barclay were trying to grab the man's arms and pull him back, but he lunged forward, his face contorted in rage. "You've no right to keep my nephew here!" he yelled. "I'll have the law on you."

The two policemen raced forward and Barnes gave him a mighty shove, extricating him from the two women and slamming him against the wall. The constable pinned his right arm to the wall just as Witherspoon grabbed the other side.

"I don't know who you are, sir." The constable used his harshest voice. "But you can't come bursting into a private home."

"I'm the boy's uncle and I've come to get my nephew." Jonathan Langston-Jones made a visible effort to calm down. "Please let go of my arms, I promise I'll not move from this spot until I've said my piece."

Witherspoon nodded assent and they released him. "Now, who are you and why have you behaved in such a fashion?"

"That's my uncle Jonathan!" Alex cried. He and Sir Donovan stood in front of the open balcony doors. "And I won't go with him. I won't, I won't."

"Shhh . . . shhh." Sir Donovan patted the child's back. "You don't have to go anywhere with this man. I promise you."

"You're hardly in a position to make such promises." Jonathan Langston-Jones sneered. "You've no legal right to keep him here. I'm his nearest relation and" — he looked at the two policemen and grinned — "as the law is here, I'm well within my rights to take the boy."

Sir Donovan stepped in front of the now sobbing child. "No, I'm afraid that's not correct. I have a signed letter from his mother appointing me guardian of the boy."

"It wasn't for his mother to say, now was it? The boy's father was my brother and that gives me more right than you. Now, if these two policemen will step aside, I'll take the child and leave. I'd like to catch the eight o'clock train for Weymouth."

"You're not taking him anywhere." Dono-

278

van started toward them. "I'll see you in hell before I let you get your thieving hands on this boy. Do you think I don't know why you want him? You want the paintings and his share of the farm. But I'm not going to let that happen. You're a drunkard and a wastrel and a gambler and you're up to your ears in debt. You're not getting control of this lad so you can rob him blind."

Langston-Jones' eyes widened but he quickly recovered. "You've no call to say that. I just want the lad to come home where he belongs. He's the only family I've got left now."

From the corner of his eye, Barnes saw a crowd gathering in the open doorway. Two little girls, their faces agog with curiosity, had squeezed between the housekeeper and the maid and were watching the proceedings with interest. Mrs. Barclay was standing a few feet in front of them and had no idea her daughters were witnessing this spectacle. The constable would have said something, but was too busy trying to take this turn of events in to worry about the sensibilities of two little girls who, judging by the big smiles on their face, were enjoying themselves hugely.

Witherspoon wondered briefly if he ought to intervene. But like the constable, he didn't want to stop what could be some very interesting revelations.

"I'm not your family!" Alex shouted. "You called me a bad name and Mama said you were going to take her to court to prove something awful, and even if you make me come with you, I'll never sign my share of the farm over to you. It's mine and I promised Papa that I'd never let you get your hands on it. You can't have his paintings, either. They're mine."

"Get out," Donovan snapped. "Get out now before I have you thrown out."

Langston-Jones looked first at Witherspoon and then at Barnes. "I'm not leaving without the child. I'm his legal guardian. I've a right to take him with me. You're the law, you've got to make him come."

"I'm afraid this isn't the sort of thing we can adjudicate," Witherspoon said calmly. "I've spoken with the late Mrs. Langston-Jones' solicitor and she did indeed appoint Sir Donovan Gaines as his guardian. If you wish to dispute that, you'll have to take him to court."

"Go ahead," Sir Donovan snarled. "Take me to court. I'll see you bankrupted and in hell before I'll let you get your hands on this boy."

"You'll regret this." Langston-Jones glared

at Sir Donovan and started for the door.

"Mr. Langston-Jones, please wait." Witherspoon spoke sharply enough to have the man stopping in his tracks. "I'm afraid you can't leave just yet. We need to interview you."

"I want that man out of my house, Inspector!" Sir Donovan cried.

"Fine. Mr. Langston-Jones, I'd like you to accompany us to the station," Witherspoon said.

"That's not a good idea, sir." Barnes fought down a surge of panic. Going to the station was out of the question.

"Really, why not?"

"That'll take time, sir," the constable said. "And you know that once we're at the station, we'll have a mountain of paperwork to sift through. You said it yourself, sir, we've a lot on our plate today. Can we use your communal garden?" Barnes directed the question to Sir Donovan.

"I don't care where you go as long as this blackguard is out of my house!" Sir Donovan yelled.

Witherspoon motioned toward the back of the house. "Let's go outside."

Myra Manley handed Hatchet a cup of tea. "I was hoping it was you," she said with a smile. She should not have been an attractive woman — her face was narrow, her teeth protruded, and her hair was liberally laced with gray. But as far as Hatchet was concerned, she was one of the loveliest women he'd ever seen. It might have been the compassion shining from her eyes or perhaps the smile that played around her lips. She was also one of the richest women in the kingdom and married to his good friend, Reginald Manley.

Hatchet had come to see them for several reasons. Reginald, a handsome man with black hair, blue eyes, and the kind of face that still turned ladies' heads when he entered a room, was also an artist. Reginald had never been a very successful painter and prior to his marriage had been subsidized by a series of wealthy women, all of whom he'd been faithful to when he was with them and most of whom remained his friend to this day. He and Myra had both been well into middle age when they'd met, had fallen in love, and against the advice of just about everyone, had married. They were perfect for each other and genuinely in love.

They were in Myra's cozy morning room. She'd dismissed the butler and was serving them herself — tea for Hatchet and good aged whiskey for the two of them.

"When the butler told us a 'white-haired gentleman had called to see us,' we were both hoping it was you." Reginald smiled at his wife as he took the glass she handed to him. "Considering we've been stuck in the most miserable of circumstances, I can't tell you how relieved I was when you arrived this evening."

"Now, Reginald, it wasn't that bad." Myra dropped into the chair next to her husband. "We've been visiting relatives," she explained to Hatchet.

"My relatives." Reginald frowned. "And they were a tiresome lot."

"That's not true. The only real bore was your cousin Maura, she did talk incessantly, but your aunt and uncle were both delightful," Myra said before turning her attention back to their visitor. "Now, wonderful as it is to see you, why don't you tell us the real reason you're here."

"I wanted to see you," he protested.

She laughed. "Yes, I'm sure you did, but I also suspect you're here because you want to ask Reginald if he knew Brandon Langston-Jones."

"So you've heard about Ellen Langston-Jones being murdered?"

"The Leicester papers reported it," she replied. "Poor woman. Was she really shot on Sir Donovan Gaines' back stairs?"

"I'm afraid so. She'd come through the communal garden and the killer must have caught her right before she reached the safety of the house," Hatchet said.

"What can we do to help?" Myra leaned forward eagerly. "No one has the right to take a human life, no one."

Both Reginald and Myra believed fiercely in justice. That was one of the reasons Hatchet didn't hesitate to ask for their assistance. Both of them had a wide circle of friends and had provided helpful information in several of their earlier cases. They were also very discreet.

"Did you know the victim?"

"No, I never met her, but I am acquainted with Sir Donovan and his family. He must have been terribly upset."

"I knew Brandon Langston-Jones." Reginald shook his head. "Sad, really. Poor fellow struggled for years and only started getting the recognition his work deserved a few months before he died."

"He was a good painter, then?" Hatchet asked.

"Very much so. Unfortunately, being good doesn't necessarily mean your work gets respect or even affords the artist a decent living. You know how the art world is —

styles and artists go in and out of fashion as quickly as ladies' hats. He struggled for years, and for a good part of that time, only the smallest galleries would handle his work. But then as so often happens, a rich collector began buying his paintings and every gallery in Paris was after him."

Hatchet put his cup and saucer down on the table. "Do you happen to know who the collector was?"

"There were rumors, of course." Reginald glanced at his wife. "Darling, I'm about to be indelicate. You may —"

"Don't be absurd. I know perfectly well what you're going to tell him and it doesn't embarrass me in the least." She frowned irritably. "Go ahead and tell him. It's all you and your artist friends talked about for months."

"That's not true, though I will admit there was a lot of speculation about it and not just a little envy." He grinned at his wife. "Forgive me, darling, I didn't mean to treat you as less than an equal." His smile faded as he turned to Hatchet. "The gossip amongst my friends was that the collector was an American from New York named Phillip Boudreau. Boudreau was well known here. He used to live in London but went back to New York just before Brandon

Langston-Jones went back to Dorset."

"They knew each other?"

"Indeed they did." Reginald tapped his finger on the rim of his glass. "Look, I'm not one to sling mud at a dead man's grave and I believe in live and let live. But well, there's no easy way to say this . . ."

"They were more than friends," Myra blurted out. "And Phillip Boudreau was devastated when Brandon left London to get married." She looked at her husband. "Go on, tell him the rest."

Reginald tossed back the rest of his whiskey. "Brandon and Ellen Langston-Jones were neighbors and they'd known each other most of their lives. The gossip going around was that she was pregnant by someone else and Brandon agreed to marry her so his father wouldn't cut him off."

CHAPTER 9

"We know you were in London, sir. We've a witness that saw you here on the day your sister-in-law was murdered." Barnes sighed in exasperation. "If needed, we can find the hansom cab driver that dropped you in front of Mrs. Langston-Jones' lodging house that morning."

"So what if I was in London?" Langston-Jones snapped. "There's no law against it. I had business here. I didn't speak to her that day."

"But you told us only a few moments ago that you weren't here, that you'd gone home right after seeing Mrs. Langston-Jones last week." Witherspoon shifted slightly as he tried to find a comfortable spot on the bench. "Which is it, Mr. Langston-Jones? We've been interviewing you for ten minutes now and you've changed your story twice. Please tell us the truth."

"Alright, alright!" he cried. "You can't

blame a man for getting confused. For God's sake, this is about murder. I was frightened and I didn't know what I was saying, and just because I was here on the day she was killed, doesn't prove anything. I didn't do it."

"What did you mean when you threatened Mrs. Langston-Jones?" Barnes looked up from the notebook he'd balanced on his knee. "You were overheard saying that if you took her to court, there were all sorts of things you could bring up."

"How do you know what I said?" He snorted in disgust. "Don't bother answering, it was that cow of a landlady. She must have been eavesdropping. I bet she got an earful. But my words didn't mean a thing. I was simply trying to get Ellen to see reason. I've a good offer for the farm, but the buyer wants the whole place, not just my half. I gave her a good price to sell Alexander's half, but she wouldn't hear of it. I hope the landlady also told you the rest of what she overheard."

"What would that be, sir?"

"Ellen complained about Sir Donovan's neighbor, a fellow that lived across the garden. She claimed he'd not paid for several of Brandon's paintings and that when she'd confronted him for payment, he'd threatened her."

"Threatened her physically?" Barnes asked.

Langston-Jones hesitated. "Well, she didn't actually say *that*. Remember, we were quarreling and it was in the context of the argument. She snapped that she wasn't scared of going to court, that she'd already engaged a solicitor to sue the other man who tried to take advantage of her. Those were her words, not mine."

"And she said this the week before she was killed?" Witherspoon wanted to make sure they were both referring to the same incident.

"Yes, I've already told you it came up when we were arguing. We were in the sitting room of her lodging house and that was the last time I saw my sister-in-law."

"When exactly did you go back to Weymouth?" Witherspoon asked.

"The day she was murdered. But I had nothing to do with it," he insisted. "I'll admit that I was angry at her so I stayed in London trying to get her to change her mind. I've been at a small hotel in Maida Vale. They can confirm when I left."

"So you stayed here and contacted her again after the two of you had argued?" Barnes eased back on the bench as a bee

289

flew past him.

"I tried to, but she refused to meet me." He laughed harshly. "Finally, I got so desperate that I even followed her. I'd gone to her lodging house that morning, but she'd already gone for the day. I knew that she had a luncheon engagement at Bailey's Hotel, so I went there and waited —"

"How did you know?" Witherspoon interrupted.

"Because she told me." He frowned irritably. "Mr. Hathaway, he's the agent representing the prospective buyer for the farm, was in London that day on business. I thought if I could get her to speak with him, it might change her mind about selling. I only wanted to talk to her, but I didn't get the chance. By the time she came out the front door and got into a hansom, the fog was so thick it was impossible to see more than two feet in front of your face. I tried following her, but it was impossible and I couldn't stay in London any longer. So I went to the station and caught the train."

The inspector frowned heavily. "Let me see if I understand this correctly. You spent several days in London trying to get her to meet with you but you gave up and went back home because of the fog?"

"No, I gave up because I had a meeting

with my solicitor and I needed to get back to Weymouth before eight o'clock. We were going to have a drink together and discuss my case." He shot a glare toward the Gaines house, where Sir Donovan stood on the upper balcony watching them. Turning back to Witherspoon, he said, "And you might ask him what he did that afternoon. He was following her, too. He came out right behind her, and when she got into her cab, he climbed into one as well. I saw him pointing towards her hansom as it pulled away from the curb. It looked very much like he was telling the driver to follow her cab."

Hatchet rapped lightly on the back door. It was getting close to dinnertime now, and knowing the household routine as he did, he hoped that it wouldn't be Wiggins who answered.

The door opened and he smiled in relief. "Mrs. Jeffries, do forgive me for barging in this late, but I need to speak to you privately. I've found out something that would be better told now rather than tomorrow at our morning meeting. It's a matter that requires a bit of discretion."

She put her hand to her lips in a silencing gesture and then looked over her shoulder to the kitchen. "Mrs. Goodge, I'm stepping out in the garden for a bit of air. I'll be back soon."

"You go and have a good think then," the cook yelled. "Dinner won't be for another hour."

"An 'our!" Wiggins cried. "But I'm starvin'."

"You're always starving." Phyllis giggled.

Mrs. Jeffries stepped out and closed the door. They said nothing until they were well away from curious eyes and standing in the center of the garden under the concealing branches of the big oak tree. He was both diplomatic and direct as he told her what he'd learned from Reginald Manley. "I thought it important for you to know this right away for two reasons. One, I've a sense that we're running out of time and it's possible this information might cast the case in a whole new light and I wanted you to have time to think about it before tomorrow."

"Yes, I can see your point," she murmured.

"Secondly, I thought if I told Wiggins privately about this, it might save a bit of embarrassment for everyone. I, too, believe in live and let live, but the subject of two men falling in love can make for very uncomfortable conversation. I thought perhaps you might want to speak to the ladies about it."

She nodded in agreement. "Your source was absolutely sure about this?"

"Indeed, Brandon Langston-Jones was in love with Phillip Boudreau. They had a small flat together in Soho and by all accounts were quite happy. Then he got a summons from his father. According to my informant, Brandon had confided to one of their mutual friends that he was certain his own brother had told their father about his relationship with Boudreau."

"And his father would have cut him off?"

Hatchet nodded. "So when his good friend and former neighbor, Ellen Arden, arrived home pregnant and in need of a husband, a quick marriage solved both their problems." He rose from the bench. "Have a good think about this, Mrs. Jeffries. I'll tell madam what I've learned tonight, and perhaps by tomorrow's meeting, you'll have an idea of how we are to go forward."

After he left, Mrs. Jeffries sat staring out across the darkening garden. She should have been more surprised by this turn of events, but she wasn't. Somehow, she'd been expecting it. Suddenly, several bits and pieces began to make sense and she had an idea about why Ellen Langston-Jones had been killed. But it would be difficult to prove, and even with this new fact tossed into the mix, there were still two possibilities as to the real motive of the killer. But her instincts were pointing toward one person and one person only. Over the years, she'd learned to trust those feelings.

She got up and went to the path. As she walked to the back door, she was mentally making a list of tasks that needed to be completed if her theory was right. But what if I'm wrong, she thought. What if the motive isn't what I think, but the other possibility? What then? She stopped on the edge of the small kitchen terrace. "Don't be a goose," she told herself. "If you're wrong, then you and the others will keep on digging until you find the truth." She took a deep breath and went inside. Tomorrow's meeting was going to be very interesting indeed. Witherspoon was exhausted by the time he walked into the front door of Upper Edmonton Gardens.

"Gracious, sir, we were beginning to get worried about you." Mrs. Jeffries took his bowler. "Is everything alright?"

He slipped off his jacket. "All is well, Mrs. Jeffries. I'm only late because there have been some substantial new developments in the case and they happened late this afternoon. Do we have time for a sherry before dinner?"

"Dinner can be served whenever you like, sir." She hung up his garments. "And I should love a sherry as well. You've obviously made some real progress on this case. But then again, of course you have. It is usually about this time in the investigation that your inner voice becomes most active."

He laughed, delighted by the compliment, as he headed down the hall to his cozy parlor. "You're most kind, Mrs. Jeffries." He stopped and sniffed the air. "Ah, that smells wonderful. Don't tell me, let me guess, we're having roast chicken tonight."

"Indeed we are, sir."

It took less than two minutes for her to get the Harvey's poured and settle down opposite him. "Now, sir, don't keep me in suspense. What has happened?"

"Hmm . . . where to begin? There's so very much to tell." He chuckled. "The morning started off easily enough. Just as Constable Barnes and I reached the cabstand on Holland Park Road, we found out from Constable Deloffre that the document we'd found in the victim's room was a shipping advice."

"Shipping advice?" she repeated. "For what, sir?"

"The remainder of her late husband's

paintings and some household goods. The actual document was a letter from a freight forwarding company; the ship is docking on the twenty-ninth." He paused and took a sip. "And as per her instructions, her goods will be delivered to a warehouse in the East End. She had the advice lying on the top of her desk as if she wanted it as a reminder. Of course, the mere fact that the goods exist is causing quite a commotion." He shook his head. "But I'll leave that for the lawyers to sort out. After that, we went back to the Montague house and had a word with Lucius Montague." He told her about his interview with their number one suspect.

She listened carefully, occasionally making a comment or asking a question.

"We cautioned Mr. Montague not to leave the city," Witherspoon said. "But I'm not sure I trust the fellow so I've assigned officers to watch the house. After that, we went across the garden and had another word with Sir Donovan Gaines." He continued with his narrative, making sure he didn't omit any details, especially about the interview with Alexander Langston-Jones. "That's when the day really got interesting." He drained his glass and glanced at the clock on the wall. "Let's have another, shall we."

"Of course, sir." She got up, taking care to keep her glass tilted away from his view. She didn't want him to see that hers was still three-quarters full. She needed to keep her head clear and another glass of delicious sherry on top of an empty stomach might impair her memory. She poured the inspector's second glass, hoping this one wouldn't affect his recollection of the day's events, and then topped up her own. "Here you are, sir." She gave him his drink and took her seat. "Now, sir, you know I'm dying of curiosity. What happened next?"

He laughed. "We were almost finished with young Alexander when who should show up but Jonathan Langston-Jones. He demanded the child be handed over to his custody."

"We've many, many things to confirm if my idea is correct," Mrs. Jeffries announced. Their morning meeting was very late. She and Mrs. Goodge had had quite a long discussion with Constable Barnes and then she'd had to tell Phyllis and Ruth about Hatchet's visit. She'd told the cook before the constable arrived. The women had taken the news with equanimity; Mrs. Goodge had shrugged, Phyllis had blushed, and Ruth had merely nodded.

Hatchet had taken Wiggins outside to the garden for a quick word, and just as he finished speaking to the lad, Smythe and Betsy had come up the path pushing Miss Belle's pram. He shooed Betsy and the baby inside and passed the information along to Smythe, trusting that Mrs. Jeffries would make sure Betsy was informed.

Smythe propped his elbow on the table and eyed Mrs. Jeffries. "You know who the killer is, don't ya?"

"If my theory is correct, then yes, I do. Yet the same facts could also indicate that any one of three people could be the murderer," she admitted. "But before we go any further, I want you all to put your thinking caps on and help me. Let me tell you what I found out from the inspector last night and what Mrs. Goodge and I learned from Constable Barnes this morning."

"Before you do that," Smythe said. "You weren't the only one with a late-night visitor. One of my sources popped in with some interestin' news."

"When did this happen?" Betsy demanded.

"When you were feedin' our Miss Belle." He grinned. "You fell asleep in the rocker, so when he knocked on my door, I made him talk to me outside. I didn't want 'im disturbin' you. You need all the sleep you can get, love. But that's by the by. What I need to tell everyone is that he found out why the Home Office is stickin' their noses into this case. For the most part, it's Neville Gaines and his sister, Martha Barclay."

Yesterday, he'd seen Blimpey Groggins, and after listening to him whine about going directly to a source, he'd found out what he needed to know. He'd not apologized to Blimpey for what he'd done. "If you'd been here, Blimpey," he told him, "I'd not have had to pay triple for Henry's information." But in the interest of continued mutually beneficial relations between himself and Groggins, he'd offered to pay double for fast information. When Angus Cleary, Blimpey's right-hand man, had shown up on his doorstep, he'd not been overly surprised.

"How'd they do it?" Wiggins asked.

"How do you think?" Smythe said. "How do toffs always do it? Family connections. Martha Barclays' godfather is Lord Symington. Apparently, she and her brother complained to him about the way the inspector was handling the case."

Mrs. Jeffries arched an eyebrow. "For the most part," she repeated.

"Inspector Nigel Nivens 'ad a hand in it

as well." Smythe looked disgusted. "That's one of the reasons Symington acted. He had more than one complaint against our inspector."

"That Inspector Nivens is a terrible man." Phyllis helped herself to another cup of tea. "Fancy him being so mean after all our inspector did for him."

"He's a snake," Luty charged. "Always has been, always will be."

"Thank you, Smythe." Mrs. Jeffries took a deep breath. "Now, we've much to do and very little time to do it in, but if I'm right —"

"Wait a minute," Ruth interrupted. "Oh, sorry, I didn't mean to be rude, but I spent half the night tossing and turning with worry and I must know. Was the inspector called to the Yard? Is he still on the case?"

"So far." She gave her a tight smile. "And Constable Barnes is going to try and keep him away from the station today as well. But it might be difficult."

"You mean they don't have another suspect yet?" Betsy asked.

"They have one. Jonathan Langston-Jones admitted he was in London when the murder took place, but they'd have a devil of a time proving anything against him," she confessed. "There is still far more evidence against Lucius Montague than anyone else. That's what we've got to discuss. Hatchet's information has cast a whole new light on the case, but getting evidence is going to be difficult. I'm going to need everyone's help."

Amanda, who'd been sleeping in her pram, whimpered. Mrs. Goodge, who'd insisted the pram be next to her chair, grabbed the handle and gently tugged it back and forth. "Then we'd best get crackin'." She looked at the housekeeper. "Don't bother tellin' all the whys and whats about it; just tell us what you need us to do. Time is getting on."

Mrs. Jeffries gave her a grateful smile. "Right. I've a task for everyone."

"Perhaps we should have stopped by the station." Witherspoon pushed his spectacles back into place. "We've not been there in two days."

Barnes surveyed the foyer of Hester Linthorp's Bayswater home. The woman wasn't a pauper; that was for certain. Straight ahead was a wide staircase carpeted in gray and gold, the walls were painted cream, and opposite the door was an intricately carved entrance table covered with a gold and lavender lace runner and a trio of Dresden figurines. "We can stop in later,

301

sir, but as you said, it's important that we interview Mrs. Linthorp as soon as possible. If Lucius Montague was telling the truth, she was overheard arguing with the victim a few days before the murder."

"True, true, and with ladies, sometimes it's best to catch them before they get out and about."

A maid appeared from the other side of the staircase. "Mrs. Linthorp will see you now. If you'll come this way, please."

She led them down a short hall and into the drawing room. The cavernous room was crowded with furniture; settees, sofas, tables, curio cabinets, and chairs were clustered together haphazardly. The windows were covered by heavy green and gray drapes, which were still closed. Witherspoon squinted in the dim light until he spotted Hester Linthorp sitting in an overstuffed chair next to the window. She did not look pleased to see them. "What do you want?"

"We need to speak with you, ma'am," Witherspoon said politely as they advanced into the huge room.

"What about?"

"About the murder of Ellen Langston-Jones." Barnes fixed her with a hard glare. "A woman you quarreled with only days before she was killed."

"Who told you that?" she demanded.

"Does it matter?" Barnes pulled his notebook and pencil out of his pocket. "Now, may I have a seat, ma'am, or would you prefer to keep us standing here?"

She stared at them for a moment and then waved at two empty straight-backed chairs. "I don't know anything about that woman's murder," she said as they sat down. "Why would I? I barely knew her."

"Then why were you arguing with her?" Witherspoon asked politely. "We have a witness that heard you."

"She'd been impertinent to me. I told her if it happened again, I'd have to go to Sir Donovan and complain about her behavior. She took exception to my comments and our conversation became most unpleasant."

Barnes stared at her, his expression deliberately skeptical, but he said nothing.

"Was that all there was to it, ma'am?" Witherspoon asked.

"How dare you, Inspector? I'm not in the habit of lying. She was impertinent and rude and I told her I'd not tolerate such behavior from a mere servant."

"Are you sure that's all you said?" the inspector asked. "Our witness said he heard you tell her, and I quote" — he repeated Montague's words — " '*that I know the truth,*

303

and if you don't take your brat and go back to Dorset, you'll be sorry,' or words to that effect."

She paled and swallowed convulsively. "That's absurd. I would never speak in such an uncouth manner."

"But we have a witness that claims you did," the constable interjected. "How do you explain that?"

"Your witness is lying and that's all I'm going to say about the matter." She started to get up.

"This confrontation took place in the communal garden," Witherspoon said. "I suspect that if we look, we can find other witnesses who overheard your conversation with Mrs. Langston-Jones. Should we do that, Mrs. Linthorp?"

"That won't be necessary." She sank back into her chair. "Alright, have it your way. Yes, it's true, our discussion was a bit more than I've led you to believe."

"What did you argue about?" The inspector pushed his spectacles back into place.

"She was behaving like a trollop and I told her so in very blunt terms. She took exception to my comments and told me to mind my own business. Unfortunately, her manner upset me and I lost my temper." She looked out the window. "I may have told

304

her to go back to Dorset and I may have used the word 'brat.' Frankly, it was such an ugly incident that I've done my best to forget it."

"What had she done that so offended your sensibilities?" the inspector asked.

"It wasn't just me. Neville and Martha thought her behavior unsuitable as well," she said defensively. "She was openly flirting with Sir Donovan. She smiled and sent him silly, inappropriate glances when she thought no one was looking. The colors she wore were wrong, too; she was widowed barely a year yet she decked herself out in reds and greens and all manner of bright colors. She was always laughing at his jokes and witticisms and you know how men love that sort of thing. It was disgusting that someone of her class even considered herself a proper partner for someone such as Sir Donovan."

"Where were you on Monday afternoon?" Barnes asked.

"Monday afternoon." She cocked her head to one side as if she was thinking.

"The day that Mrs. Langston-Jones was murdered," he reminded her. "If you'll recall, you came rushing over to Sir Donovan's home as soon as you heard about the tragedy."

■ ■ ■

Wiggins waited till the crowd thinned before heading toward Mr. Calder's bench. "Remember me?" he said cheerfully as he sat down next to the elderly gentleman.

Calder stared at him through watery blue eyes. "I can't place you, lad. Do we know each other?"

"We met 'ere a few days ago. You told me about the lady that were killed over in the communal gardens behind Portland Villas," Wiggins explained. Cor blimey, he thought, has the old gent gone off his head this quick? Last time they spoke, his memory seemed fine.

Calder studied him for a moment and then broke into a broad grin. "Now I remember. You bought me a pint."

"And I've a mind to buy you another if you can spare me a few minutes."

"I can spare you more than that. My niece likes it if I'm out of the house in the afternoons when she does her cleanin'. I live with my niece and her husband. He's a nice enough bloke, 'e works hard. He's under-gardener at Kensington Palace."

"I'll get us somethin' to drink, then." Wiggins went to the bar, got two pints, and came back to the bench. "Here you are, Mr. Calder. Now, if you don't mind, I'd like a word about Mrs. Langston-Jones."

Calder smiled sadly. "It's a pity she's gone. She was such a pretty lady. She was nice, too, always had a kind word for me. She was always asking what kind of flowers and plants was what as she walked about the garden. I hope they catch whoever killed her. I hope they catch 'em and hang 'em till they're as dead as one of Mrs. Guinever's chickens."

Wiggins had no idea who Mrs. Guinever might be, but he understood the sentiment. "That's the reason I've come to see you, Mr. Calder. You see, I'm thinkin' you might 'ave some information that would be of 'elp to some people that are 'elpin' the police."

Calder drew back and studied him. His expression hardened and his eyes narrowed. "I've not seen the woman in years. How could I know anything? I had naught to do with her murder. I liked the lady."

"Don't get all het up, Mr. Calder. I wasn't sayin' you knew anything about her death." Wiggins feared he was handling this all wrong. He didn't want to scare the fellow into silence. On the other hand, he could think of no other way to find out what he needed to know. "I know you had naught to do with it. You were 'er friend."

Calder's face softened and Wiggins continued speaking. "It's not about what you know now, sir. It's about what you might 'ave seen years ago when she was workin' as a governess."

"My memory isn't what it used to be." Calder shrugged. "But as long as you keep buyin' me pints, I'll tell you what I can."

Mrs. Jeffries flattened herself against the side of a post and studied the face of the young boy holding the hand of the tall, well-dressed man she was certain was Sir Donovan Gaines. She'd slipped through a side door into St. James Church prior to Ellen Langston-Jones' funeral because she needed to have a good look at young Alex. As she watched the man and boy make their way down the center aisle to the front of the church, she realized her suspicions were correct.

Her attention fixed on the group coming in behind Sir Donovan. There were two well-dressed people, a man and a woman with sour expressions, followed by a retinue of what were obviously servants. She waited till they'd taken their places in the pews and then left the way she'd come.

Cutting through the churchyard, she came

out onto the road, took a good look around to ensure that there weren't any police who might recognize her, and then made her way to Portland Villas.

Five minutes later, she was standing in front of the Gaines house. She looked around to make sure no one was watching her before ducking into the walkway between the homes. Mrs. Jeffries hadn't told the others her plans because she was afraid they'd try to stop her. Her actions were illegal and, if she were perfectly frank, rather frightening. But she could see no other way and this was the kind of task she wouldn't ask anyone else to do.

She moved slowly down the concrete path toward the back of the house. She peeked into every window as she passed. She was sure the place was empty, but she was taking no chances. When she reached the servants' door, she looked around for the key she hoped would be hidden nearby. Even in grand houses, housekeepers didn't want to risk being locked out, and everyone, even responsible people, could lose keys. Standing on tiptoe, she stretched and ran her fingers along the top of the door, but the key wasn't there. It took her another ten minutes of careful searching but she finally found it wedged in a crack between two bricks along the top of the wall.

Mrs. Jeffries gathered her strength, put the key in the lock, and went inside. As she'd hoped, the kitchen was empty. Moving quietly, she went up the back stairs, and to her great relief, she found herself alone. She checked the rooms on the first floor first. Two single beds, both with white ruffled coverlets and pink and green curtains at the windows, meant this was the twins' room. Next door was a nursery cum schoolroom, and directly across the hall was a large bedroom with an attached sitting room. Martha Barclay, she thought, as she closed the door and went to the next one.

She continued searching till she came to a suite of rooms on the second floor and knew it belonged to Sir Donovan. She went inside and tried to recall exactly how Wiggins had described his conversation with Tommy Wheaton. She crossed the huge room, walking past the big, four-poster bed with its maroon coverlet to another door that led to a gentleman's dressing room.

Suits, trousers, jackets, and shirts hung along one wall; shoes, boots, slippers, and hats were on shelves opposite the doorway; and a wardrobe with an ornate carved hood stood beside the door. The box Wiggins had described was on the top.

From outside, she heard a carriage pull up to the pavement and her heart almost stopped. She raced to the window and saw that it was a hansom. A woman stepped out and went into the house next door. Mrs. Jeffries sagged in relief, allowed herself a few seconds to still her racing heart, and then rushed back to the dressing room. She grabbed the box and took it to the bedroom. So she could see properly and have a bit of warning if the household came back, she laid it on top of the table by the window. Opening the lid, she looked inside and then smiled.

As she'd hoped, what she was looking for was on top. She pulled out the pen and ink drawing and studied the faces of the two children.

Three minutes later, she locked the door behind her, wedged the key back into its hiding place, and hurried out to the street. But her heartbeat didn't slow down until she was safely back at Upper Edmonton Gardens.

"Really, Inspector, we've just come from a funeral," Neville Gaines complained as he walked into the drawing room. "What is it you want now?"

"Just a quick question for you, sir," Witherspoon replied. "You said that on the afternoon of the murder you were looking at property in Fulham. Is that correct, sir?"

He sighed in exaggeration. "That's correct."

"May we have the address of the property?" Barnes asked.

"What for?"

"We need to confirm your whereabouts, sir." The constable gave him a cool smile. "It's standard procedure."

"I don't see what good the address will do you. I was on my own when I inspected the property."

"But surely someone in the area would have seen you going in or out," the inspector pointed out. He had no idea why the constable had insisted they come back here and have another go at everyone's alibi, but he trusted his colleague.

"Hardly, Inspector. If you'll recall, there was a thick fog," Neville said sarcastically.

"And the fog lifted by three o'clock and you claim you were there until four that day so there should have been someone who noticed you," Barnes said. "Most people in Fulham do have eyes."

"Have it your way then. I was at the old Quigley Building. It's at the end of the high street right before you get to the bridge."

The door opened and Martha Barclay burst into the room. "What is the meaning of this? I couldn't believe it when Mrs. Metcalf said the police were here. Why are you disturbing us again? Uncle Donovan is in a terrible state. The funeral upset him greatly."

Barnes ignored the woman and kept his gaze on Neville. "How did you get into the building, sir?"

"With a key, Constable, and it was given to me by the owner's agents. They sent it over by messenger Monday morning."

"I'm sorry, ma'am." Witherspoon smiled apologetically. "We're only doing our job. Just a few more questions and we'll be on our way. By the way, what time did you go up to your room to rest on Monday?"

"I don't know, Inspector, it was after lunch sometime. I had a headache."

"This is ridiculous," Neville snapped. "We've told you all this before —"

Barnes whirled and looked at Martha Barclay. "If you were in your room resting, then why was the hem of your dress wet and muddied, as if you'd been out in the garden?" This was a shot in the dark, but he'd had a hunch from the start that she was lying about going up to her room for a lie down.

She gaped at him in stunned surprise and

he knew his shot had hit the mark. So he increased the pressure. "Mrs. Barclay, it was very foggy but even the worst haze clears for moments, and during one of those moments, someone saw you outside."

"I only stepped out for a second. I needed to get a bit of fresh air before I went up to lie down."

"Why didn't you tell us this to begin with?" Witherspoon asked.

"Because I didn't think to!" she cried. "I'd forgotten all about it."

"We've told you everything we know, Inspector. How many times must we go through it?" Neville put a protective arm around his sister.

Sir Donovan Gaines stepped into the room. "As many times as necessary. I want Ellen's killer found and punished, Neville. I thought I'd made that perfectly clear."

"Where have you been, ma'am? We were getting worried." Hatchet chided his employer as she hurried into the kitchen.

"I know, I know." Luty pulled off her black lace gloves as she headed for her chair. "I didn't mean to be late, but I couldn't get that clerk to talk any faster. He was talkin' a blue streak, and as I'd bought and paid for his time, I didn't want to shut him up just so I'd git back here on time." She plopped down in the chair that Hatchet pulled out.

"I take it you were successful then," Mrs. Jeffries asked. "You learned about Sir Donovan's plans?" She held her breath, praying that Luty had found out what she was certain was one of the keys to this crime.

"I found out most of what you asked." Luty was breathing hard. "But not all of it. My sources knew some of it, but not everything. Should I go first then?"

"Have a cup of tea and catch your breath." Mrs. Goodge poured a mug of tea and put it in front of her.

"Much obliged." She closed her eyes, dragged in a deep lungful of air, and then grinned broadly. "You were right, Hepzibah. He's really selling up."

"Everything?"

"Lock, stock, and barrel." Luty chuckled. "All of it, including his house."

Mrs. Jeffries could have cried with relief. Thank goodness she was on the right track. "Your source was sure of this?"

"Both my sources were sure of it," she replied. "Mind you, the one thing neither of 'em knew was who in Sir Donovan's family or circle of friends might have known about it. He played it close to his chest and warned both the solicitor handling the conveyances and the clerks at the exchange to keep quiet about it."

"Has he sold everything?" Mrs. Jeffries asked.

"That's the other bit I couldn't confirm." She took a quick sip from her cup. "All the stocks and bonds have been sold, most of the commercial property is gone, but neither of the sources knew if the house had sold yet. My sense is that it hasn't. No one seems to know it's on the market, and with a place like that, someone would know if it had changed hands. But then again, he's had six months to get rid of everything and he could have sold the place on the quiet."

"Six months?" Mrs. Jeffries repeated. "Are you sure?"

"Yup, he started selling up in January with a block of commercial properties in Shoreditch. Anyway, I hope that's what you needed to know because that's all I found."

"Thank you, Luty." Mrs. Jeffries wasn't sure how this fit in with her theory. But she pushed her doubts aside and decided to plunge ahead. "Who'd like to go next?"

"Let me." Phyllis smiled self-consciously. "I've not much to tell, but I did like you asked and went to Bayswater. But I couldn't find anyone who knew anything about Mrs.

Linthorp. I tried talking to the shop clerks but no one knew anything about her comings and goings on the day of the murder. I'm sorry."

"Don't be," Betsy said quickly. "Sometimes we find things out and sometimes we don't. That's just the way it is so stop worrying about it. You did the best you could."

Phyllis smiled gratefully. "I did try and I'm willin' to go out and try again if need be."

"I know you are," Mrs. Jeffries said.

"I found out something," Wiggins blurted out. "You were right, Mrs. Jeffries. The two of 'em did know each other eight years ago. It took me a couple of pints and I'm goin' to 'ave a right old 'eadache later, but it were worth it."

"I thought you looked a bit bright eyed and bushy tailed when you came in." Mrs. Goodge snorted delicately. "I hope you didn't drink too much; it's bad for your liver. But when we've finished here, I'll fix you up with a nice potion that'll put you right as rain."

Wiggins grimaced slightly. "That's alright, I'm fine. It were only two pints. Anyways, I got Mr. Calder chatting and he finally admitted that when Mrs. Langston-Jones was workin' as a governess, she and Sir

Donovan used to meet in the garden early of a morning. At first they were just friendly like, because they was the only ones there, but then Mr. Calder said he noticed they got to be more than friendly."

"More than friendly," Betsy repeated. "What on earth does that mean?"

"He saw them kissing," Wiggins explained. "But he didn't like to say anything about it, even after all these years, because he felt so sorry for both of them."

"How so?" Hatchet asked.

"Sir Donovan's wife had been ill for years," he continued. "She'd not been out of her bed in months and hadn't been in the garden for over a year. Mr. Calder said they were both such lonely people that even though what they was doin' was wrong, he still felt bad for 'em."

"Why did he feel sorry for Mrs. Langston-Jones?" Luty asked. "She's been described as a pretty woman. If she was lonely, she could've found herself a feller."

"She were shy around men," Wiggins said. "She'd spent years nursing 'er old mum, remember."

"So she had a romantic relationship with Sir Donovan," Mrs. Goodge mused. "No wonder he hired her to tutor his nieces."

"He wasn't like that," Ruth said. "I'm

sorry, I didn't mean to speak out of turn."

"I'm done." Wiggins put his hand up to stifle a burp.

"Go on, Ruth, tell us what you found out," Mrs. Jeffries said.

"I did what you asked and spoke to two different women, both of whom moved in the same social circles as Sir Donovan and his late wife." Ruth laughed. "They were both rather surprised by my just showing up, but were polite enough not to let it show too much. What was interesting was both of them said the same thing, that Sir Donovan had been devoted to his wife. He never even looked at another woman."

"He did more than look at Ellen Langston-Jones," Smythe murmured.

"Yes, but his wife had been ill for many years by then," Ruth continued. "Laura Penworthy told me that the saddest thing of all was that both Lady Gaines and Sir Donovan desperately wanted a child. They were going to adopt, but then she fell ill and that was the end of that. That's all I found out."

"I'll go next," Betsy offered. "I took the baby and we went to Bailey's Hotel. I told the manager my sister had been dining with a gentleman at Monday lunchtime and she'd lost her earring. No one reported finding it, of course, but he did call the waiter over, and that's where I got lucky. There was some sort of trouble in the kitchen and the manager got called away. The waiter and I had quite a nice chat." She broke off and glanced at the housekeeper. "You were right, Mrs. Jeffries, Ellen Langston-Jones was dining with Sir Donovan. He lied to Martha Barclay about sending her on an errand to the bookstore. But according to the waiter, their manner together indicated they were happy. Jerome wasn't sure . . ."

"Jerome?" Smythe repeated. He frowned ominously.

Betsy took no notice. "Don't interrupt. That's the boy's name and he was no more than a lad. Jerome said that when he was serving their coffee, he distinctly heard Sir Donovan say that they wouldn't have to wait much longer." Betsy sighed. "I think Sir Donovan proposed to her."

"Did the waiter say that?" Mrs. Jeffries clarified. She wasn't certain how this fitted in with her theory.

"No, but he said they weren't bothering to be discreet and that Sir Donovan waved at several acquaintances as he and the lady came into the restaurant, so he wasn't hiding the fact that they were dining together. Was this what you thought we'd learn?" she asked.

"I'm not sure," Mrs. Jeffries replied slowly. "But I think so." She looked at Hatchet. "Did you have any success?" She wasn't sure if his information would help or hinder her theory, but she needed to hear what, if anything, he'd learned.

"I spoke to both the owners at the Arnold and Boxley Gallery," he replied. "You were right, Mrs. Jeffries, those paintings are worth a fortune. They already have buyers for every painting done by Brandon Langston-Jones."

CHAPTER 10

Mrs. Jeffries poured two glasses of sherry, turned, and went toward where the inspector sat in his favorite chair. He'd arrived home a few moments ago and she'd not even waited for him to suggest they have a drink. "You look so tired, sir," she'd said as she ushered him down the hall. "A nice glass of Harvey's will do you good." It was time to take the bull by the horns, she thought as she handed him his drink. Before they ran out of time and he was yanked off the case, she needed him to find sufficient evidence proving that someone other than Lucius Montague was the killer. The man was odious, but he hadn't murdered Ellen Langston-Jones. If Inspector Nivens got this case, the first thing he'd do would be to arrest Montague.

"Thank you, Mrs. Jeffries. One hates to admit it, but I sorely need this tonight." He took a quick sip and sighed happily. "It's been a very tiring day, but I feel a most successful one."

"Are you close to making an arrest, sir?" She took her spot across from him.

"I'm not certain. We did learn an enormous amount of information though I'm not sure what to make of any of it."

"Now really, sir, you're teasing me." She laughed. "But I'm on to you, sir. It's always at this point in the investigation, at the place where you think you've so many pieces of the puzzle, that you'll never fit it all together. But you know very well that it's when you feel the most muddled that your true brilliance shines through."

He laughed delightedly. "Really, Mrs. Jeffries, you give me far too much credit. I'd hardly say I'm brilliant."

"Now, now, sir, you mustn't be overly modest. You've solved more murders than anyone in the history of the Metropolitan Police Department." She reminded him of this fact whenever his confidence seemed to be waning. "I must say, sir, it was rather clever of you to realize that you needed to look at the case in a completely different way."

"Well, yes, I suppose it was." He paused and cocked his chin to one side. "Er, exactly how was I clever?"

"It was the comment you made at the beginning of the case, sir. You said and I quote, *'Not all killers are intelligent, Mrs. Jeffries. As a matter of fact, by and large, criminals are rarely clever.'* Remember sir?"

"Of course, but —"

"Obviously that comment started you thinking that the evidence against Montague was deliberately staged because not only was the man arrogant, but there were many indications that he simply wasn't very bright. Only a genius would have had the foresight to arrange evidence against himself that could then be argued by a defense barrister that he was being framed for a crime he didn't commit." She was deliberately muddying the waters within the context of their original conversation, but she had to steer him toward the suspect she was certain was guilty. She beamed at him proudly. "Of course, once you verified that Montague wasn't clever enough to set himself up in such a manner —"

"I realized that as soon as we interviewed him," he interrupted. "The fellow is thick as two short planks."

This was patently untrue, but she certainly wasn't going to point it out. "Precisely, sir. Now, do tell me about the rest of your day."

"As I said, it was very, very busy. Mrs.

Langston-Jones' funeral was today, so after the Constable watched the congregation file into the church, we went to Bayswater and spoke to Mrs. Linthorp. Neither Constable Barnes nor I thought it likely that she'd be one of the mourners, and we were right."

"She and the victim had a terrible quarrel just a few days before the murder, didn't they," she commented. It was important to keep reminding him that there were suspects other than Montague.

"Indeed they did and it was quite a nasty confrontation as well. At first, Mrs. Linthorp tried to pretend she was only chastising a servant for stepping out of her place, but then we quoted back her exact words and she finally told us what we hope is the truth."

She listened closely as he told her about the interview. "I believe she was very jealous of Mrs. Langston-Jones' relationship with Sir Donovan," he concluded.

"I've heard the same thing, sir," she blurted out, then she held up her hand in apology. "Oh dear, I'm repeating gossip but you know how everyone loves to discuss your cases. I'm sorry, sir. I assure you I only listened to Mrs. Kendall when she cornered me at the draper's shop. I certainly didn't say a word about the case to her."

Witherspoon smiled graciously. "Come now, Mrs. Jeffries, I know you'd never be indiscreet." He leaned forward eagerly. "But exactly what did you hear?"

Mrs. Jeffries repeated the conversation she'd had with the imaginary Mrs. Kendall and hoped that he never asked to meet the woman. But this was the only way she could think of to get Witherspoon moving in the direction that would catch the real killer before he lost the case. "Apparently, she had her sights set on becoming the next Lady Gaines, and because of the gossip surrounding Alexander's parentage, she was terrified that Mrs. Langston-Jones had the advantage." She paused and took a drink, watching him over the rim of her glass and hoping that he'd ask the obvious question.

Witherspoon's expression was puzzled. "What gossip?" he finally asked.

She almost cried in relief. "Oh sir, I'm not sure I can credit the rest of what Mrs. Kendall told me, but as you've often said, sometimes it's an inconsequential bit of talk that steers you toward the killer." She chose her words carefully, making sure she didn't tell too much or too little, but she needed him to know much of what the household had learned today, and more important, she needed him to act upon the information.

By the time she was finished, he was nodding in agreement. "So you see, sir, why I was hesitant to repeat everything she said. Add to that your theory about how the killer could have gained access to the Montague house —"

"My theory," he interrupted.

"Montague couldn't keep a cook," she reminded him. "You said so yourself." She gave him her own idea of how the killer had gained access. When she'd finished, she stood up and reached for his empty glass. "I believe that dinner is ready now, sir."

"Are you goin' to tell us who you think it is?" Luty demanded.

"You know she won't," Mrs. Goodge complained. "She wouldn't even tell Constable Barnes this mornin'. Just give him a long list of bits and pieces he and the inspector needed to do today."

Mrs. Jeffries looked at the faces around the table. Even Amanda Belle, propped in her mother's arms, looked disapproving. "I'm not being deliberately vague. The truth is, I'm not sure who killed her."

"You say that every time," Wiggins complained. "I think you just like keepin' us in suspense."

"That's not true. There could easily be

two very different motives for this murder, and the truth is, I'm leaning toward one, but I could be wrong. I didn't sleep well last night," she admitted. "Frankly, the more I went over all the bits and pieces, the less confident I felt about my conclusion, and even worse, according to what Constable Barnes told Mrs. Goodge and I this morning, we really are out of time."

"But he's done a splendid job of keeping the inspector away from the station. Can't he manage one more day?" Hatchet inquired.

"It wouldn't matter if he could," Mrs. Goodge answered. "One of Barnes' sources sent word last night that they're bein' pulled off the case today. Chief Inspector Barrows is goin' to be called to the Home Office this afternoon and given his orders. He'll not have a choice in the matter."

"So we've got until this afternoon," Phyllis said.

"I don't think that's enough time." Mrs. Jeffries shrugged wearily. "We've done our best —"

"And we're not giving up now." Ruth stared at Mrs. Jeffries. "This defeatism isn't like you."

"If I could think of a way to discover which motive got the poor woman killed, we could turn the tide on this one, but for the life of me, I can't."

"Then try harder." Mrs. Goodge frowned at her friend. "You gave the inspector an earful last night about what needs doin' —"

"Yes, but that was before —"

"Before you spent the rest of the night second-guessin' yourself and worrying about being wrong," the cook interrupted. "Stop it right now. You've got the inspector and the constable out doin' this, that, and the other to sort this mess out, so just tell us what it is you need us to do. As Phyllis just said, we've got until this afternoon."

Mrs. Jeffries said nothing; she simply sat there with her mouth slightly open while they all stared at her. Finally, she laughed. "Ye Gods, I suppose I had that coming. You're right, I'm being ridiculous. Regardless of which motive is right, we can't stop now."

"You're never ridiculous, Hepzibah," Luty said. "But you were beginnin' to act like a ninny. Now, what do we need to do?"

"Inspector, you know I can't divulge that sort of information." Richard Dorrington of Dorrington and Naismith, solicitors for Sir Donovan Gaines, frowned at the two policemen sitting in front of his desk. He was a tall man with close-cropped steel gray hair, a bristle-like mustache, and piercing blue eyes.

Witherspoon nodded. He'd known this was most likely a wild-goose chase. Sir Donovan hadn't been arrested nor was he legally related to the victim, so his lawyer was under no obligation to answer any of their questions. Nonetheless, he felt he ought to try. "You do understand this is a murder inquiry."

Dorrington sighed heavily. "I'm aware of that, Inspector, and I would like to help with your inquiries. However, I must respect my client's confidentiality. So unless Sir Donovan himself gives his permission for me to speak to you, I'll have to decline to answer." He rose to his feet. "If you'll excuse me, gentlemen, I've work to do."

The inspector stood up, but Barnes sat where he was. "Look, I know you're in a bit of a spot, sir, but can you at least tell us if Sir Donovan is likely to gain custody of Alexander Langston-Jones?" the constable asked. He'd known they wouldn't get any particulars out of the fellow about the changes in Sir Donovan's will, but that wasn't what he was really after anyway.

"I've no idea, Constable. That depends on how hard Mr. Jonathan Langston-Jones fights to regain custody of the child. He is, after all, a blood relative." Dorrington looked pointedly at the clock on the wall.

"What if it could be proved that he wasn't?" Barnes pressed.

"Wasn't what?"

"A blood relative to the boy. What then? Would Mr. Langston-Jones have a strong case if it could be proved he wasn't his uncle?"

"I'm not an expert on domestic law," Dorrington replied. "But if Brandon Langston-Jones was married to the mother at the time of the birth and he acknowledged the child to be his, then he is the father regardless of what can or cannot be proved about actual physical paternity."

"So Jonathan Langston-Jones would have a stronger case for custody than Sir Donovan, despite the mother naming Sir Donovan in her will?" Witherspoon asked.

"As I said, domestic law isn't my area of expertise, but that would be my conclusion. Now, if you'll excuse me . . ."

"Did Sir Donovan know he could lose custody?" Barnes closed his notebook and, to buy a few more seconds, fumbled at putting it in his pocket.

"Of course he did. I told him so yesterday at the poor woman's funeral," he snapped

331

irritably.

Barnes shot to his feet. "Thank you, sir."

"You've been very helpful, sir." Witherspoon slapped his bowler on his head and they headed for the door.

Luty pulled a roll of pound notes out of her pocket and put it on the table next to the glass of gin she'd ordered. She and her companion, a pudgy young man with thinning blond hair and a ruddy complexion, were at the back table of the Chase and Stag Pub. "Sorry, I hope I ain't insultin' you with cold hard cash, but I believe in payin' for what you need."

"I'm not insulted," Michael Brooks assured her. He didn't take his gaze off the wad of bills.

"You're Mr. Gaines' clerk, right?" She was fairly certain she hadn't made a mistake, but it paid to make sure. Sometimes, even a supposedly trustworthy source such as the street lad who claimed he did errands for the commercial firm of Mason and Tynley might not be honest. The lad had pointed Brooks out to her, grabbed the coin she'd tossed him, and taken off faster than one of Snyder's hounds.

"I am." He looked at her and then reached for his pint. "What can I do for you?"

She noticed he didn't ask her name, and her estimation of his intelligence went up a notch. What he didn't know, he couldn't tell. "I need some information and I'm hopin' you're goin' to be able to provide it."

"What kind of information?"

"The kind I'm willin' to pay five pounds to hear," she replied.

"Five quid. That's a lot of money." He glanced around the room, searching the faces of the people at the other tables and along the bar.

Amused, she grinned when he finally turned back to her. "You're smart. But don't worry — even if someone you know sees us talkin', it'll never come back to nip you on the heel. I'll make sure your name is never mentioned."

"I don't know if I can be of any help to you." He took another sip. "I'm just a clerk. I'm not privy to any transactions that may be on the horizon. The senior partners keep that sort of information to themselves. So if you're wanting to find out what's being bought or sold so that you can make a bit more of that" — he nodded toward the stack of bills — "you're out of luck."

She laughed. "At least that's honest. I don't care what your company is fixin' to buy or sell and I'm goin' to pay you the fiver whether you know anything or not. Now let's get down to business."

He tilted his head, his expression puzzled, then he shrugged. "Alright, we'll have it your way, down to business."

"How close do you work with Neville Gaines?" She ran her finger along the top of her still untouched gin.

"I'm his assistant so I do most everything he doesn't fancy doing." He took another drink. "I take care of all the correspondence, handle his appointments, make sure all the keys to various properties are available when one of the senior partners needs them."

"Does he ever have ya doin' personal stuff for him?"

"Rarely, though he did once send me downstairs to fetch a street lad. He needed to send a message home and that is usually the fastest method."

"He went to see a property in Fulham on Monday last?" she asked.

"That's right and he was in a foul mood all morning because the keys didn't turn up until a minute or two before he wanted to leave."

"What time was that?"

"Just before one o'clock, but by then he'd already worked himself into a state. He was viewing the place on his own, so I didn't see why he was in such a rush. He wouldn't let me accompany him."

"Do you usually go with him?" she interrupted.

"Yes. But this time he said he didn't need me. I kept offering to go get the keys, but he wouldn't hear of it. He just paced back and forth across his office. Finally, the lad from the seller's agents showed up with the wretched things. Mr. Gaines snatched the keys out of the lad's hand and ran out of the office. I had to chase after him because he'd forgotten the file and I only just caught him as he was climbing into a hansom cab." He frowned. "That was odd, too. He didn't tell the driver to take him to Fulham; he told him to drive to Gloucester Road."

"Gloucester Road?" she repeated. "Are ya sure?"

"There's naught wrong with my hearing." He stared her straight in the eye. "It's bothered me ever since I heard about that woman that was murdered. But there's naught I could say because I need my position and he's a rich man, the nephew of a knight. If I said what I knew and the police did nothing, I'd lose my job. I can't afford that. I've got my mum to take care of."

Luty said nothing. She simply stared at him expectantly.

"But I know he didn't like that lady, the French tutor."

"How do you know?"

"Right after the New Year, he found out from one of his colleagues, someone in the property business like him, that his uncle was selling everything and he blamed Mrs. Langston-Jones. He said it was her fault."

Smythe elbowed his way through the Dirty Duck toward the fireplace. The pub was already crowded. Day laborers, bread sellers, van drivers, and stevedores from the nearby commercial docks were three deep along the bar, and there wasn't a bare spot at any of the benches along the wall. The tables, save one, were all full, and it was to this one that he headed.

He grinned at Blimpey Groggins and then slipped onto the stool across from him. Blimpey did most of his business from this rickety table. "Glad you didn't take it into your head to go gallivantin' off to the seaside with the missus again," Smythe said.

Blimpey was a short, rotund man with a ruddy complexion and ginger-colored hair. He was dressed in his usual attire of a white shirt that had seen better days and a checked jacket. On the stool beside him was his brown porkpie hat and red scarf. "One day off and I've heard nothin' but complaints from you lot. My Nell enjoyed our day out, thank you for asking. Now, you wantin' a pint?"

"Not today, I don't 'ave time. I need whatever information you've got for me and then —"

"I've got plenty," he interrupted.

"And I've somethin' else I want you to find out and I'm goin' to need it fast."

"Let me tell you what I've got before you 'ave me sussin' out something else. My people are good, but they can't pull information out of their backsides at a moment's notice." Blimpey paused and waited till Smythe nodded. "My man at one of the steamship lines found out something that may be of interest."

Blimpey had become a rich man brokering information. He was successful because his sources were everywhere: at police stations, law courts, steamship lines, custom house brokers, docks, insurance companies, hospitals, and half the members of Parliament. "Last month, Sir Donovan Gaines made reservations for two staterooms on the *American Patriot* sailing from Liverpool to New York on July eighth. The reservations were for himself, his wife, their son, and a nanny."

"But he's not married."

"Not then, but he planned to be." Blimpey leaned closer. "He was going to marry none other than Mrs. Langston-Jones. He proposed to her at Bailey's Hotel the day she was murdered."

"How'd you find that out?" he blurted out. When Blimpey merely raised an eyebrow, he said, "Stupid question, I shouldn't 'ave asked."

" 'Course not. My sources are reliable, and that includes the lad that waited their table. Charged me a pretty penny for the goods, too, but that's neither here nor there."

"Did she accept 'im?"

"She did, according to young Thomas. He was their waiter. The two of 'em were cooin' like a couple of lovebirds, especially when he slipped that big, sparkly diamond engagement ring on her finger."

Smythe frowned. "But she wasn't wearin' a diamond ring when 'er body was found and there weren't one in her rooms, either."

"Then your killer probably took it." Blimpey looked over Smythe's shoulder toward the door. "Oh, blast and tarnation. Wouldn't you know 'e'd bloomin' come early." He cut his gaze back to Smythe. "I've another appointment and 'e's just shown up."

Smythe started to get up, but Blimpey waved him back to his seat. "Sit back down for a minute, there's more." He held up his hand toward the newcomer, signaling him that he wasn't ready yet. "I'd better be quick about this, Lord Stimson's not a patient fellow. Sir Donovan didn't wait to wed the woman before he started actin' like a married man. He'd already changed his will, making her and the child his heirs months before he proposed."

"Now that she's dead, I wonder if he's planning on changing it back," Smythe muttered more to himself than Blimpey.

"I doubt it. He canceled the two staterooms for the July sailing and booked on another ship. He reserved a double bedroom stateroom on the *Empire.* She sails tomorrow evening with the tide to New York. The passengers listed are himself and Alexander Langston-Jones."

"Would you care for tea?" Fiona asked as she waved Mrs. Jeffries toward one of the rose-colored wing chairs.

"Sorry, no, I don't have time." She sat down. They were in Fiona's morning room and she was hoping against hope that she'd get the answer she needed. There were two possibly three details they needed to learn, so in the interests of efficiency, she'd doubled up and sent more than one person out looking for a specific fact. "I have to get back. I've come to see you about Lucius Montague. If we're going to stop him from being arrested, there's some very important things I need to ask you."

"Thank you, Hepzibah." Fiona closed her eyes briefly and sank back against the seat cushion. "I was so afraid you were going to, oh, I don't know, let this one go on as it would."

Mrs. Jeffries took a deep breath. "Please don't thank me. I'm the one that ought to apologize. You came to us in good faith, seeking help for someone you felt was innocent, and I cast aspersions on your motives. I'm deeply sorry. But rest assured, your visit made all of us and me in particular see that if we truly believe we're working for the cause of justice, then we can't turn our backs on any innocent person, even those we don't approve of or like."

Fiona stared at her for a moment and then burst out laughing. "Oh my gracious, we are a pair, aren't we. We both want the same thing but we have a very difficult time believing one another's true motives are altruistic. I wish I could change our pasts — I think you and I might have been good friends if I'd handled things differently. But what's done is done, and all we can do is move forward. I know you'll do your best for Lucius and I'm very grateful, not because he's a friend — as I told you before, I don't much like him, either — but because he's innocent, and after what might have happened to me, I've developed a horror at the thought of anyone, even terrible people, being condemned for crimes they didn't commit."

"And in that vein, I'm hoping you'll have the answer to a very important question." The clock on the mantelpiece chimed, reminding her that time was passing. "A few months ago, Lucius Montague was at a dinner party. I don't know who was the host, where it was, or exactly when it took place, but what is important is that the subject of firearms came up in the conversation. Montague bragged that he owned an Adams Beaumont and that his initials were monogrammed in gold on the weapon. What I need to know is who else might have been at that dinner party."

Fiona thought for a moment and then shook her head. "Oh dear, I'm afraid I'm not going to be much help. We go to so many dinner parties." She got up and began pacing the small room. "But let me think for a moment."

"Take your time." Mrs. Jeffries forced herself to be patient. She'd take a hansom home, and hopefully she'd make it back before the others did. Ruth was also trying to find out this particular bit of information.

"Wait a minute." Fiona stopped. "Yes, yes, now I remember. It was at Lady Rumford's in Mayfair. But there were a dozen guests at that dinner party."

"We're only concerned with certain people who might have been there," Mrs. Jeffries said. "Specifically, Sir Donovan Gaines, Hester Linthorp, Neville Gaines, and Martha Barclay. Were any of them present?"

"Yes, as a matter of fact, some of them were."

Phyllis had been sure that she'd be the one at the afternoon meeting admitting that she'd failed at her task, but she'd gotten lucky when she arrived at Portland Villas. She'd only had to walk down the street twice before she'd spotted a housemaid coming out the servants' door on the lower ground floor. The girl carried a shopping basket over her arm and Phyllis had wasted

342

no time in making contact. She'd pretended to be lost.

"Thanks so much for your help." She smiled gratefully as she fell into step with the maid. "I was so afraid my mistress would scold me for getting lost. I have to meet her at the chemist's, but sometimes I get confused. I'm new to London, you see."

"It can be a frightening place, but you'll soon learn your way about. You come with me. The chemist shop is at the end of the high street and I'm goin' in that direction."

Phyllis nodded at the wicker basket the girl carried. "They let you do the household shopping? How wonderful. My mistress only lets me carry her packages."

"Me do the shopping?" The girl gave a harsh bark of a laugh. "Not likely. They're only sending me out because the household's been turned upside down and the cook's run out of butter for the mashed potatoes. Otherwise, Mrs. Metcalf would see to it."

"I'm sorry, I hope there's nothing wrong." Phyllis slowed her pace and did her best to look sympathetic.

"Wrong? Well, I might be losin' my job, but then again, we all might be gettin' the sack." She gave Phyllis a grim smile. "Sorry, it's just everything is up in the air. I liked working there but now I might have to find another position."

Phyllis threw caution to the wind. "What happened?"

"At lunch today the master announced that he was leavin' the country." She laughed harshly. "He's takin' the boy and getting on the evening train to Liverpool and tomorrow they're sailing for America. He's sold everything, all his properties, his stock and bonds, and now he's even selling the house. Mind you, he did tell those of us losin' our jobs that he'd give a reference and a whole quarter's pay when the house sells, so I suppose I'll be alright. Mrs. Barclay had hysterics right there at the dining table and would have screamed the house down if Mr. Gaines hadn't told her to shut up."

"Are they employed there as well?" she asked. She dug in her pocket and made sure she had plenty of coins. If necessary, she'd see if she could get the girl to stop for a cup of tea.

"Not likely," she snorted. "Mrs. Barclay and her two snotty brats are the master's nieces, and Mr. Gaines is his nephew. They're brother and sister. They've been sponging off the master for ages. You should have seen their faces when they found out they'd have to leave."

"Do we know where Constable Barnes and the inspector are now?" Mrs. Jeffries asked as she took her seat at the head of the table.

"They're searching Mrs. Langston-Jones' flat again," Wiggins said. His assignment for the day had been to shadow the two policemen. If the case was coming to a head, it was imperative that they be able to locate the inspector if need be. Barnes had told them he and the inspector were seeing Sir Donovan's solicitor first thing this morning, and Wiggins had caught up with them there. For the rest of the day, he'd stayed back but kept them in his sights until he'd left them searching the victim's flat. "I've got a street lad keepin' watch. 'E'll come runnin' if they go anywhere else."

"Where did they go after leaving the solicitor's office?" Ruth asked. She felt just a tad guilty; it seemed strange to have anyone, even Wiggins, watching the inspector. It was almost as if they were spying on him and she'd had to remind herself several times that it was for a good cause. Justice.

"Fulham." He helped himself to a piece of brown bread and butter.

"Is that the building where Neville Gaines was inspecting?" Mrs. Goodge asked.

Wiggins nodded as he took a bite, chewed, and swallowed. "They didn't get inside so they spoke to a lot of the local people, but I don't think they found anyone that saw Neville Gaines."

"That doesn't mean he wasn't there," Mrs. Jeffries mused. "Remember, there was an awful fog that day."

"There's one coming in now." Phyllis pointed to the window over the sink.

"Oh dear." Mrs. Jeffries tried to think and realized that, even with her new information, there were still two possibilities. There was only one thing to do — get on with it. "Right, everyone, we don't have time for a lot of discussion. Let's do our reports. Who would like to go first?"

"I will," Ruth volunteered. "I've nothing to say. I visited the two most likely people to have been at that dinner party. One wasn't home and the other couldn't recall the last time she saw Lucius Montague." She smiled apologetically at Mrs. Jeffries. "I hope you did better."

"I did actually, but please don't feel yourself a failure. I had the advantage, you see, of going to someone who we know is in Lucius Montague's social circle."

Hatchet gave Ruth a sympathetic smile. "I didn't have any luck, either, so I might as

346

well go next. None of my sources had any idea who, if anyone, in the Gaines household knew of Sir Donovan's plans." He glanced at Luty. "I suspect by the smug look on your face that you did have some success in obtaining this particular bit of information."

Luty grinned broadly. "That ain't all I found out." She told them about her meeting with Michael Brooks. "So it seems to me we ain't really narrowed it down much. Both Neville Gaines and Martha Barclay were aware of what he was doing."

"The real question is did they know he'd changed his will and they weren't his heirs?" Smythe said. He repeated what he'd learned from Blimpey.

When he'd finished, there was a stunned silence.

"Sir Donovan is leaving this evening?" Mrs. Jeffries clarified.

"Taking the night train to Liverpool and from there he and the lad are sailin' to America."

"We should tell the inspector," Mrs. Goodge declared.

"His household was turned upside down when they heard the news," Phyllis said.

Mrs. Jeffries looked at the maid. "What? He told them? They know he's leaving?"

She nodded. "That's what I was goin' to

report when I had my turn." She told them what she'd found out from the housemaid.

As she listened, Mrs. Jeffries' mind worked furiously. "Were both Neville Gaines and his sister present today when Sir Donovan made his announcement?"

"Yes. Susan, that's the housemaid who told me all this, said they were in a state, that Mrs. Barclay had hysterics so bad that her brother told her to shut up at the dinner table."

Mrs. Jeffries stared at her, her expression troubled. "Oh dear Lord, we've got to do something." She looked at Wiggins. "How fast can you get to the inspector and Constable Barnes?"

"Twelve minutes or ten if I run." He got to his feet.

"What's wrong, Mrs. Jeffries?" Smythe asked as he and Hatchet both shoved back from the table simultaneously and got up.

"There's going to be another murder and I'm not sure we'll be in time to stop it."

"What can we do?" Hatchet asked.

"You and Smythe need to get to Portland Villas and keep watch. There's a policeman on guard at the Montague house so be at the ready to get him if need be."

"What are we looking for?" Smythe asked. He and Hatchet started for the back door.

"I'm not sure, but I know you need to be there." Mrs. Jeffries knew it sounded nonsensical, but she didn't have time to explain what she knew to be true. Something was going to happen.

"Be careful." Betsy adjusted Amanda so the baby could see her father. "Both of you."

"Should I get the inspector?" Wiggins asked.

"In a minute." She looked at Phyllis. "Are your forging skills still up to par?"

The maid was a surprisingly good forger; not that she'd ever used the skill for personal gain. One of her previous employers was an alcoholic miser and his wife had insisted Phyllis forge notes to the bank manager for the money to run the household.

"Just tell me what to write," she replied.

Barnes and Witherspoon walked out to the street and came face-to-face with a scruffy lad. "Oy, you Constable Barnes?" he asked. The boy stood on the pavement in front of number 14. His trousers were frayed at the hem, his shirt was patched in two places, and his face was dirty.

"I am," Barnes admitted. He silently prayed this wasn't the summons to the Yard that he'd been trying to avoid all day. If it was, there was no getting around it now;

the inspector would insist they go and see Barrows immediately. "Who are you and what do you want?"

"I want to do what I was bloody 'ired to do. I've been chasin' you 'alf the day." The boy pulled a crumpled piece of paper out of his pocket. "This old gent paid me a bob to give this to you. Said you'd know who it was from."

"Good gracious," Witherspoon exclaimed. "How on earth did you know where to find us? We've not checked in at the station."

The kid snorted. "Don't be daft, you're coppers. Findin' you is a lot easier than findin' a hot dinner." With that, he turned on his heel and dashed off, disappearing into the gathering fog.

Barnes held his breath as he unfolded the paper.

Barnes, the toff on Portland Villas, is leaving tonight and taking the boy with him. I've kept watch and with this bit, we're square, I don't owe yu nuthin.

"You'd better read this, sir." Barnes handed Witherspoon the note. "It's from one of my informants. It looks like Sir Donovan is making a run for it." He deliberately used the words most effective in getting the inspector to move quickly. As he'd not had an informant watching the Gaines house, he knew this was from Mrs. Jeffries by way of Phyllis, whose forging skills he admired on an intellectual level.

The inspector read the note. "Gracious, you've had someone watching the Gaines house?"

"Only since you mentioned you were suspicious about some of the goings-on there, sir," he replied. Like Mrs. Jeffries, he'd learned the fastest way to achieve his goals was to let Witherspoon think everything was his idea. Women apparently did this sort of thing all the time with their husbands, but he found it tedious. However, as he enjoyed the benefits from being associated with the inspector that had solved more homicides than anyone in the history of the Metropolitan Police Department, he'd do whatever it took to solve the case. "My informant, sir, he owed me a favor so I had him not only keep watch, but he made a connection to someone in the household and it's paid off, sir. Sir Donovan is doing a bunk."

"Thank goodness you thought ahead, Constable." Witherspoon hurried to the curb and waved at a hansom dropping a fare at the corner. "Let's get over there. I'd not considered Sir Donovan a suspect, but now that he's trying to leave the country, we'd best have another chat with the fellow."

Lucius Montague was hungry. He stared at the two pieces of limp brown bread, the slice of ham that smelled slightly off, and the stale bun that the housekeeper had brought him for tea. For the first time in his life, he didn't dare complain. "Thank you, Mrs. Redman." He gave his housekeeper a weak smile. "I appreciate that you're doing your best. Uh, what will you be serving for dinner?"

"Cold pork roast." She crossed her arms and stared at him. "That's all there is unless you'd like to go out and do the shopping. Since the cook and both the maids have walked out, I didn't have time. Perhaps, sir, you'll think twice about shouting at those trying to serve you, sir. People generally don't take kindly to being called pathetic half-wits that couldn't find their way out of a corridor with one door. Will there be anything else, sir?"

Montague had just enough brains to realize if he said one word, she'd be out the door, too, and he'd be stuck here taking care of himself. He had no idea how to do such a gargantuan task, so he nodded meekly.

"Nothing else, Mrs. Redman, I'm fine."

"Very well, sir." She left him to his food.

Montague felt like crying but knew that it was unseemly. So he took a deep breath and picked up a slice of bread. Taking a bite, he grimaced as he realized it was not only stale, but had a strange, overly yeasty taste as well. He wondered if one of his former servants was trying to poison him. He couldn't understand what had happened. This morning, he'd awakened as usual. When his breakfast tray was late, he'd gone down to the kitchen and been informed that his meal would be later still. He'd rather foolishly said several things he'd since come to regret, the result of which was the cook and both housemaids taking off their aprons and stomping out the back door.

He nibbled a bite off the crust. The day had gotten progressively worse. After choking down a badly boiled egg and burnt toast, his lunch had consisted of tepid tomato soup, overcooked cod with boiled potatoes and sprouts (both so undercooked that he'd almost chipped a tooth trying to chew them), and no pudding. Add to that, a policeman was still standing right outside his front door.

He sighed and poured his tea from the pot on the tray. He stirred it properly and took a sip. It was lukewarm. Lucius wanted to scream in rage, but he didn't dare. Without Mrs. Redman, he'd be completely on his own. But perhaps there was something he could do, someplace where he'd be welcomed and where, if he were very lucky, he could get a decent cup of tea and a hot meal.

He glanced toward the windows and frowned. The fog was back. Lucius hesitated and then picked up his serviette and wiped his mouth and hands. He shoved the tray to one side and got to his feet.

By God, he'd show them. He was descended from a long line of kings on his mother's side. He wasn't a coward. If he had to brave the fog to get something substantial to eat, so be it. He'd just go out the back door and across the garden. There was no need for that stupid policeman to be apprised of his whereabouts; he certainly didn't answer to the likes of the Metropolitan Police Force. That fellow could just stand out front until hell froze over.

Lucius smiled at his own cleverness, checked his clothes to make sure he didn't have any crumbs on his suit, and then hurried toward the back of the house. He didn't bother to inform Mrs. Redman of his actions; let the cow figure it out on her own, he thought, as he opened the back door and stepped outside.

CHAPTER 11

Barnes banged the brass knocker against the front door of the Gaines house. Inspector Witherspoon and Constable Rivers, who had until two minutes ago been standing guard outside Montague's house, stood at his shoulder. Inspector Witherspoon had decided that, with this new development, it might be wise to take him along with them.

Mrs. Metcalf opened the front door. "Oh, it's you." She sighed and tucked a strand of hair behind her ear. "You've come at a bad time. The master is getting ready to travel and we've had no time to prepare."

"That is precisely why we've come." Witherspoon stepped forward. "We don't mean to inconvenience anyone, but nonetheless, I must insist on speaking to Sir Donovan."

There was a crash from inside the house and she looked over her shoulder. "Be careful with those cases!" she yelled. "Just leave them there before you break every vase in the place."

"I'm afraid this isn't a request." The inspector spoke loudly in order to regain her attention.

"Oh, what do I care?" She opened the door wider. "Come on in. Sir Donovan is in the drawing room trying to keep his family from having hysterics. A pointless task if you ask me."

The three policemen stepped inside. On the staircase, two young men were struggling with a huge trunk while another lad was shoving traveling bags and suitcases up against the wall.

They followed Mrs. Metcalf toward the drawing room.

"You can't be serious about this." Martha Barclay's voice carried through the closed doors. "This is ridiculous. What about us? What about your great-nieces? What's to become of them while you and that boy go gallivanting off to parts unknown?"

"You'll be taken care of," Sir Donovan said. "I've already promised you a generous allowance and I've instructed Neville to find a flat for all of you. For God's sake, Martha, he's in the business. He can find you a decent place."

"A flat!" she yelled. "I don't want to live

357

in a flat. I want to live here. You said this was our home."

"It's been like this for hours," Mrs. Metcalf told them. She rapped sharply on the door and, without waiting for a response, opened it. "Excuse me, sir, but the police are here to see you."

"He's busy," Martha Barclay snapped. "Tell them to go away."

Barnes reached out and gently eased the housekeeper away. "Thank you, Mrs. Metcalf, but we'll handle this." She shrugged and moved to one side as the three policemen entered the drawing room.

Sir Donovan Gaines stood in front of the fireplace with his hands clasped behind his back. Martha Barclay sat on a wing chair a few feet away. One of her daughters, dressed in a white frock with pink ribbons on the neck and sleeves, played on the rug at her feet. "Mama, those policemen are here." She tugged at her mother's skirt.

"Sir Donovan," Witherspoon said. "I'm sorry to barge in like this, but I must speak with you."

"Don't you have any manners," Martha snapped. "I told you quite clearly that we were busy."

"Martha, be quiet," Sir Donovan ordered. He raised his eyebrows as he stared at them.

"You've brought reinforcements, Inspector. There's three of you now. Did you think I'd make a run for it?"

"I certainly hope not, sir." Witherspoon advanced into the room. "But we have had some information that is rather disturbing. Are you leaving the country?"

"I am."

From a door on the far side of the room, another little girl dressed exactly like the one on the rug ran into the room. She flopped down by her sister and whispered in her ear.

Witherspoon wasn't sure of his next step. The man wasn't under arrest so he had no right to stop him leaving. Nonetheless, he could be considered a suspect. "I was under the impression that you very much wanted to help us find Mrs. Langston-Jones' murderer. That won't be possible if you're not here."

"Even if you find her killer, it won't bring her back," he said bitterly. "And my first priority has to be Alexander. That's what Ellen would want."

One of the little girls swiveled around and tugged at her mother's skirt. "Mama, we want to go outside and play."

Martha ignored her and kept her attention on her uncle. "You're making a fool of yourself over that child." She sneered.

"Sir Donovan, I don't understand why you want to leave the country, but I assure you that if you're worried about the boy's safety, there's no evidence that he's in danger," Witherspoon said.

"Mama, why can't we go outside and play with Uncle Neville? He took Alex out to play." The girl tried again and again, but her mother ignored her.

Barnes looked at the child. "What did you just say?"

"You don't understand, Inspector." Sir Donovan's hands clenched into fists. "If I stay, I might lose him. Ellen's wretched brother-in-law wants custody of the boy. He doesn't care about him; he just wants control of Alexander's estate. He's threatened to take me to court and times have changed. Just because I'm a knight doesn't mean I'll win. I can't risk losing Alexander so I'm taking him far away, to America." He turned his back on the room, cradling his head against the mantelpiece.

"Mama, that policeman asked me a question." The little girl kept her eyes on Barnes as she tugged at her mother's skirt again. "Am I allowed to answer him?"

But Martha brushed her aside and leapt up, her gaze fixed on her uncle. "You're

360

abandoning your own family for that little bast—"

"Shut up." Sir Donovan rounded on her. "If you say one word about Alex, I'll cut you off. Do you understand? You'll not get so much as a penny from me, and I doubt that your loving husband will bother sending you anything to live on."

"Of course you can answer me," Barnes said sternly. "Now, what did you mean when you said that Alexander went outside with your uncle?"

"You've no right to talk to my child," Martha yelled. She glared at her daughter and pointed to the door. "Both of you, go up to the nursery."

Sir Donovan whirled around. "Cecily, what did you say?"

"I said that he went outside to play with Uncle Neville," she repeated. Her lip trembled and her eyes filled with tears. "I don't like all this shouting. That's why I wanted to go out and play. I don't care if it is foggy."

"He did no such thing," Martha said. "Neville would hardly take that brat out to play."

"Don't call him a brat!" Sir Donovan roared.

"I'll call him what I damned well please,"

she retorted. "You're tossing us out in the cold so I don't have to kowtow to you anymore."

"When did your uncle take Alex out to play?" Witherspoon interjected. Something was wrong, very wrong. He glanced at Barnes. He looked worried, too.

"Mrs. Meese, this really isn't a good time to speak to the master." Mrs. Metcalf's voice came from the corridor.

"I don't care. That knife belongs to me." The doors burst open and a thin woman wearing a cook's cap and apron burst into the room. Mrs. Metcalf and two maids trailed after her.

"Your nephew is a thief!" the cook cried. "He stole my knife, my personal knife, the one I've cooked with for thirty years. It was lying on my worktable and Liddy here saw him grab it."

"Why on earth would Neville want your blasted knife?" Martha shouted.

"Mama, can we go out now? Uncle Neville is outside with Alex," one of the twins whined. "Why can't we go play, too?"

"He's not playing with that boy!" she yelled.

"But he took his coat off, like he does when he plays with us," the other twin said.

"Are you saying that young Alex is outside

with Neville Gaines?" Witherspoon spoke loud enough to make them all shut up. He had a bad feeling about this.

"What of it?" Martha snarled.

"I want you to tell him to give me back my knife!" the cook cried. "He's no right to it. It's my personal property."

"I don't like this, sir," Barnes muttered.

"Neither do I. Let's go," he said. He sprinted toward the French doors that opened onto the upper balcony. The constables were right on his heels.

"Where are you going?" Sir Donovan charged after them.

They ran out onto the fog-enshrouded terrace and dashed down the stairs.

Outside, Smythe crouched behind a hedge. Wiggins had taken the front of the house and he'd opted to climb the fence and take the garden. He couldn't see a blooming thing but he could hear voices and footsteps coming toward him.

"Come along, boy," a man said harshly. "We've not got all night."

"Where's Mama's rosebush?" a child asked plaintively. "You said you were bringing me out here to take a cutting from Mama's favorite rosebush. But it's so foggy I can't see anything. Ow, that hurts, don't squeeze my hand so hard."

"Stop acting like a baby," the man ordered. "It's just over here. It's hard to find in the fog."

"I don't like this." The boy sounded scared now. "Let go of me. I want to go back to the house."

Smythe knew something was terribly wrong. He stood up but all he saw was a sea of whiteness. He turned in a circle, no longer caring if anyone saw him. He could hear footsteps, shuffling noises as the boy dug his heels into the ground.

"Quit pulling back."

"Let me go, Mr. Gaines, I want to go back to the house."

"It's just down here, boy, I've told you. Don't you want a souvenir of your dear mama? Quit dragging your feet, you little sod . . . stop that, that hurts. You bit me, you disgusting heathen. Get back here, boy, now I've got you."

Smythe heard a scuffle, whirled in the direction he thought it had come, and charged forward into a privet hedge. "Run, lad!" he shouted as he tried to regain his feet. "Run for your life and scream to high heaven as you go."

Startled by the sudden voice, Neville Gaines relaxed his hold on Alex enough for the boy to jerk free. Alex shrieked and stumbled backward. Gaines slashed at him, but he dodged to one side and the knife slashed the side of his bare arm.

Alex yelped with pain, turned, and raced for what he hoped was the house. "Help, help, he's trying to kill me!" he yelled. He didn't know who the unknown voice in the fog might have been but it had given him a chance to escape.

Lucius Montague couldn't see, either, as he crossed the garden, but once the shouting started, he realized he was trapped in the fog with a madman. Panicked, he turned twice, got completely mixed up, and then when he heard even more horrifying sounds and someone shouted they were being killed, he started running. He charged through a sea of white mist, as all around him there were ominous shouts, screams, and footsteps pounding after him. The screams got louder and louder, and to Montague, it sounded as if someone was being murdered.

Witherspoon, Barnes, and Rivers raced onto the path and stopped dead as they heard a bloodcurdling scream. "Alexander, are you alright, hang on, we're coming." Witherspoon raced forward and then changed direction as Rivers cried, "It's this way, sir." He pointed toward the center. "I know it."

"Help, help, help . . ."

"Blast a Spaniard!" Smythe swore as he finally regained his footing. He charged toward what he hoped was the right direction, but he couldn't see anything and he didn't trust navigating through a fog by sound alone. Yet he couldn't stand by without trying to save the lad.

"Where are you, boy?" Barnes bellowed.

"I'm over here, help, help . . . I'm bleeding . . ." The voice rose in a wail of anguish. "Let go, let go . . ."

The boy twisted away and dashed farther into the garden, into the fog. Gaines went after him, holding the knife high. Footsteps shuffled on the path amid grunts and screams. "Get back here, you little bastard."

Montague was so frightened he couldn't do anything but keep going until suddenly he ran smack into another body, sending the knife flying out of Neville Gaines' hand and both of them sprawling onto the ground.

Just then, the fog lightened. "There, sir!" Rivers cried. Gaines lunged for the knife. His fingers closed around the handle when the inspector's foot suddenly slammed onto his hand, forcing it to the ground. Gaines screamed.

Barnes rushed to the boy. Alex was holding his hand over his bleeding arm and sobbing. "He tried to hurt me. He hurt me with the knife." The constable gently lifted Alex's hand and examined the wound. The cut wasn't much more than a deep scratch. "Is this the only place he got you?" he asked.

Rivers raced to Gaines' other side. Montague moaned. Everyone ignored him.

"That's the only place." Alex's eyes filled with tears. "I moved just as he brought the blade down, and then when I saw he was going to do it again, I ran, but he chased me and kept trying to grab me."

"Alex, Alex." Sir Donovan materialized out of the fog. Martha Barclay, the twins, the housekeeper, the cook, and several housemaids trooped behind him. They fanned out in a semicircle around the path.

Sir Donovan rushed to the child and knelt on one knee to look him in the eyes. "Are you alright, son? Oh dear God, this is all my fault. I should never have brought you into this house."

"No, you shouldn't have." Martha snarled. She glared at her uncle and Alex.

Alex pointed to Gaines. "He tried to hurt me. He told me we'd come out here and he'd get me a cutting from Mama's favorite rosebush. I wanted to take it with us to

America, to San Francisco. Mama wanted to go there so badly. But then he tried to stick the knife into me."

"He's lying." Gaines snarled. "You can prove nothing; it's his word against mine. He's only a child."

Moaning and holding his head, Montague stumbled to his feet. "Oh dear, what happened? What is everyone doing out here? Neville, you owe me an apology. You ran into me."

"You stupid sod." Neville glared at him and tried to pull his hand out from under the inspector's foot. "You ran into me. This is all your fault."

"Thank God." Sir Donovan rose and pulled the boy close. "You saved my son's life. Thank you, Lucius. I'm forever in your debt."

Witherspoon motioned for Rivers and Barnes to pull Gaines to his feet. "Neville Gaines, you're under arrest for the murder of Ellen Langston-Jones."

"You can't prove it." He smiled smugly. "This little incident can be interpreted in several different ways. The boy grabbed the knife from the kitchen and I saw him. I followed him out to take it away before he hurt himself. But he wouldn't hand it over and he got cut when I tried to take it away."

"That's not true," the scullery maid interjected. "The lad didn't take the knife; you did. I was there and I saw and heard you." She looked at the inspector. "I did hear him. He told the boy they were goin' outside to take a cuttin' and then I saw him grab Cook's special knife and I knew there'd be trouble. Cook don't allow anyone to touch her knife and she was already in a state because we're losin' our positions and the house is to be shut up and sold."

Smythe, who'd come as close as he dared, realized the fog was starting to lift so he eased back toward the gate, taking care to stay on the grass to muffle his footsteps. He wasn't needed here now. The lad had the life scared out of him, but he was safe now and three policemen should be able to handle Neville Gaines.

"Neville Gaines tried to kill Alexander Langston-Jones," Wiggins announced as they rushed into the kitchen. He'd joined the other two men in keeping watch after getting a street lad to deliver the bogus note to Constable Barnes.

"Oh dear, is the boy alright?" Mrs. Jeffries, who'd been pacing the kitchen, stopped in front of the cooker. Fred raised his head and stared at her.

"He's fine." Hatchet took off his hat and laid it on the table in front of his chair. "Frightened, but safe, and you're not going to believe who he'll have to thank for it — Lucius Montague."

"Lucius Montague," she repeated, her expression incredulous.

"You were right, Mrs. Jeffries." Smythe grinned as he dropped into his spot next to Betsy. "We stopped a murder. Well, we didn't so much as the inspector and Montague did."

"We can't read your minds. Tell us what happened," Luty demanded.

"I'll pour your tea as you tell us," the cook offered. Phyllis was already on her feet and getting the cups.

They all began to speak at once.

"That ruddy fog was both a curse and a blessin'," Smythe began. "I almost got caught out because I shouted at the lad to run when I heard Gaines goin' after him."

"We could hear what was going on but we couldn't really see," Hatchet said.

"It were right scary if you ask me," Wiggins declared.

"One at a time, please," Mrs. Jeffries insisted. "Wiggins, you start. I take it you were able to track down the inspector and Constable Barnes."

"They was right where I left 'em and the lad give 'em the note when they came out of her flat." He nodded his thanks as the cook passed him his tea. "Once the constable showed the note to the inspector, they were off right quick to the Gaines house. I waited a few seconds and then followed 'em. Just like you told me, I kept watch on the servants' door, but it was bloomin' 'ard. The fog kept driftin' in and out so that I couldn't see properly."

"I'll tell it from here." Smythe told them about being in the garden and hearing the boy and Gaines come outside. "I wasn't sure what to do. I knew the lad might be in danger but I couldn't see anything."

"I was still out front at this point, but I did see the inspector and Constable Barnes get the constable that had been in front of the Montague home and take him with them," Hatchet said. "I'm afraid I wasn't of much use. But I did manage to make my way inside the garden when I heard the boy screaming."

Smythe took a quick sip. "Let me tell you what happened, at least what I think happened."

"What do you mean?" Betsy shifted the baby so she was facing forward. "I thought you were in the garden."

"I was, but like I said, I couldn't see." He told them everything he'd heard, and the small bit he'd actually seen. "So between Lucius Montague knockin' into him and the inspector slappin' his foot on Gaines' hand, the lad was safe and Neville Gaines was arrested," he finished.

"Gerald is so very brave." Ruth sighed happily.

"I knew we could do it." Phyllis giggled. "I just knew it."

"Once again, justice prevails," Hatchet said.

"You're very quiet," Mrs. Goodge said to Mrs. Jeffries. "What's wrong?"

"Nothing is wrong," she replied. "I'm just grateful that we managed to help find the killer once again."

"How did you figure it was him?" Luty asked.

"I wasn't precisely sure," she admitted. "As I told you, there could have been two possible motives for this murder. One of them, of course, turned out to be the one that was true."

"You mean that Neville Gaines killed that woman to keep her from marryin' Sir Donovan and becoming his heir?" Phyllis guessed. "Is that right?"

"That's correct. I suspect that Neville

Gaines saw Sir Donovan and Ellen Langston-Jones together very soon after she came here from France. He'd have remembered her from when she worked as a governess to the Furness family."

"But he didn't live with Sir Donovan then," Mrs. Goodge pointed out.

"True, but I'm sure that he knew all about her." She nodded toward the footman. "It didn't take Wiggins long to find out they'd had a previous relationship and I suspect that once he saw her, the child, and Sir Donovan together, he made it his business to find out everything he could. When he realized that Alexander was Sir Donovan's child, he knew he had to get rid of them. That was the only way for him and his sister to continue being the heirs to a vast fortune."

"How did you suss out that Sir Donovan was Alex's father?" Wiggins asked.

"There were several strong signs. The old gardener, Mr. Calder, claimed she loved London yet all of a sudden, she goes back to Dorset. Why?"

"Because she was expecting and hoped to go back home and fob herself off as a widow," Betsy guessed. "More than one poor woman has had to walk that path." She dropped a kiss on Amanda's head and the baby gurgled happily.

"That was my assumption as well." Mrs. Jeffries smiled approvingly. "Luckily for her, she didn't have to go that far. Hatchet's source told him that Brandon Langston-Jones was in a spot himself and a sudden marriage was just what he needed to hang on to his inheritance. So they married and moved to France, she had the child, and by all accounts, they lived fairly happily together."

"Brandon Langston-Jones loved the boy and raised him as his own," Hatchet murmured. "He was a good man, a true man."

"But if Sir Donovan wanted a child so badly, why did he let her go away?" Phyllis crossed her arms over her chest. "Why not just keep her and the baby here in some quiet neighborhood in London? By then, his wife was already ill, so he must have known it wouldn't be too many years before he'd be a widower."

It was Ruth who answered. "Because she didn't tell him." She looked at Mrs. Jeffries, who nodded. "They were honorable people, both she and Sir Donovan. She didn't want him to abandon his wife because of her predicament so she simply left."

"If she got a baby, they weren't *that* honorable," Wiggins muttered. "I know his wife had been sickly, but still, if you love someone, you need to stay true to 'em."

"Quit bein' so holier-than-thou." Luty frowned at the footman. "Even good people make mistakes. You'll make a few yourself before they plant ya six feet under and you're one of the most honorable people I know."

Wiggins sulked for a moment and then grinned. "That's right nice of you. But I don't understand how Neville Gaines figured out that Alexander was Sir Donovan's son. She didn't even come and ask Sir Donovan for a position when she came back to London. He saw her in the park and offered 'er one."

"I'm sure that Gaines saw the three of them together, and once he saw Alexander, he suspected the child was Sir Donovan's. He confirmed it by going through Sir Donovan's personal box. Remember what the footman, Tommy Wheaton, told you? That he'd seen Neville Gaines snooping through Sir Donovan's things and that a drawing of Sir Donovan and his sister done when he was a child about Alex's age had dropped on the floor. Alexander Langston-Jones is the spitting image of Sir Donovan as a child."

"How do you know that?" Betsy demanded. "You've never seen the boy." Her eyes widened. "You went there, didn't you?"

"I got a look at both Alex and Sir Donovan before the funeral and then I went to the Gaines house. I was certain that Sir Donovan would insist his entire household go to the service so I knew the place would be empty. I didn't want to say anything because I didn't wish anyone other than myself to be involved in what was, well, a crime. But that's neither here nor there; it did confirm my suspicions, though. If I could see the resemblance, then Neville Gaines most certainly could."

"Do you think it was then that Gaines began askin' his connections in the property business to keep their ears open for anything that Sir Donovan might be up to?" Mrs. Goodge asked. "It seems a coincidence that he'd find out that Sir Donovan was sellin' up right after he'd figured out the boy was a danger to him."

"I think that is exactly what happened." Mrs. Jeffries took a sip of tea. "Once he had confirmation of what his uncle was going to do, he knew he had to act. The first thing he and his sister did was to start pushing Hester Linthorp toward Sir Donovan. As several of your sources pointed out, prior to that time they were barely civil to the woman, but once Mrs. Langston-Jones was in the house every day, Mrs. Linthorp became an honored guest and they encouraged her dislike of the victim."

"I don't understand why they did that," Wiggins announced. "I mean, it's not like Sir Donovan was suddenly goin' to fall in love with the woman. She was 'is wife's friend and 'e'd known her for donkey's years."

"She was insurance," Mrs. Jeffries said. "Neville Gaines wanted the finger of guilt pointing to as many people as possible, so he made certain Mrs. Linthorp was available as a suspect. We've learned that, at least twice, Sir Donovan became annoyed with her for overstepping her bounds with Mrs. Langston-Jones, and in both of those incidents, Martha Barclay was there adding fuel to the fire. I don't believe that's a coincidence."

"You think Mrs. Barclay is a coconspirator?" Hatchet asked.

"I do, even though her brother will take the entire blame." She sighed. "But the evidence clearly suggests she was in on it from the beginning. I imagine she was the one that came up with the idea of framing Lucius Montague for the murder."

"Why do you think that?"

"Because she was sitting next to Montague at the dinner party where he foolishly bragged about owning a gun," she replied. "Luckily for us, Fiona was at the same party as was Neville Gaines, but he was at the far end of the table, and according to Fiona, he couldn't have heard anything Montague said. But Martha could and it was at this point that they came up with their plan. Not only would they get rid of Ellen Langston-Jones and her son, but it would also give Neville Gaines a chance to revenge himself on Montague."

"That's right. Gaines hated Montague because his advice had bankrupted him," Ruth said.

"Precisely. So I asked myself why would Mrs. Barclay keep up such a strong friendship with the man who'd literally sent her brother to the poor house? Fiona told me that it was only recently, since Christmas, that Mrs. Barclay had begun inviting Montague over for dinner and tea. Prior to the holidays, Montague had been nothing more than Sir Donovan's friend and neighbor. But if the plan was going to work, they needed to be close to him so they could steal the gun and the pillow."

"Which they didn't even need," Mrs. Goodge muttered. "The pillow, I mean.

They didn't need it because the boy next door had his trumpet lesson, and accordin' to the maid, he was loud enough to wake the dead."

"Excellent observation, Mrs. Goodge." Mrs. Jeffries smiled approvingly. "Which was one of the reasons we knew Montague wasn't the killer."

"He lived on the garden so he'd have known he didn't need to use the pillow to muffle the gunshot," Betsy said.

"Agreed," Mrs. Jeffries said. "And that's when I realized the only reason for using it was to frame Montague. He's an odious man and not well liked, the kind of person one might take pains to avoid. Yet someone hated him enough to want him to hang. The only person that fit that description was Neville Gaines. Of course, when Gaines realized that Sir Donovan was moving up the timetable and proposing marriage to Ellen, he knew he had to act fast. He pretended he was going to inspect a property in Fulham, but he wouldn't let his assistant go with him, and when he left his office on the day of the murder, he told the cab driver to take him to Gloucester Road."

"To Bailey's Hotel," Betsy murmured. "I'll bet he went in and watched Sir Donovan and Mrs. Langston-Jones."

"I suspect he did, and that's when he saw him slip the ring on her finger. Add to that he knew they were going to leave early in July, and he couldn't risk them marrying. He'd already stolen the gun and the pillow, so he followed her back to the garden and killed her."

"What I don't understand is how did Mrs. Langston-Jones get a key?" Ruth tapped her fingers against her cup.

"I'll bet Sir Donovan gave it to her," Luty said. "He and Mrs. Langston-Jones wanted some quiet time together and the only place they could git it was early in the mornin's in the garden. Remember, the boy said that sometimes the neighbor lady in the lodgin' house took him to school because his mama had to leave."

"That was my thought as well," Mrs. Jeffries said. "I think they were very much in love and Neville Gaines realized this and knew he had to stop the marriage. However, what he didn't count on was Sir Donovan going on with his plan to sell up and leave the country immediately."

"So he panicked and tried to murder the boy," Hatchet mused. "But surely he didn't think he'd get away with it."

"Oh, but he did," Mrs. Jeffries argued. "Remember, he'd no idea anyone was in the kitchen when he took the knife. Smythe said the maid saw Gaines but he didn't see her."

"So you think he was going to stab the boy and then make it look like an accident?" Phyllis guessed.

"I think that's what he hoped to do, but he bumbled it. His first murder was well planned to some degree; he'd stolen the gun and the pillow. All he had to do then was wait for an opportunity to murder her. This attempt was born out of desperation. He probably felt that with the heavy fog, he could claim he saw the boy take the knife and he went out to take it away . . ."

"But he was too late," Betsy guessed. "He was going to try and make them believe that Alex ran, tripped, and fell on the knife."

"You said there was a second motive," Ruth reminded Mrs. Jeffries. "What was it?"

"It occurred to me that Sir Donovan might have murdered her to keep the boy for himself," Mrs. Jeffries said. "She'd become financially independent, you see. Brandon Langston-Jones' paintings are worth a fortune and that coupled with the fact that she'd already planned on taking the child and leaving the country might have prompted him to try and stop her. If you'll remember pamphlets and ships schedules were found in her room as well. Then, of course, she was threatening to sue both Montague and her brother-in-law, and she might have told Sir Donovan she wasn't interested in a life with him. From what we know of her character, she was a very independent woman and not all women enjoy being married."

"But Sir Donovan loved her," Ruth protested.

"And she loved him, but I suspect that one of the reasons he was moving so quickly to get them married and out of England was because he was frightened she might decide to carry on with her own plans." Mrs. Jeffries' expression was thoughtful. "But in this case, it turned out to be good old-fashioned greed."

"Neville Gaines was stupid as to try to murder the boy right under everyone's nose. That was a foolish, stupid mistake. Why not wait a few months and then arrange an accident?" Hatchet took a sip of tea.

"There's a very simple explanation for his behavior," Mrs. Jeffries replied. "He was afraid that Sir Donovan suspected he'd murdered Ellen."

"So the minute he showed up for a nice little family visit, Sir Donovan would watch him like a hawk and make sure he never got near the boy," Hatchet finished.

"Were they going to live in America?" Ruth asked.

"San Francisco," Phyllis said quickly. "Sorry, I forgot to tell you this bit, but right after Sir Donovan told everyone he was leavin', he told Mrs. Metcalf to tell the servants he and Alex were goin' to eventually settle in San Francisco, and that if anyone from the house came there, he'd give them a job."

"But why go all that way?" The cook poured herself more tea. "There are plenty of civilized towns in America. What's wrong with Boston or Philadelphia or New York?"

"I bet I know." Luty chuckled. "You're all forgettin' that Alex might be Gaines' son, but Sir Donavon wasn't married to his mother. Out West, especially in a town like San Francisco, those kinds of things don't matter so much to us."

"So he was going there in case anyone found out about his parentage?" Betsy murmured. "Good for him. But he wouldn't be a 'sir' in America."

"True," Luty agreed. "But he'd still be rich in America — that's what counts."

"What do you mean, you've no idea where he is?" Inspector Nigel Nivens glared at the duty sergeant manning the front desk at the Ladbroke Road Police Station. "Witherspoon is assigned to this station, isn't he? Isn't it your job to know where he might be?"

The duty sergeant, an old warrior who'd handled the likes of upstart twits like Nivens for years, smiled politely and played dumb. "Yes sir, come to think of it, he is assigned here. But he's investigating the Langston-Jones murder, sir, and when he's on the case —"

"He's no longer on that case." Nivens slapped his hand on the counter. "It's now been assigned to me. I'm taking over and I demand to see the senior officer in charge here."

"The senior officer, sir, let me see, that would be . . ." He trailed off as the front door opened and Witherspoon came inside. Barnes and Rivers were right behind him, flanking Neville Gaines as he entered the station. "That would be Inspector Witherspoon, sir, and he's just arrived." He pointed in their direction.

Nivens looked around. "Witherspoon, it's about time you got here. We've no time to waste. Chief Inspector Barrows has taken you off the Langston-Jones case and passed it to me. I'm going to need all your reports and case notes." He appeared not to notice the disheveled but well-dressed man standing between the two constables. If he had, he might have realized the case was already solved.

Barnes stifled a snicker, ignored Nivens, and grinned at his inspector. "We'll take him back and book him, sir," he said. He and Rivers ushered Gaines toward the door leading to the interior of the building.

Witherspoon turned to Nivens. "I'm sorry, I didn't catch what you said."

"I said I'm taking over this case so I'll need all the reports and your notes." Nivens' attention was caught by the trio retreating toward the back door and he frowned. "Who is that?"

"Neville Gaines," Witherspoon said. "He murdered Ellen Langston-Jones. We suspect his sister was in on it as well, but as he's made a full confession and insists he acted alone, there isn't anything we can do about that."

Nivens made a strangled sound in the back of his throat and then glared at Witherspoon's back as the inspector moved toward the duty sergeant.

"Good evening, Sergeant Prior." The inspector pulled a sealed envelope out of his pocket and handed it across the counter.

"We'll need this logged into evidence and then put somewhere safe. It's very valuable."

Behind him, Nivens' face flushed beet red and his hands balled into fists.

"What is it, sir?" Sergeant Prior asked.

"A diamond ring," Witherspoon replied. "It belonged to the victim. Sir Donovan Gaines gave it to her on the day she died. It was found in Neville Gaines' room this evening."

"I don't believe this," Nivens muttered. "This can't be happening . . . it can't be happening." He kept saying it over and over as he walked out the door.

Witherspoon didn't often have tea in the kitchen, but when he'd arrived home, Mrs. Jeffries had insisted.

"I can tell by the look on your face that you've had a most successful day, sir," she'd said.

"Indeed I have. We've arrested Ellen Langston-Jones' murderer."

"What luck, sir, then you must come downstairs. Luty and Hatchet have dropped by for a late tea and Lady Cannonberry stopped in to invite you to dinner. They're all downstairs, sir, and they'll be terribly disappointed if you don't tell them what happened."

"Well, one hates to disappoint anyone," he'd said as he followed her downstairs. The only new information the inspector was able to add to what they already knew was that Ellen's engagement ring had been found in Neville Gaines' bedroom and that he'd confessed to being the sole perpetrator of the crime.

Mrs. Jeffries was very proud of everyone. They asked intelligent questions, made all the right comments, and did a wonderful job of pretending ignorance as he gave his account of the circumstances surrounding the arrest. When he'd finished, he held out his arms to Amanda. "May I hold her?"

Betsy handed him his goddaughter. "Do you think he did act on his own?" she asked.

"Oh no, I'm sure Mrs. Barclay is as guilty as he is, but we'll never prove it." He cuddled the baby close and stroked her cheek. "But sometimes justice is served in other ways. I think Sir Donovan suspected she was part of it as well. As we were taking Gaines away, I overheard him speaking to Mrs. Barclay; he told her that it would be best if she made arrangements to go to the East, to her husband. From the tone of his voice, I rather got the impression that regardless of what happened in the future,

Mrs. Barclay was definitely out of the will."

"Thank goodness you were there." Ruth patted his arm. "If you hadn't been, that poor child would have been brutally murdered. You were so brave."

Witherspoon shrugged self-consciously and smiled. "It's nice of you to say so, but I was simply doing what any other officer would have done. Which reminds me, the oddest thing happened when we went back to the station."

"What, sir?" Mrs. Jeffries asked.

He shifted Amanda into a more comfortable position on his lap. "Inspector Nivens was at the station. Apparently, he was going to take over the case. He seemed a tad upset when I told him we'd made an arrest. One could almost say he stormed out in a huff."

"Why was he goin' to take over the case, sir?" Wiggins asked. He wanted to see if Witherspoon realized he had enemies in high places.

"Apparently someone at the Home Office was annoyed that I'd not arrested Lucius Montague."

"Thank goodness you didn't, sir," Mrs. Jeffries said. "He sounds like a horrible person but it turned out he was innocent."

"Indeed he was." Witherspoon stroked the baby's head. "As I've always said, Mrs.

Jeffries, in a decent society, justice must be blind, even for people like Lucius Montague."

The employees of Thorndike Press hope you have enjoyed this Large Print book. All our Thorndike, Wheeler, and Kennebec Large Print titles are designed for easy reading, and all our books are made to last. Other Thorndike Press Large Print books are available at your library, through selected bookstores, or directly from us.

For information about titles, please call:
  (800) 223-1244

or visit our Web site at:
  http://gale.cengage.com/thorndike

To share your comments, please write:
  Publisher
  Thorndike Press
  10 Water St., Suite 310
  Waterville, ME 04901

Discard
NHCPL

CPSIA information can be obtained
at www.ICGtesting.com
Printed in the USA
FFOW04n2346190514
5474FF

9 781410 462374

mL   6-14